Daniel was pouting.

He was bored.

B.

O.

R.

E.

D.

Bored.

Mal was in a snit and had ignored everyone and then disappeared entirely.

Desmond was in his rooms with his latest bottom.

Daniel would have thought someone would be interested in topping him after the show he'd put on the other night, but that didn't seem to be the case.

And he was looking fine, too. Damn it.

He all but stamped his foot.

His hair was loose, falling around his shoulders. His eyelashes were darkened and his lips reddened. His body was displayed to great effect in the violet skin-tight jumpsuit he wore.

So why was he alone and bored? He wandered over to the bar. "I want a Purple Passion Explosion."

A soft chuckle sounded, the noise deep and rumbling and low. "I don't know, Poppet. You're already purple enough, aren't you?"

He turned his head and saw a massive bald man, dark eyes sparkling under heavy brows.

"You think?" he asked, wriggling a little. "So what would you suggest then?"

One eyebrow arched. "Whiskey, Jim. Two. Neat."

"Whiskey? Are you trying to get me drunk?" He gave Baldy a long once over. He wouldn't mind this one getting him drunk, or not, as long as there was advantage taken of him.

This is a work of fiction. Names, characters, places, and incidents either are the product of the author's imagination or are used fictitiously. Any resemblance to actual events, locales, organizations, or persons, living or dead, is entirely coincidental and beyond the intent of either the author or the publisher.

Velvet Glove Volume II
TOP SHELF
An imprint of Torquere Press Publishers
PO Box 2545
Round Rock, TX 78680

Cover illustration by Anne Squires
Published with permission
ISBN: 978-1-60370-272-0, 1-60370-272-5

www.torquerepress.com

First Torquere Press Printing: February 2008
Printed in the USA

If you enjoyed Velvet Glove Volume II, you might enjoy these Torquere Press titles:

Bent by Sean Michael

Love Runes by Jay Lygon

Deviations Series by Chris Owen and Jodi Payne

Hyacinth Club by BA Tortuga

Secrets, Skin and Leather by Sean Michael

Velvet Glove Volume II
by Sean Michael

Torquere Press Inc.
romance for the rest of us
www.torquerepress.com

Table of Contents

The Misadventures of Daniel and Zane

Daniel Meets His Match

Daniel was pouting.

He was bored.

B.

O.

R.

E.

D.

Bored.

Mal was in a snit and had ignored everyone and then disappeared entirely.

Desmond was in his rooms with his latest bottom.

Daniel would have thought someone would be interested in topping him after the show he'd put on the other night, but that didn't seem to be the case.

And he was looking fine, too. Damn it.

He all but stamped his foot.

His hair was loose, falling around his shoulders. His eyelashes were darkened and his lips reddened. His body was displayed to great effect in the violet skin-tight jumpsuit he wore.

So why was he alone and bored? He wandered over to the bar. “I want a Purple Passion Explosion.”

A soft chuckle sounded, the noise deep and rumbling and low. “I don’t know, Poppet. You’re already purple enough, aren’t you?”

He turned his head and saw a massive bald man, dark eyes sparkling under heavy brows.

“You think?” he asked, wriggling a little. “So what would you suggest then?”

One eyebrow arched. “Whiskey, Jim. Two. Neat.”

“Whiskey? Are you trying to get me drunk?” He gave Baldy a long once over. He wouldn’t mind this one getting him drunk, or not, as long as there was advantage taken of him.

“No. You’ll only have one. I’m not interested in having you sloppy drunk.”

Sure, firm. Absolute. Sexy as fuck.

“Well how are you interested in having me, then?” Oh, suddenly he wasn’t bored anymore. Not one little bit.

“Spread out on the sofa in my suite. Saw you the other night, but I don’t want sloppy seconds and I want you to know when I fuck you. Drink your whiskey.”

“Oh, it’s like that is it?” He gave Baldy his best, sassy look, but he took the whiskey from Jim and took a sip, looking up at the man from over the rim of his glass.

“It is.” Baldy took his own drink in one smooth shot, not flinching, not grimacing. “You’ve got a hungry little hole, Poppet. I think I can make you scream.”

He was mid-preen when he realised what Baldy had said earlier. “Wait a minute. You called me sloppy seconds.”

Daniele shot back his own whiskey and slammed his glass on the bar. A flip of his hair and he was heading off, grand exit entirely ruined by his gasping chokes. Damn, that was strong stuff.

"You're making a mistake, Daniel." He spun around to see a key card being laid on the bar. "I've been watching you. Learning you. I'll be upstairs, if you decide to come play."

Calling him sloppy seconds and then walking off without him? Oh.

Oh.

Daniel was livid.

Just... oh.

He'd spent over an hour wandering through the club before admitting he was well and truly bored.

Again.

Still.

Whatever.

The only thing that had interested him all evening was... well Baldy. How dare the man call him sloppy seconds?

He'd show him.

Daniel marched back up to the bar and held out his hand.

Jim grinned at him and pulled the keycard out of his shirt pocket.

"Thank you, Jim."

He was in the elevator on his way up when he wondered if he should change his outfit. Baldy had been rather disparaging about it, on top of everything else.

No.

He wouldn't go out of his way even an inch for that man.

Daniel used the card to open the door and walked in as if he owned the place. If Baldy was asleep, not there or with someone else? It was over.

No matter how bored he was.

Or how intriguing those dark eyes had been.

Heat pressed against his back as a blindfold covered his eyes, sending the plain room black. "Hello, Poppet. Thank you for coming."

Oh....

"It was a slow night." His heart wasn't in the insult though and it was everything he could do not to melt into Baldy's heat.

"Mmm..." One long hand stroked down his chest, unfastening his jumpsuit, fingers just teasing along his shaft.

"I don't even know your name," he breathed, a ripple going through him.

"You'll remember me, though. I promise you." The heat against him intensified, Baldy's body hot and hard and fine behind him.

He did melt against the man this time. He had a suspicion Baldy was right. His whole body was tingling, waiting, anticipating.

His ear was nuzzled, his clothes slowly worked off, the heat behind him solid, the touches to his belly light and infuriating and arousing.

"You said you were going to make me scream and all you're doing is teasing me."

"Daniel? Shut up and pay attention."

They took a few steps forward, Baldy moving him easily.

Bending him over a soft settee.

Fastening his wrists with leather.

"Oooo, kinky." A pillow was slid under his hips, then his ankles were bound, Baldy not saying a word. "Very kinky." His words were a little less sassy, a little more husky and he was forgetting just why he was talking back to Baldy in the first place.

"Do you need to be gagged, Poppet?" The words came

as two hands landed on his ass, thumbs pressing at his hole.

He shivered, whimpered. "No. I'll be good."

"Good boy." He felt the slick touch around his hole. "Very good boy."

He moaned, pushing back into the touch. Baldy's hands were big, fingers large. It felt good.

Two slick fingers slid deep, pushing in hard and then disappearing, only to slam in again.

He whimpered, tried to spread his legs, but couldn't.

One hot hand settled on the small of his back, hard and sure, thumb and forefinger holding him open. So strong. God. One-handed, holding him open with one hand and fucking him with the other. Baldy was right -- if he'd missed this he'd have regretted it.

Then. Oh, Lord. Hot and so wide and stretching him inexorably. His groan was pushed out from him by that huge cock. Sparks flashed behind his eyelids as Baldy filled him, spreading him wide and pressing in so fucking deep, branding him. His fingers grasped at the cushions, his mouth open on soundless breaths.

Then Baldy started moving -- deep, hard motions that pushed that hot cock over his gland again and again. His body didn't want to let the thick length go, but the man didn't ask what he wanted, just gave him what he needed.

He started meeting the thrusts as best he could, breath groaning from him now. Oh God, oh fuck, oh wow.

"Yeah. Yeah, Daniel. Sweet fucking ass." Hands wrapped around his hips and pulled him into the thrusts over and over.

He couldn't do anything but take it, and take it he did, loving every second of it.

One of those hands wrapped around his prick, holding it, stroking it as that cock slammed into him. The pleasure slammed through him and he held onto his sounds by the barest margin.

"I want to hear you, Poppet. Want to hear how good it feels."

A shudder went through him and he moaned. "Very good. 'S very good."

"Just good?" A low growl filled the air and that cock pushed harder, faster, deeper. "Then you haven't had enough of me."

He groaned again. "Not bad."

"Not bad?" The motion of that hard cock stopped, the tip just held by the ring of his body.

"That's what I said," he whimpered.

"Mmm." Baldy didn't move, fingers simply rubbing around his hole, cock spreading him wide.

Oh, fuck.

Oh, sweet fuck it was pure torture.

He would stay right here forever if he could. Right here where there was nothing but ass and cock and heat and darkness. One fingertip slid in alongside that still cock and disappeared, another pushing in on the other side. Daniel moaned and whimpered, shudders working their way along his spine.

The quiet touches continued, the cock simply throbbing inside him, holding him open.

Oh, Baldy was good. Really, really good.

"Not bad at..." He cleared his throat. "At all."

Two fingers pushed inside him, he could feel Baldy rubbing the tip of his own cock.

He screamed, body rippling around Baldy's fingers and cock.

"There we go." That heavy cock slammed into him, fingers still spreading him wide.

He screamed again, unable to hold anything back.

"Yes. Yes, Poppet. Show me."

Again and again he was fucked and fucked hard. The man was a fucking machine. He lost everything but that cock fucking him raw. His screams eventually faded, throat growing hoarse.

"Yes, Poppet. Yes. Come for me. Come on my cock now."

Daniel obeyed, coming hard, body squeezing the huge prick inside him. He barely registered the heat inside him, flooding him, the soft moan sliding through the air. He was boneless, limp. Floating.

F.

L.

O.

A.

T.

I.

N.

G.

Yeah.

The thick cock slid from inside him, only to be replaced by a heavy plug, those thick fingers rubbing his back and thighs as soon as it was seated inside him.

Another shudder went through him, his nerves screaming. "Oh, fuck."

"Yes, Poppet. Again and again and again." A soft kiss brushed his hip.

Oh, he was so fucked. So. So. Fucked.

Cool.

Zane Begins To Woo Daniel

Zane slicked his hands with spiced oil and began working it into Daniel's skin, warming it. The oil wouldn't burn, but it would tingle, set those nerves alive.

Make sure he kept the little shit's attention.

He'd decided that he wanted Daniel and he'd spent the last two cycles studying.

Talking to Mal.

Watching.

Waiting.

And now. Now he had the pretty ass right in front of him, filled with his come. Daniel wriggled and shivered, arching beneath his touches. He didn't speak, just purred softly and kept rubbing, stroking, awakening nerve after nerve.

Daniel's breath was audible, interrupted by gasps and moans, his Poppet shivering again and again.

He focused on the wrinkled patch of skin between filled ass and hanging balls -- fingers stroking and pinching, pulling and lightly scratching.

Sweet sobs began to fill the room, Daniel's body shaking now, his toes digging into the soft carpeting, his fingers tearing at the couch.

Yes. Yes, that wass what he'd needed. Pure need and all for him. Zane leaned down and pressed his tongue against the soft skin. That earned him a scream, the scent of Daniel's come sharp on the air.

He backed away and put his clothes back on, hiding himself in dark, heavy layers. Mal had taught him that, had told him after one of the dozens and dozens of training sessions he'd been to.

"Make him earn everything, Z. Every kiss. The chance to look at your body. To be held. Danny knows he's beautiful, knows how much people want him. The secret with him? Make him want it, and then?" Mal had given him a slow, breathless kiss that made the aches in his back and ass worth it. "Make him earn it."

Zane went and poured an icy cold glass of juice and then settled on the floor near Daniel's head, holding the straw up to those parted lips.

Daniel whimpered softly, red lips closing around the straw and sucking in the juice.

He let Daniel have about half and then took the straw away, rubbing a stray drop off Daniel's bottom lip with his thumb.

Daniel's tongue came out to briefly, tip touching his thumb.

"Thank you." Daniel's voice was rough from use.

"You're welcome, Poppet. You did beautifully." He gently unfastened Daniel's wrists, then ankles.

Daniel didn't move once he was free, just lay bent over the settee, hands opening and closing.

Zane carefully helped Daniel up, the man sitting gingerly, gasping as the plug shifted. Then he removed the blindfold.

Daniel blinked in the soft lighting, eyes watering slightly. "I always hate this part."

He used the soft blindfold to wipe Daniel's eyes. "Yeah? Too bright?"

"Yeah. And the whole coming down thing." A shiver went through Daniel, his arms wrapping around his middle.

"What do you need, Poppet?" Zane wanted to hold Daniel, but knew Daniel was going to have to ask.

The lovely green eyes looked shyly up at him, all the earlier sass and flash gone, though he suspected they'd return soon enough. "What's your name?"

"Zane."

"Zane." Daniel nodded and shivered. "I'm cold."

"Are you? Would you like to sit with me or would you prefer a blanket?" He would out-stubborn this man. He would.

"Are you warm?" Daniel asked him, a hint of that humour already returning.

"I am. Very." He winked over and held one arm open.

Daniel grinned and shifted over to him, gasping. "Oh. Somehow I'd forgotten it was there."

"Well, I can't have that." He pulled Daniel into the curve of his body, one hand just cupping the curve of Daniel's ass.

Daniel melted against him, head on his chest, hand on his belly, another soft shiver shaking the slender body. "You are warm."

"Yes, Poppet. I told you I was." He petted gently, easing Daniel from passion to lazy pleasure.

"Yeah, you did." Daniel pushed into his touches, like a cat, not quite purring.

He rewarded the trust with soft, careful warm strokes, humming softly. The shivers soon disappeared altogether, Daniel rubbing against him, cock oh so slowly filling again. He jostled the plug, shifting it, rocking it.

Daniel gasped, jerking against him and pressing closer.

"How does that feel, Poppet?" He knew exactly how it felt. Mal had fucked him with it not a month ago, then moved onto its bigger, heavier brother.

"Good." Those green eyes rose slowly, met his. "Not as good as your cock."

He arched an eyebrow and gave Daniel a smile. "You like to be fucked. I've watched you."

"You have, have you?" Daniel preened, fingers stroking his belly. "You obviously liked what you saw."

"I knew I could send you flying in a way the other men couldn't."

"Oh, you did, did you, Zane?"

He nodded, sliding his finger against the plug again. They'd either continue tonight or Daniel'd get mouthy and leave. Either way, Zane knew he'd made the man soar, knew Daniel'd be back for more.

Daniel Finds His Match

Daniel writhed, the plug inside him shifting, hitting his gland and making his cock fill completely. God, Baldy was confident.

Zane.

God, Zane was confident.

Sure.

Bold.

It was very sexy.

He closed his eyes, breath leaving him with soft, needy pants as he tried to worm his fingers under Zane's sweater.

"What do you want, Poppet? What do you need?" God, that low voice spoke right to his balls.

"I want you to suck me," he murmured. He wasn't trying to push... well, it was a side benefit, but he'd actually said the first thing that had popped into his head.

Zane chuckled, cupped his balls in a huge, gentle hand. "I'm no star-eyed newbie, Poppet. Do you think you've earned my mouth?"

He moaned softly, moving between Zane's hands, the one making his whole ass zing, the other pulling pleasure straight from the source. "You asked what I wanted..."

"I did." Zane chuckled again, the sound vibrating against him. "Now, what do you need?"

He bit his tongue over the flippant words that sprung to mind. If he hadn't had that plug in him he might have risked it. Instead he looked at Zane, thinking carefully before answering. "Whatever you need to give me."

"Oh, that was a good answer, Poppet." The plug was jostled, hard, the fingers rolling his balls enough to make him twist.

He grabbed onto Zane's sweater, gasps and shivers rocking him. He had a feeling behaving was going to be very rewarding when it came to Zane.

Zane fingers slid up to circle the base of his cock, circling it and pumping in short jerks.

Daniel moaned, eyes dropping closed. He tried to move with the movements of Zane's hand, but the strokes weren't even and he kept jostling the plug inside him, so in the end he just went with it, let Zane do what he would.

"Touch your body for me, Poppet. I want to set what you like."

"I like it when other people touch me," he informed Zane a little tartly. After all, if he liked touching himself best, he could do that any old time, right? Nevertheless he ran his hands over his body, rubbing his belly and stroking his nipples.

The hand on his cock stopped moving, went back to holding, fingers wrapped loosely around the base.

"Tease," he accused, hands sliding down his body toward his prick.

"Not at all." Zane tilted his prick away from his hands. "You get the pleasure you earn, Poppet. No less."

He glared. It looked like Zane wasn't going to let him get away with anything. There was always a different way to pluck a chicken. He wriggled his ass, jostling the plug inside him, making sparks shoot up along his spine.

"And no more." With those words he was spun, ending ass-up in Zane's lap, wrists caught in one hand.

He gasped at the speed and strength Zane displayed, moaning as heat filled his belly, made his cock jerk hard.

One huge hand cupped his ass, the touch feather light. "You'll get what I give you, Poppet."

He wiggled his ass. "Then give it to me, Zane."

God, the man was magnificent.

He got a firm, hard swat. "Tell me why I should, Daniel. What have you earned?"

"I'm here."

"You are. So am I." Those fingers traced the bundle of nerves in his lower back, driving him mad.

"You want me to suck you? To let you fuck me again?" His voice wasn't steady, Zane's touches spiking his need.

"I want you to quit fighting me so hard and relax." Zane tapped against those nerves, then against the plug. "I want you to be honest, Poppet."

"Ah, but Zane that's what you have to earn."

He heard Zane's soft laughter. "I know that, Daniel. That's why I'm different from the rest. I know." His ass was cupped again, the plug base gripped and his hole slicked again so that Zane could slide it in and out of him.

He moaned, fingers trying to wrap around Zane's hand, needing something to hold onto. "I like the real thing better because it's alive, hot, personal," he whimpered, giving Zane a little piece of himself.

Zane gave him fingers, those big ones twining with his own, holding on. "Thank you, Daniel."

Then the plug slid free, three thick fingers taking its place.

He cried out, holding on tight to Zane's fingers, glorying in the warmth that filled him.

"Oh, Poppet, you are so fine." Another finger joined the three, spreading him wide.

Oh, Zane's hands were large, just like that prick and he moaned loudly, spreading his legs as best he was able.

"Yes, Daniel. Yes. Your pleasure sounds sweet."

"More, Zane. Please." He shook, unable to do more in the position he was in except take what Zane chose to give him.

"Let me get more lube, Poppet. I won't tear you."

He whimpered, clutching at Zane's fingers. "Please." His fingers were released, then more cool slickness hit his hole, easing the burn. Then Zane was pushing in, so hot.

So big. So fucking insistent. He grabbed onto the cushions, using them as leverage to push back against Zane's invasion.

"Yes. Open for me, Poppet. Let me in deep." The low growl was so intimate, so rich, sliding over his skin as that hand filled him.

He bore down, one cry after another torn from his throat as Zane filled him.

Zane pushed inside, his body snapping around Zane's wrist, that hand burning inside him like coal. He closed his eyes, face pressed into the cushions, hands opening and closing. One whimper after another left him, building into a keening cry.

"That's it, Poppet. Let it out. Nothing left but you and me."

His cry build into a scream, the silence left behind loud. He was quiet and full, at peace.

Zane stroked his spine, rubbed the back of his neck, easing him. So still, so sure. Inside him. Deep.

He purred, the pleasure heavy on his skin, in him.

The fingers inside him moved slowly, rubbing his gland, drawing up his pleasure slowly. The quiet slowly grew noise again, whimpers and moans and soft, keening sounds that came from deep inside him.

He lay there, Zane's hand deep inside him, the man controlling every part of his pleasure, his need.

"I'm going to make you come again, Poppet, and then we can go soak in the tub. Relax. Together."

"You'll hold me?" he asked, need making his voice low, husky.

"Yes. Yes, Poppet." Zane sounded happy, growling low, fingers nudging his gland.

He moaned again, body beginning to ripple around Zane's hand. The pressure inside him started moving, the fist sliding deep and moving faster and faster. Sounds were pushed from him, along with pleasure, wave after wave of it.

"I want you to come, Poppet. One more time. Come with my hand inside you."

With no more than a soft sigh he obeyed, the pleasure overwhelming, making everything else fade away.

He barely felt the ache when Zane's fingers slid away, just noted the soft cloth cleaning him up. "Come on, Poppet. Let's go soak in the tub."

Daniel would have agreed but he had no voice left, nothing left to give.

Zane slid from beneath him, stripping down, then gathered him up into warm arms. He was carried down a hall into a warm bathroom and down into a hot tub. He curled into Zane, hands sliding randomly over strong muscles.

"Can I kiss you?"

Oh, God, yes. He raised his head, looking up into dark eyes as his mouth opened.

Zane's kiss was slow and deep and sweet and hot. So hot. And those eyes never once looked away from his.

When the kiss was over he sank back against Zane, utterly undone. Zane reached over and turned on the bubbles, holding him close, keeping him warm and safe and near as he floated. He had a feeling he wasn't going to have much of a chance to be bored anymore.

Daniel Earns His First Punishment

Zane woke up slowly, blinking as he tried to figure out why he was so warm and so blinky and so... Snuggled against.

Oh. Oh, right.

Daniel.

Pretty Poppet.

He ran one hand down Daniel's spine, enjoying the peace and silence. Daniel stretched beneath his touch like a cat, curling harder against him. Such a sensual thing. So hungry for contact, for touch. He petted and held, hands learning his Poppet's form.

Daniel rubbed against him, cock full and hot against his side.

Oh, someone woke hungry. He cupped Daniel's balls, stroking the velvet soft skin. That earned him a purr, Daniel's leg sliding overtop of his. Zane nuzzled Daniel's throat, breathing in the rich, sweet scent. The lovely green eyes slowly blinked open, sleep and hunger twined together in them.

"Good morning, Poppet." He leaned in and licked Daniel's lips, keeping the contact light.

Daniel kept rubbing against him. "What's that mean - Poppet?"

"Some places it means doll. Where I grew up, it meant dear." His first lover had called him that, years ago and the phrase meant lover and pleasure to him.

"I'm no doll," Daniel told him, moving slowly but surely against him.

"No. No, not at all." Zane chuckled. "Dolls are nowhere as interesting as you."

"As long as we're on the same page," murmured Daniel, fingers starting to slide over his skin, starting at his breastbone and slowly working down.

"I think we are, Daniel." He took a kiss, making this more about love-making, about two people touching each other, than about games and control. Daniel opened to him, met him in the kiss, tongue sliding along his as those teasing fingers continued to slide down toward his cock. His fingers tangled in Daniel's hair, tilting his Poppet's head back.

Sweet moans filled his mouth as Daniel's hand wrapped around his prick. He pushed into the touch, his prick hard and hungry, heavy with wanting. Daniel whimpered and began to stroke him, from root to tip.

"Mmm... feels fine. Your hands." He gasped, shivering.

Daniel didn't say anything at all, just rubbed harder against him, hand moving faster.

He bent his head, licking and sucking at Daniel's shoulder. Oh, shit. Sweet. So good.

"Zane... Hot. You're hot."

His fingers found Daniel's ass, fingers just sliding over the tender ring of muscles, just stroking. "Poppet..."

A shudder moved through Daniel, the hand on his cock tightening. They moaned together, green eyes meeting his own. He stroked again, fingertip slid over the hot ring. Daniel twisted, humping frantically against him, breath coming hot and fast against his skin. Their mouths met, his tongue pressing deep inside those red lips, tasting deep. All it took was one last scratch of his fingernail against Daniel's hole and his Poppet was coming, heat splashing on his skin.

The scent of musk and salt and Daniel filled his nose, making his balls tight. His own orgasm hit like a freight-car, come pumping right into Daniel's hands.

Daniel purred and curled against him, fingers slowly rubbing his own come into his belly, his cock, his balls.

He held Daniel close, keeping his Poppet warm, bringing them down.

"Well you're fucking sexy -- I'll give you that."

"Yes? What else would you give me, Poppet?" Ah, the smell of power games in the morning.

Oh, those green eyes gleamed wickedly at him. "I wouldn't kick you out of bed for eating crackers."

He pinched Daniel's ass. "Oh, you have a wicked tongue, Poppet."

Daniel yelped rubbed his ass. His Poppet looked undaunted though. "How would you know, you haven't had it yet." Daniel stuck his tongue out

He reached out and grabbed that tongue, holding it between two fingers.

Daniel laughed, eyes dancing at him.

He chuckled, sliding his fingers on that tongue. "Mouthy, mouthy."

Daniel couldn't speak, but his shrug spoke for him.

"Be good, Poppet, or I'll put that mouth to work."

"Promise, promise," Daniel muttered around his fingers.

He pulled Daniel's face down to his crotch. "Are you testing me?"

The green eyes turned up to him, Daniel's affirmative reply unmistakable.

Zane shook his head. "If I feel your teeth, Poppet, we'll go visit Mal's playroom. Clear?"

Daniel nodded, hands sliding along his thighs.

"Good." He spread, drawing Daniel's mouth down to his groin. "Clean me up, Poppet."

Daniel's mouth surrounded his prick, taking him almost all the way in without hesitation and then those green eyes looked right up at him as Daniel drew back his lips and slowly and carefully, but surely pulled back up along his cock with nothing but teeth.

He sighed softly and pulled away, sliding out of the

bed and getting into his clothes. He pushed the comm-unit, dialing Mal. "I need a discipline area. I'll be down in a moment."

Then he looked at Daniel. "Do you need to be bound, or can you be trusted to walk?"

Daniel immediately held out his arms wrists together.

Those green eyes watched him.

Zane took Daniel's hands and spun him, lashing the thin arms together palms to elbow. Then balls and cock were bound in leather and steel, Zane fastening a leash on a conveniently placed hook.

Not even a tremor shook the beautiful body, Daniel just watching, testing, pushing.

He found a leather hood in his supplies, solid leather without eyeholes and a zipped closed mouth. He brought it up from behind Daniel, sliding it on and lacing it up along the back without warning.

Daniel's entire body clenched, staying tight for nearly a full minute before slowly relaxing.

When he was sure Daniel was ready, he took hold of the leash and tugged, jostling the heavy balls. They would work out which of them was boss, whether Daniel wanted to or not.

Daniel and the Hood

Daniel walked silently behind Zane.

Well, he hardly had a choice on the silently, he was wearing a hood. He couldn't see, his hearing was muted, and the mouth was closed so he couldn't speak.

The hood went all the way around his head, enclosed him completely.

Daniel hated it. He didn't mind the binding of his arms behind him from his elbows to his wrists. He didn't mind the elaborate contraption around his cock and balls from which he was led on a leash.

But the hood.

He hadn't been prepared for it.

He might even not have been quite so sassy if he'd known it was coming.

Maybe.

He'd panicked when it had gone on and it had taken a long time before he'd calmed enough to breathe and stand normally. He was still on edge, following where he was led with tentative, stiff steps, his usual grace having abandoned him.

He would not panic.

He would not panic.

He would not.

Zane never spoke to him, didn't tug him hard or hurt him, just led him inexorably down the halls and into the lift.

It was like he didn't exist. No one could see him like this. Daniel couldn't even see himself. He could feel them going down, feel it in his stomach. He knew where the discipline rooms were, had heard Zane ask for a private room. Not that it mattered, he couldn't be seen. He moved from tile to carpet to tile again, then he was stopped and he heard Zane murmur softly.

Gloved hands stroked over his skin, impersonally helping him into a sling. His wrists were unbound and retied to the thick straps, his legs splayed and bound.

Then he was left, swaying in the air.

He closed his eyes and started counting his breaths, forcing himself to go slowly. It was that or try to hear through the hood and that was going to make him crazy. He would just pretend he was in bed. Sleeping. Trying to sleep. Whatever. The wait went on and on, the silence deafening, the air chill around him.

Daniel was at 647 when he started to panic, tugging at the bonds that held him, wanting the hood off, now. It was like he was immersed in nothing. He didn't do nothing. He wasn't nothing.

He wasn't.

He wasn't.

He wasn't.

He wasn't.

He wasn't.

Then a hard, solid hand landed on his belly.

Hot. Sure. Real. Touching him. Feeling him.

Zane's hand.

He stilled immediately, taking a sobbing breath and then another.

Zane's hand.

Zane's hand.

Zane's hand.

One hand slid along his spine, the other caressed his stomach, his ribs. "Where are you, Daniel? Are you here with me?"

"Zane."

Hands.

Touching him.

Zane's hands.

"Zane." He said it louder, unsure if he could be heard through the hood.

"Yes, Poppet." The lips of the mask were opened, fingers sliding in to touch his mouth.

A shudder moved through his as he gasped for breath, for fresh air. It was an illusion of course -- the hood had adequate breathing holes, but it felt better, having access.

"I see you fighting me, I see you trying to push me away. I won't let you. Do you hear me, Poppet?"

He heard.

He knew sooner or later Zane would go, it was what people did, but he heard. "Yes, Zane."

"Tell me what you need, Daniel." His body was touched, limbs massaged.

Oh, that was easy. "Hood off."

"Okay, Poppet. Close your eyes." The mask was unlaced and removed, his sweaty face wiped with a soft cloth.

Oh.

Oh, yes.

Tears began to leak from his eyes, his relief a physical sensation.

Zane's hands stroked his face, his shoulders. "I see you, Poppet."

Another shudder went through him. Yes, please. Zane saw him.

One soft kiss, then another, the heat of Zane's body pouring over him, touching him. Soon instead of shudders, it was shivers, pleasure beginning to insinuate itself along his nerves. Zane touched him everywhere. Fingers touching here and there, stroking his skin, his hair.

He floated on the sensations, keeping his eyes closed, focusing on the large, warm hands that moved over him.

"There we are, Poppet. There we are." Zane's voice

whispered over his skin, low and rough. He purred, body rippling. He became aware of his cock, bound in leather and metal, throbbing against its bindings. Zane's hands and voice and his own cock became his whole world. Warm slick fingers pressed into his body, lips brushing over the bare, exposed tip of his cock.

Keening softly, he would have spread his legs wider, rocked between the sensations, but he couldn't, he couldn't move at all.

"Yes, Poppet. Feel. Trust me and we'll fly."

He whimpered softly, wondering if Zane knew what he was asking. Oh, Daniel trusted the people who were members of the club, but he only trusted so far. He could hear in Zane's voice that the man meant entirely, completely. Full and total trust.

"I will not give up, Daniel. I am a patient man and I am here to stay." His cock was taken in a soft, hot mouth, sucked gently, almost too gently, those fingers inside him driving him to madness. He whimpered and keened, shivering from pleasure. He bit his lip to keep from begging for more, to keep from demanding the strange cock glove be removed.

The slit of his cock was licked, then the tip of Zane's tongue touched him there, pressing in. Touching him even there.

Daniel began to babble, unaware if words came from his mouth or just sounds, not caring. His muscles tensed and pulled as he tried to writhe. His cock was freed and then swallowed down to the root. He screamed, coming down Zane's throat.

Zane drank him down and then moved up his body, hot, wet lips whispering in his ear. "I have your flavor inside me now, Poppet."

Oh.

He whimpered softly.

"Would you like to come home with me, Daniel? Have a meal? Relax." His temple was kissed, softly. "No games. Just resting together."

He nodded. "Yes, please."

Zane helped him out of the sling and wrapped him in a soft, heavy robe that smelled sweet. His face was tilted up and he was given a kiss. "Come on, Poppet. Let's go enjoy our day."

"Yes, Zane."

Zane took his hand and led him the way they had come.

He could see, but more importantly, he was seen.

Zane and Daniel

He'd been off-planet for business. It worked out well -- gave Daniel some breathing room, a chance to decide whether or not to accept his offer of another evening together. Another session together.

Zane had known it was going to be intense. Known it, because he'd been watching and waiting and learning what Daniel liked, what Daniel needed. Still, the man's response over the hood had scared him, worried him, and it had only been a few long contacts with Mal that convinced him he'd done the right thing.

He was home now, though. Warm and clean and relaxed in his rooms. Waiting and wondering if he'd hear from his Poppet.

There was a knock at the door, one of the wait staff's voices calling out. "Your evening meal, Sir."

He arched an eyebrow and went to the door; he hadn't ordered his meal yet.

When he met pretty green eyes, he smiled. "Poppet. Good evening."

Daniel smiled back, the look eager and warm and honest, though the coquette came out when his Poppet spoke. "I ordered food. So that we could eat together. You aren't busy are you?"

"No. Not at all. I just got back in this afternoon. Come in." He offered Daniel a warm, genuine smile. He'd come to truly enjoy Daniel's company in the evening they'd spent playing and relaxing and learning each other outside the game.

Daniel's hand was warm on his arm, his Poppet walking with a lazy sensuality he'd come to expect. "You've been away a very long time," Daniel complained with a soft pout.

"Yes. The atmosphere on Veron IV is nowhere as

pleasant as here, either." The waitstaff set the food out with a quiet professionalism and left them to settle on the sofa.

"I ordered all my favorites," Daniel told him, one hand reaching to the table and gracefully snagging a piece of fruit. Papaya by the looks of it, cut into long, slender slices. Daniel put it in his mouth and slowly went down on the piece of fruit, eyes watching him.

"You are a flirt, Poppet." He chuckled and caught a drop of juice from the full lips on his finger. Licking it clean, he grinned and winked. "One day I'll have that mouth on my cock."

"It's worth waiting for, I promise you."

"Yes. And when you've earned the right to suck my cock, you'll feel the same way." He took a piece of pineapple and ate it. Spoiled little tease.

Daniel's eyes went wide, but he recovered quickly, shrugging nonchalantly. "It's a nice-sized prick."

"Your ass sure thought so."

Daniel laughed, eyes twinkling. "It did indeed. It would like to think so again."

He laughed in return, drawing Daniel in for a kiss. Daniel purred, slender body pressing against him. Zane ran his hands along Daniel's back, fingers finding nerves they'd discovered earlier. His touches made Daniel writhe and the slender fingers clutched at his shoulders for a moment before beginning to explore, pushing beneath his shirt for skin.

"Greedy Poppet." He leaned Daniel back, nipping at the soft, parted lips.

Daniel arched sensuously and put his arms up over his head. "I'll wait until you tell me what to do then."

He shook his head and reached down, finding the restraints and sliding them over Daniel's wrists. He didn't fasten them though, in fact he left them almost dangling open. “Don’t let them fall off, Poppet, or I won’t fuck your ass when I’m done playing.”

“They won’t fall off,” Daniel told him with a purr.

“You make sure of it.” Then he began exploring -- tickling and nuzzling, working Daniel’s skin with teeth and nails and fingers.

Sweet gasps and soft moans began to fill the air, Daniel writhing for him, arms still enough the restraints didn’t move at all.

He slowly worked Daniel’s pants off, lips and hands beginning to tease balls and cock and hole, occasionally traveling to pinch a nipple or trace the curve of Daniel’s lips. As soon as his pants were removed, Daniel’s legs spread for him, one foot on the floor, the other over the back of the couch. He took one of Daniel’s ankles in hand, fingers trailing over the sole and ball of the foot. Stubborn, beautiful man.

Daniel cried out, foot jerking, hands catching the restraints and keeping them in place.

“Careful. You’d hate to drop those.” He gave Daniel a grin and a wink, then repeated the action.

Daniel shuddered and shook. “I would.”

He met Daniel’s eyes, serious and sure. “I would, too.”

A small whimper sounded, passion and need, honest and true, flaring in Daniel’s eyes. He rewarded that honesty with a long, deep kiss, holding Daniel’s eyes with his own. Daniel pushed up against him, mouth opening wide to him. Zane poured himself into the kiss, wanting Daniel to feel his passion, his heat.

Sweet moans filled the kiss, Daniel responding beautifully to his passion. He slid his hand beneath Daniel’s back, stroking the long spine, cupping that pretty ass. Daniel’s legs came around his waist, pulling him close as that sweet body pressed into his hands.

Zane rubbed against Daniel, knowing the slight scrape of his clothes on bare skin would be maddening. Daniel's whimpers grew noisy, the slender body writhing beneath him.

"What do you need, Poppet?" The question was growing more and more familiar.

"Tie me properly. Blindfold me. Fuck me. Hard." The answer was simple truth this time, unadorned by sass or humor, just plain need.

"Come to my playroom." He stood up, held out his hand. There he could bind Daniel and send him flying.

Daniel took his hand, eyes dark, a fine sweat sheening the sweet body.

He led Daniel to the only room they hadn't played in yet, a simple room with a massage table and a low bed. Zane moved over to a cabinet and pulled out a leather blindfold. "On the table, Poppet."

"Front or back, Sir?"

It was the first time Daniel had used the honorific with him.

"On your back, Poppet." He rewarded Daniel with a soft caress of the flat belly, heat blazing inside him.

Daniel purred at the touch and then climbed onto the table, lying still with his hands by his sides, looking up at the ceiling. Zane leaned over and kisses each eye closed, then tied the blindfold on. "Do you need your cock bound, Poppet?"

"As you wish, Sir."

"I wish you to control your need, Poppet, and come on my request." He found the thick thigh straps, slowly and carefully wrapping Daniel's legs and drawing them up and back, spreading his Poppet wide.

Daniel licked his lips, hands opening and closing. He knew the choice his Poppet was making was between giving up total control and losing himself in the pleasure or proving himself.

"I... bind my cock, please. I'm sorry."

He brushed his thumb across Daniel's bottom lip. "For your honesty, Poppet? Never be sorry."

Then he found a soft, buttery leather sheath, carefully binding Daniel, controlling that need.

"Thank you, Sir."

Daniel's hands relaxed, his Poppet's breath evening out as Daniel centered himself. He carefully bound Daniel's wrists, then began the pleasurable job of touching and stroking Daniel's skin, sensitizing it to his touch.

Sweet moans and soft gasps escaped Daniel, shivers of pleasure running through the lean frame. He dipped his fingers in heated oil, letting it drip over Daniel's cock and balls, letting it slide to cover the tight hole waiting for him. Daniel purred, shifting the minute amount he could.

He gently squeezed the tip of Daniel's prick, opening the tiny slit, letting the oil drip inside. A soft, keening noise filled the air.

"Oh, yes, Poppet. Feel for me." He stroked over the slit with one finger. "One day I'll fill you here, fill you everywhere."

Daniel jerked, gasped, body pulling against the bonds toward his touch.

"Yes." He stroked again, pressing, letting the touch burn.

A shudder went through Daniel, his Poppet's breath coming quickly, noisily.

"Today, though. Today, you get what you need." He slicked his thumbs, pressing them suddenly into Daniel's ass.

Daniel shouted out, body rippling around his thumbs. He gave Daniel only a heartbeat to catch his breath, then started moving his hands, spreading Daniel.

Daniel's moan sounded pushed out of him, the slender body twisting. "Yes, Zane. Please. Oh. Please."

Removing his thumbs, he pulled his prick from his slacks. Then Zane dropped the bottom of the table away so he could step up, bringing his hard cock to Daniel's hole.

Daniel's hole winked open and closed, his Poppet's body straining toward him. He stroked the tip of Daniel's prick one more time before slamming into his Poppet, filling him deep. Daniel screamed, the sound filling the room.

"Again. Oh, Zane. Again."

"Yes, Poppet." He growled, pulling out and slamming back in again, burying himself to the root.

Daniel screamed again, body grasping at his prick, holding him tight. "Again," whispered Daniel. "Please, Zane, again."

Zane leaned down and dropped a soft kiss on Daniel's breastbone. "Yes. Until you fly."

Then he started fucking Daniel with hard, bone-shaking thrusts. Daniel screamed and shouted and rode his cock with such pleasure. Eventually, his Poppet grew hoarse, full body shudders shaking the slender body.

He eased open the sheath holding his Poppet's prick, fingers so careful. "Now, Poppet. Come. Come for me and let me feel you."

It was a sob rather than a scream, his Poppet's body tightening around his cock as heat sprayed from Daniel's freed prick.

"Yes." He moaned low, taking his own pleasure, driving into the tight heat again and again until he shot, filling Daniel with heat.

Daniel was babbling, head moving from side to side, nonsense sliding from the red lips. His Poppet's body was limp, relaxed. He rested his forehead against Daniel's chest, breathing slowly, coming back to himself.

"Zane." The soft murmur was a caress.

"Yes, Poppet." He slowly stroked Daniel's thigh.

Daniel purred softly. Zane held Daniel, slowly unfastening the bond, stretching muscles, touching. When Daniel was relaxed, he stripped and then carried them both to the tub for a warm soak.

Daniel was quiet, relaxed against him, soaking up his heat and his peace. If he could help it, Daniel would never shiver and whimper after a scene again.

Daniel Explores Zane's Rooms

Daniel woke up warm and snuggled against a solid, hot body.

Oh, yes, Zane.

It was only the second time he had woken with the man, but he already knew that he liked it, he liked it a lot.

He also had to piss, so he snuck out of bed and headed for the lavatory, taking care of business, brushing his fingers through his hair and giving his teeth a quick finger brush as well before wandering back to Zane's bedroom.

The man was still asleep, so he decided to explore, to look at the place and see what all there was. Without the extremely distracting presence of Zane to keep him from noticing anything but the long, pretty muscles and the fascinating bald head.

The rooms were all decorated simply, the lines and colors and textures very rich, very clean, very male, but not at all sterile. The art was rustic -- different masks and fetishes and such from more places than he could name. There were three real books in the case in the front room, a hawk's wing seeming to hover over them.

The playroom was more simple -- he found the damnable hood, the blindfold. He found a ton of different bindings and plugs. Sounds, clamps, a glove covered in tiny spikes. Oddly enough, he didn't find a single crop or flogger. No whips. No paddles.

And he looked for them, opening every cupboard and searching every nook and cranny.

Interesting.

"Looking for something particular, Poppet?" Zane's voice was low, deep, almost amused.

He jumped up and whirled. Damn, the man was quiet. Especially for someone so big.

"You don't have anything for hitting. I couldn't believe you didn't have even one paddle. So yeah, I was looking." He tossed his hair off his face, and looked defiantly at Zane. After all, the man had never said he couldn't look through Zane's things.

"No, I don't need one." He got a smile, warm and happy and terribly disconcerting. "Good morning, Poppet. Did you sleep well?"

He blinked, a slight shiver going through him. "Yes, I did. You're good to sleep with. Warm. And you let me snuggle." It was amazing how many tops weren't interested in showing a soft side, in letting themselves being exposed in sleep.

"You feel good in my bed." Zane leaned against the wall, stretching slowly. "What are your plans today, Daniel?"

He purred, moving slowly toward Zane, eyes traveling the length of the naked body. "You tell me, Zane."

Zane's arms opened and pulled him into that heat. "As you wish, Poppet. First we're going to share a good morning kiss. Then? I'm going to fuck that pretty little hole of yours until you scream. Next, I'll plug you well, so that you keep my come inside you. Then we can get dressed and go to brunch. Then, a nice long swim."

He shivered. "Okay." His voice was breathless, face tilting for the good morning kiss.

"Excellent. Good morning, Poppet." His mouth was taken in a sure, hard kiss, those huge hands holding him close. He moaned into Zane's mouth, arms wrapping around Zane's neck. Oh, he did enjoy a good, solid man who knew what he was doing.

Zane didn't hold a damned thing back either, just took his mouth with a fierce intensity, stealing breath and sense. He pressed hard against Zane, opening as wide as he could. Zane demanded everything from him and he wanted to give it. Most of the time.

Walking them to the low mattress, Zane slowly eased him down, settling between his legs. He wrapped his legs around Zane's waist, heels digging into the firm ass. Oh, Zane was lovely and solid and big and hot and saw him. Saw him.

That big body rocked against him, huge, hard cock sliding against his belly, making promises. He met the movements, moaning happily.

"Mm... Poppet. I want to fuck that sweet hole of yours." Lube was pressed into his hand. "Get me slick."

"Yes, Sir," he purred, opening the tube and spurting out a lot of lube into his hand. He pressed between them, moaning and bucking as his hand wrapped around Zane's huge cock.

Oh, fuck him blind.

Zane gave him only a few seconds to touch, then his legs were pushed up and back, that cock splitting him wide. He gasped, tilting his hips, taking everything Zane gave him.

The thrusts were hard and deep, sending him flying, making his bones rattle. "So tight, Poppet."

"For...oh gods... for you." He held onto the solid shoulders and rode the amazing sensations.

"Yes, Daniel. Yes." His mouth was taken in a hard kiss, Zane's tongue pressing in deep. Oh, yes, it felt so good, Zane's tongue and cock invading him, fucking him, taking him. The pressure and heat grew and grew until Zane lifted his head. "Come on my cock, Poppet. Show me your need."

"Zane!" He shouted his lover's name, ass squeezing the huge cock as he came hard.

"Yes. Yes, Daniel!" Zane's bald head was thrown back, those hips pistoning as heat filled him. He moaned, hands and feet clinging, body holding Zane tightly inside him.

Zane petted him, stroking his skin, taking slow, easy kisses. "Morning."

"Mmm... morning." He purred, arching into Zane's touches. Oh, he felt good. Alive. Zane's hands keeping his skin sensitized.

Zane reached beside the mattress, bringing up a thick plug, eyes twinkling. "For you, Poppet. Then we can go eat and play, yes?"

He licked his lips, wriggling on Zane's cock. "I'm going to feel that even when absolutely still." How fun!

"Yes, and I'll know." That fat cock slid away, the plug pushing in its place.

His eyes rolled up as his body rippled around the plug. Oh, Zane had the wickedest ideas, said the naughtiest things. Zane seated it well, twisting it inside him. He whimpered, hands opening and closing on Zane's shoulders.

"Beautiful Poppet." A kiss dropped on his lips, his nipple, the tip of his cock. "Shall we go dine?"

"Yes, Sir."

Oh, yes, Sir.

He purred.

That earned him a smile and a warm hand helping him upright, sliding down his spine and cupping his ass, jostling the plug. He gasped. "Oh, you're going to do that a lot aren't you?"

"Oh, yes, Poppet. Again and again and again." Each again was punctuated by a jiggle. He gasped each time and then purred, pushing his ass back into Zane's hand.

Zane lapped at his lips, then stepped back. "Come, Poppet. Let's find some clothes."

"Yes, Sir." He peeked up at Zane from beneath his lashes, smiling. Oh, it was going to be a wonderful day.

Daniel and Zane Go Swimming

Brunch had been delicious, the long walk after perfect and lazy and sensual, Daniel's hips rolling with that heavy plug jostling inside. Zane had taken kisses on the balcony overlooking the river, jostled the plug as often as possible, loving the happy little moans and gasps he got in return.

Then they got into the one of the private pools.

Now this? Swimming and chasing and floating with his Poppet? This was fun.

Daniel was currently lying over a floating board, legs relaxed and slightly spread in the water. Those pretty eyes were heavy lidded, dark, gazing at him whenever he floated into view.

He floated over, hands sliding up Daniel's legs. "So pretty."

Daniel purred. "I know. But it's lovely to hear. Especially from you."

He nuzzled Daniel's inner thigh, wanting to make his Poppet moan. "I'll remember that."

Daniel's breath hitched. "Oh. Zane... so sensitive there now."

"Are you? The skin there is so soft, just barely flushed." He nuzzled again. "It needs my mark."

Daniel moaned softly, legs spreading wider for him.

"Yes, Poppet. Right there." He set his lips to the soft skin, pulling the blood up to the surface. Soft whimpers met his ministrations, Daniel's hands splashing. The boy's legs remained still though. His hands slipped up, jostling the base of the plug.

Daniel cried out, jerking. "Oh, Zane... Zane."

"Yes, Poppet?" He licked up, tongue pressing against the soft skin behind Daniel's balls.

That noise was definitely a strangled scream. Oh, he

liked that. He licked again and again. "You know, I think I could see a ring right here." He pinched Daniel's skin lightly.

Daniel's whole body jerked and then a shiver rippled through his sweet boy. "Oh... " Daniel whimpered.

"Oh, yes. A pretty little ring with a 'Z' etched in. One that I can take in my teeth and tug." He pinched again, harder.

Daniel screamed, full out this time, body jerking hard. "Zane!"

"Yes, Poppet." His finger circled the base of the plug. "Yes." He was purring, hard, so happy and addicted to the man in his hands.

Whimpers echoed off the water, doubling the noises Daniel made. "Please, Zane. Please."

"Yes, Poppet. Tell me what you need." He pulled the plug out, moving slowly, watching the tight ring stretch.

Groaning, Daniel shook and it was another scream that bounced off the walls as the plug left his body entirely. "You. Please, Zane."

"Yes." He found the raised step on the edge of the pool, pulling Daniel down to ride his cock, pushing in deep. Slamming in.

Daniel screamed again, body squeezing his cock hard. "Again!"

His muscles clenched, hands hard on Daniel's hips as he pulled out and then slammed deep. Daniel's hands scrabbled at his arms, holding tight once they were found, the sweet back bowed in front of him.

Zane turned all his focus on simply fucking -- fast, hard, deep, determined to give Daniel all he had. Daniel's screams faded to breathless gasps, the grip on his arms growing harder and harder, the muscles squeezing around his cock rippling over and over again.

Then Daniel shook and Zane could smell the sharp

scent of come, even as his name was uttered in a broken whisper.

"Oh, yes. So fine, Poppet." He arched, fucking harder, searching for his own completion.

Daniel rippled around his cock a few more times and then his Poppet bore down hard, squeezing him tight, all but demanding his orgasm.

"Daniel!" He dropped his mouth to Daniel's shoulder, biting down as he shot, filling Daniel with his heat.

More sweet whimpers were thrown around the room, Daniel collapsing back against him. Zane held Daniel close, keeping his Poppet warm and near as the aftershocks faded. Daniel began to hum and murmur, nuzzling and rubbing against him like a great big, lazy cat. He purred, hands stroking over Daniel's belly, petting, lips nuzzling over the curve of Daniel's shoulder.

"Mmm... you're something else, Zane."

"You're very special yourself, Poppet."

Daniel purred and wiggled. "Thank you, darling."

He carefully turned Daniel around, smiling into those beautiful eyes. "Thank you."

Zane took a long, sweet kiss, their limbs tangling as they floated.

Daniel and Zane Have a Conversation

Daniel and Zane left the pool to have a light supper together in Zane's rooms. The food was impeccable, as always, and Zane's choices suited him well. It made Daniel hum and vibrate, to think that Zane had been watching him, learning him.

Well, having that plug inside him all day and then getting fucked raw didn't hurt either.

Now his hungers were satiated and he felt loose and easy in his skin and he wanted to go dance. To put on his most outrageous outfit and go boogie. Preferably with a hot stud at his side. Well, not just any hot stud -- Zane. He turned to Zane, rubbing lightly. "Take me dancing, lover."

Zane chuckled, hand stroking down his spine. "Mmm... I think I would enjoy that. Dancing with you, even if you are a sweet, demanding Poppet."

He raised an eyebrow, even as his body rippled from the touch. "I could have just left you to your own devices and gone."

"That is always your choice, Daniel." The warm fingers didn't falter, simply kept touching him.

"Yes, it is," he snapped, unaccountably upset with Zane's easy acceptance of the thought of being on his own for the evening.

One of Zane's eyebrows rose up. "Is there something you'd like to discuss, Poppet?"

"Like what?" he asked tartly.

"Like what's made you so angry." Zane's hand traced his jaw.

"I'm not angry." And he wasn't, not angry. Maybe... hurt.

"Then what are you? Pissed? Hurt? Mad? Frustrated?" Zane's eyes were warm, sure, watching him closely.

He turned away from those all-seeing eyes, sniffing. "Well..." He traced a knot in the wood of the coffee table. "If you must know, I'm hurt."

"I think I must know, Daniel." Gentle fingers turned his chin. "What hurts?"

He peeked up at Zane. "My heart, Zane."

"Why, Poppet?" One large hand stroked his chest, petting.

"You don't care if I go out without you. You don't care what I do." He sniffed again. He wouldn't cry. It hadn't been long enough to truly get entangled, no it hadn't. He'd go find Mal and let the man whip the memory of Zane right out of him.

He'd just thought Zane was different.

Special.

"Daniel." Zane waited until he looked up. "Do not misunderstand me. I would be deeply hurt if you chose to go out without me. I want nothing else than your trust, your heart, but I will only take it if you wish to give it to me. It is your choice to be with me, it is always your choice. I can only hope you choose to stay."

"You seemed so casual." Part accusation, part question, he looked Zane right in the eyes.

"Do you believe you are the only one who defends their heart, Poppet? The only one who wants this thing between us to grow?"

He laughed. "Oh, Zane look at you. So self-assured and confident and handsome. You could have any man you choose, do anything you want to him."

How could Zane even compare them?

"I choose you, Daniel. I have wanted you from the moment I saw you." Zane's voice was deadly serious.

"I know I'm a sweet little thing, Zane. Everyone wants a piece."

"I don't want a piece, Daniel. I want everything. I want

you to wear my mark, to wear my collar. I would sign a commitment agreement with you right now, if you would agree to it."

Oh, wasn't that a lovely thought. "It's all right, Zane, you don't have to make promises. I'll be good until you're ready to move on. Live in the moment, right?"

"Move on?" Zane chuckled and shook his head. "I trained for almost a year before I approached you, Poppet. I know my own heart. You'll have to try very hard to be rid of me and one day, you will agree to be mine and allow me to be yours."

He blinked back sudden tears and turned, staring sightlessly at the wall. "I want to believe that that is how your heart truly feels, Zane."

There had been too many, though, who had come and promised to stay and then gone again. The first blush always wore off.

"You will believe and I will be here. Until then, Poppet, I promise to trust you enough to bluster and growl when you dare suggest you will dance with another." He was gathered in warm arms and held. "And you will not hurt alone anymore than you will come down from a scene alone. This, we can do together."

He clung to Zane, nuzzling into the warm body and daring to believe for the moment that this would last.

Zane's hands cradled him and that strong heart beat for him, a sweet cadence under his ear.

Maybe he didn't feel like dancing after all. Maybe he wanted to stay right where he was as long as he could.

He thought maybe, maybe Zane would let him.

Zane Invites Daniel Along

They spent days sleeping and playing and eating -- slowly building trust between them. The playroom was used some, but most of their play was casual, easy -- in the pool, in the bed, in the kitchen. It had been luscious, delicious. He had learned that Daniel's sense of humor was wicked, that the man was remarkably fragile in many ways, that his Poppet needed attention and care.

Now he had to return to his job and responsibilities, much as he wished to stay and play for another whole season.

He looked down at Daniel, who was resting lazy in his arms. "I must return to my work, tomorrow, Poppet. I will be gone five days. I have reset the palmlocks for you, should you wish to stay here." He'd not even seen Daniel's rooms

"What? Gone? Five whole days?" Daniel sat up and away from him, hurt sharp on the lovely face. "No. No, you cannot."

"I must. I must work, Daniel." He took Daniel's hand, hating the pain on that lovely face. "However, if you wish, you may come with me. It will be dull, during the days, but we will have the evenings to explore, to play."

"Well I can always use more beauty sleep." Daniel leaned in and looked hard at him. "Can I really come with you? You would bring me along?"

He met Daniel's eyes, letting his confidence show. Trust me, Poppet. I will not abandon you. "I would. You can. I will book passage for you while you pack a bag."

Daniel clapped his hands, hurt giving way to excitement. "A trip! How exciting!"

"You'll need to bring something warm. We're going to the ice floes on Columb XII." He leaned close, tweaking one pretty little nipple. "I don't intend to have any of my Poppet frozen off." In fact, he quite intended to have the most relaxing, peaceful business trip of his life, knowing his Poppet was plugged and waiting for him.

Daniel gasped softly, pushing against him. "They do keep the rooms warm, don't they? Completely covered isn't my best look."

"I'll make sure they're warm, but I want to show you the floes, Poppet. They sparkle and glitter in the starlight." He tweaked again, purring as the flesh tightened for him. "Oh, Poppet. You tempt me to have a ring embedded there, just for my fingers to tug."

Daniel gasped again, eyes going wide. "I've never been decorated before."

"No? Good." He let his growl out, let Daniel hear his want. "I'd like to see that, pretty little rings in your nipples keeping them hard, a ring here." He stroked behind Daniel's balls, the spot he'd found when they'd first swum together.

Daniel's eyes got wider and he moaned, head dropping back

"Mmm... so wanton, Poppet." He leaned in, nipping Daniel's throat, nails scraping the sensitive flesh.

Daniel cried out, legs spreading for him. "Zane!"

"Yes, Daniel?" He smiled, fingers sliding back to circle Daniel's hole

"Oh, Zane. You make me want."

"Good. You make me need, Poppet. Make me hard." He pressed one finger into Daniel's body, easing it in.

A sweet moan was pushed from Daniel as his finger slid in. "Such a beautiful big cock you have, Zane. I love it when you fuck me."

"Mmm... You have a sweet tight hole, Poppet. So responsive. So hot." He took a kiss, purring into Daniel's lips.

Daniel writhed for him, pushing back against his finger, sweet whimpers filling his mouth.

His own cock was aching, full. "I haven't had your mouth yet, Poppet. I want you to suck me and then I'll give you what you need."

"Oh." A shudder went through Daniel and then his Poppet's eyes turned up to him. "Blindfold me, Zane? I want to taste and hear you without any distractions."

He nodded, pleased deep inside. "Come to the playroom, Poppet. It has all we need."

Daniel nodded, standing, as eager as the prick that was already full and reaching up to lie against Daniel's belly.

Zane stood too, hand sliding into Daniel's as they moved through the rooms. "Get the blindfold, Poppet, and I'll meet you on the mattress." He turned down the lights and turned up the temperature, making the room comfortable and intimate. Daniel moved eagerly, going to the drawer where the blindfolds were kept and coming back with the silk-lined leather one.

He took the blindfold and kissed it, then kissed Daniel's eyes before covering them. He brought Daniel's hands to his body. "Undress me, Poppet."

"Yes, Sir." murmured Daniel, hands sliding up his chest to the top button of his shirt. The slender fingers slowly worked each button open.

His own hands were busy, sliding over Daniel's hair, down the flat belly, petting gently. Daniel's nostrils flared as his shirt was opened, his Poppet breathing in deeply, moaning softly. Stepping close, Daniel pushed the shirt off his shoulders

"Tell me what you feel, Poppet. I want to know all of you."

"Heat. You're so hot, your skin is like a fire that I want to burn me. And smooth." Daniel moaned softly, fingers trailing down his belly.

His muscles rippled and he leaned toward Daniel's touch

"Oh. I can feel you feeling me."

"Your hands make me hard, Poppet. My fine lover." He purred, nuzzling Daniel's temple.

Daniel's head tilted up toward him, a soft noise sounding. The sweet hands teased around his waistband and then began to work the buttons of his pants open.

He took a long, slow kiss, tongue sliding deep into Daniel's mouth. Daniel opened to him like a flower turning to the light, silently begging his kiss, his touch. He put all he was into that kiss, arms wrapping around his Poppet and holding tight. Daniel's fingers were trembling as they undid the last of his buttons.

His cock throbbed and he sank to the mattress, bringing Daniel with him into the soft warmth. Daniel followed easily, trusting that he wouldn't let his Poppet fall. They ended up cuddled together, lips clinging, hands exploring and stroking. He slowly drew Daniel's hand to his cock. "I want your mouth, Poppet."

"Oh, oh yes." Daniel wriggled down, sliding against him all the way. Then his Poppet used those warm fingers to feed his prick into Daniel's waiting mouth.

There wasn't a hint of teeth this time, only lips and tongue and eagerness

"Oh... Oh, Poppet..." He arched and cried out, toes curling as he sank in deep.

Daniel took him right in, swallowing around the tip of his cock, moaning around him. It was heaven, hot and tight and fine and he groaned, letting Daniel hear how much he needed. That made Daniel suck harder, head bobbing slowly, lips and tongue exploring. His hips rocked steadily, pushing up, cock dragging on Daniel's tongue.

Long fingers slid between his legs, stroking his balls

"Close, Poppet..." He warned, balls drawing up, cock throbbing. Daniel sucked even harder, head bobbing enthusiastically.

He jerked as he shot, hips pumping furiously, pleasure shooting down his spine. Daniel cried out around his cock, sending vibrations to chase the pleasure. "Oh, Poppet..." He melted back into the cushions, moaning low.

Daniel's fingers continued to explore him, the blindfolded face turned up to him, looking like the cat that got the cream.

Zane chuckled and drew Daniel up, licking those pretty lips. "How do I taste, Poppet?"

"Mmm, like the best thing ever, Zane."

"Oh, nice answer, Poppet." He rolled his Poppet, kissing hard, drawing the long, thin arms up over Daniel's head.

Daniel purred, stretching. "Oh, Zane..."

"Yes, Daniel. Keep your hands up for me. You made me feel so good, Poppet." He licked his way to Daniel's nipples, taking one in between his teeth and rolling it.

Daniel cried out, breath shaky. "Yes, Sir."

He purred, hands sliding down to spread Daniel, teeth teasing the hard nipples. So fine, his Poppet. Daniel bucked up into his mouth, legs spreading at his touch, offering him everything.

Zane licked his way down Daniel's belly, avoiding the long, needy cock and mouthing the sweet soft balls instead, thumbs spreading Daniel wide. Sweet, sweet sounds poured down on him, Daniel moving like a sylph.

He reached for the lube, slicking his thumbs as he licked, then pressed deep, pushing into his Poppet's body

"Zane! Oh..." Daniel's body rippled around his thumbs

"Yes, Daniel." He licked the sensitive skin behind Daniel's sacs, spreading the tight hole

"Zane. Zane." Daniel repeated his name in soft, breathless gasps, over and over.

He nodded, blowing against Daniel's skin, tongue lapping at the spread hole. Oh, that was a sweet noise, a strangled cry

"Mmm... Yes, Poppet. Feel me. Feel me." He licked again, thumbs moving harder, deeper

"I do." Daniel's body rippled around his thumbs

"I'm inside you." He nipped the place where he was going to get Daniel pierced.

Daniel jerked, gasped. "Inside me."

"Yes, love. Inside you." He was hard again, cock thick and heavy between his legs. Zane pushed up, covering Daniel with his body, pushing his prick deep. "Inside you."

Daniel cried out, hands fisting above his head.

Pushing hard, deep, Zane slammed into Daniel with all he was, fucking the tight hole desperately. Keening, Daniel legs wrapped around his waist, holding him tight.

He leaned down, kissing hard, slamming Daniel with all he was. "Poppet!"

"Zane! Oh! Yes!" Daniel moved with him, meeting each thrust, body rippling beneath him, arms still above his head

"Come for me. Now, Daniel. Now." He was close, needing, aching.

Daniel cried out, the sound loud in their quiet rooms. The hot body squeezed tight around his cock as Daniel came, heat splashing between them. Zane let Daniel's need carry him over, let the motion and heat draw his pleasure out so that he filled his Poppet with seed

"Oh, I can feel you! Inside me. So deep."

He nodded, moaning low. "Yes, Daniel. Inside you. Always."

Daniel's body rippled around his cock again, his Poppet stretching, hands open and loose above his head. "Mmm..."

He echoed the sound, nuzzling Daniel's neck, staying close, staying warm. "We can't fall asleep, Poppet. You need to pack for our trip."

"May I hold you?" Daniel asked him

"I would like that. Very much." His heart was pounding. So happy.

Daniel's arms came down, sliding around him. Zane purred, cuddling in, rubbing against his lover, his Daniel

"You're really taking me with you, aren't you?" The words were soft

"I am really taking you with me, Daniel. We are going to see the ice floes and you are going to be with me every night." He could hear the truth in his own words

"Thank you, Zane." Daniel's hand slid over his head and down his neck to his back and then his Poppet snuggled in

"My pleasure, love." He relaxed in, breathing in Daniel's scent. They could pack in the morning.

Daniel Experiences Interplanetary Travel

Daniel had never been out of the city, let alone off planet.

It was exciting and scary and he was clinging quite hard to Zane's hand with both of his, just trying to catch his breath. He might even have been bouncing slightly. It was cold aboard the transport, but Zane had bought him a lovely fauxfur coat and only his toes and his nose were very cold.

Zane leaned over and kissed him. "Are you well, Poppet? Comfortable?"

He nodded. "It's very cold." He smiled up at his bald lover. "But exciting! I've never been so far away from home before."

"Well, I travel often. There are many places I would show you." Zane drew him close, draping a blanket over their legs.

He snuggled in close. "Tell me about where we're going today."

"Columb XII is cold, covered in ice. My Corp mines the rose star gems that the seers use -- the focus stones?" Zane smiled at him. "I have to check the mine books and deal with a labor dispute. We'll be staying in a beautiful place -- the Palace. You'll be warm enough there."

"You'll keep me warm." He nodded as he said it, faith in Zane's ability to do that complete.

Zane's hand slid over his thigh. "I will, Poppet."

Daniel took a nice long look from Zane's head down his leather coat clad body, to the boots that completed the simple, elegant and very hot outfit.

He pressed closer.

"Mmm... sweet wanton." Zane smiled for him, tilting his face up for a long kiss before closing the privacy screen that left them alone in the soft seats.

A thrill of excitement slid along his spine and settled in his belly, in his balls. "I always have been. Wanton, I mean."

"Yes?" Zane's tongue slid over his lips. "Have you always been sweet?"

He followed Zane's tongue with his own. "Oh, come now, Zane. You already know I have a tart side."

"No..." Zane's chuckle was warm, playful, hands sliding into his coat to stroke his belly.

He chuckled, pushing into the warm touches. "I've never met anyone like you."

"My mam said I was one of a kind. Perhaps she was right." He got a wink, Zane's eyes playful, happy. Focused on him.

He laughed at that, happiness full and real. "I don't think she and I see you in quite the same way..."

Zane laughed, leaning in to nibble at his neck. "No. No, I would hope not."

He tilted his head back, giving Zane more room to work up a mark. Silly coat getting in the way and hiding his skin. A soft purr sounded and Zane's lips fastened onto his skin, pulling hard. He gasped. It was like Zane's mouth had a direct line to his cock and each pull made his prick throb. One of Zane's hands worked around to his ass, tugging him close, the steady pulls driving him mad. He wriggled and pushed into Zane's lap, straddling the strong thighs. There were far too many clothes between them -- he couldn't even press his aching cock against Zane's belly. Well, he could but there was so much cloth separating them.

"Mmm... Poppet..." Zane squeezed his ass, tugged him closer. "You're wearing my mark."

"And too many layers." He pouted, trying to rub.

"You were cold, remember?" Zane brushed his throat with soft, warm lips.

"I don't feel cold anymore." Granted he didn't want to freeze anything... necessary off, but he was counting on that being either in Zane's mouth or snug against the man's belly or in the tunnel of that big hand.

One of Zane's hands cupped his cock through his pants, the hard heel rubbing firmly. "Oh. No, Poppet. You're not cold."

A shudder of pure pleasure shot through him and he moved against Zane's hand.

"My wanton." The low growl vibrated through him.

He whimpered. "Say it again."

"Mine. My wanton. My Poppet. My Daniel. My love." Zane's eyes met his, blazing. "Mine."

He came with a cry, body shaking, mind high on the words and the pleasure that moved through him.

Zane purred, lips covering his, tongue pressing deep and tasting him.

He wrapped his arms around Zane's neck, holding on tight, pushing as close as he could. Zane loved him. Zane saw him. He'd been trying to guard his heart against when that was no longer true, but it was too late, he belonged to Zane wholeheartedly now. Maybe he would get lucky and Zane would not tire of him for a very long time to come.

Zane produced a cloth, cleaning him easily before wrapping him in arms and coat and blanket and settling him against the wide chest. "Look out the port, Poppet. The Angelic lights."

Out the port he could see dozens of lights -- reds and blues and purples, all dancing and bright.

"Oh, how pretty!"

He rested his cheek on Zane's chest, listening to the solid heartbeat as he watched the beautiful lights.

"Yes. Very much so." The words were husky and warm, Zane's thumb brushing the mark on his throat.

A shiver went through him at the touch, warmth flooding him anew.

A kiss brushed the top of his head, then Zane settled, holding him, keeping him warm.

Keeping him close.

He decided he very much liked traveling.

Daniel and Zane enjoy their offplanet adventure

Zane got them settled in the room, pleased at the view. The starshowers would light the room all night, fascinating his Poppet, decorating the pretty skin. The food here was passable, the service polite and quiet. The room had a huge tub, big enough for them to relax in. Best of all, the bed was big enough for four.

"There's a vidfeed in the wall, plus a communit to order food. We should be comfortable, Poppet."

Daniel's arms slid around his waist, his naked Poppet pushing close. "You'll make sure I'm comfortable, I'm sure."

"I will, Poppet." He lifted the thin chin and took a deep kiss, tasting the sweet flavors of his lover.

Daniel moaned sweetly, opening to him, giving him everything. And he took all Daniel had; tongue pressing deep, licking and lapping at the parted lips. Those slender hands moved up his arms and latched onto his shoulders, holding on.

He drew them across the room, pushing Daniel onto the bed before stripping down to his skin.

"Ooo, someone's hungry." Daniel wriggled on the bed.

He pinched Daniel's hip, grinning. "Just testing the mattress."

Daniel yelped. "That's not the mattress!"

"No? You're sure?" He pinched again.

Daniel shrieked and giggled, trying to wriggle away.

Zane laughed, letting his happiness and pleasure show as he kept Daniel close, tickling and teasing and playing. Daniel's hands slid over his head and his shoulders, the touches soft and loving despite the way his Poppet was trying to get away.

He started sharing long, deep kisses as his tickling turned to caressing. Daniel's laughter faded, turned to moans and the attempts to escape turned into attempts to press closer.

"Still hungry, Poppet? Always so responsive." His hand slid down, curling over Daniel's hip.

"Mal says I'm insatiable."

He nipped Daniel's bottom lip. "Mal is a good friend, but you deserve someone who can focus on you alone."

"Does it make you jealous when I mention him?"

He gave it a moment's thought. "Not jealous. Protective. Jealousy would mean that I believed he could give you what I do."

Daniel purred, hand sliding over his head. "Such confidence. It's very sexy, Zane."

"I just know what I want." He brought their lips together, the kiss hard and hungry.

Daniel pushed up against him, arms wrapping around him, mouth open wide to his invasion.

His body throbbed, want driving him. He had wanted since the transport, since the scent of Daniel's pleasure had filled his nose. Daniel's hands slid over his skin, fluttering and teasing with gentle touches.

"Don't tease the bear, Poppet. I bite." He offered Daniel a grin and a wink, then nipped Daniel's bottom lip.

"Oh... promise?" Those lovely eyes gleamed up at him.

He leaned down, biting the curve of Daniel's shoulder. Oh, Daniel did make him laugh.

Daniel jerked beneath him, hips bucking up and sliding the hot, wet-tipped cock along his belly. "Oh, Zane..."

"Mmm..." He bit again, moaning low, his own cock pressed along Daniel's thigh.

A soft gasp sounded, Daniel moving beneath him again.

He lifted his head, admiring the dark marks. "Mine."

"Am I?" Daniel asked, eyes twinkling even as that lithe body moved against him.

"You are." He was serious, sure.

Daniel laughed softly, but his eyes were dark and needy and the body moving against him did not lie. He did not need to hear the words.

He knew.

Even if Daniel did not.

"You going to prove it?" Daniel asked, wriggling.

Heavens, he loved this little asshole.

Zane slicked two of his fingers in his mouth, then slammed them into Daniel's body, pushing them deep. Daniel shuddered and screamed, fingers biting into his shoulders as Daniel clung to him.

He grinned, pushing another finger it, drawing out another scream. "Mine."

Daniel's laughter was thready, needy, wanton. "Make me fly, Zane."

"Through the stars, pushy Poppet." He pulled his fingers away, nudging the tight hole with his cock.

"You're the pushy one," murmured Daniel, the words ending on a long moan.

He laughed, pushing deep, stretching Daniel's hole with two long strokes. Daniel's hands slid restlessly over his back, the slender body bowed, Daniel pushing into his thrusts.

They fucked, bodies slamming together, heat ratcheting higher and higher.

Daniel's legs wrapped around his waist, his Poppet's hands finding purchase around his biceps. Sweet cries that grew progressively louder filled the air, Daniel's pleasure undeniable.

He growled low, pushing deep and rolling until Daniel was resting on top of him. "Ride me."

Daniel purred and began to move, using his knees for leverage as he raised and lowered himself wildly.

"Yes." He spread his legs, eyes fastened on Daniel's body as he moved.

Daniel's skin was flushed a dark pink, his Poppet moving gracefully, urgently. The slender hands reached out toward him, giving Daniel balance.

Their fingers twined together, squeezing, soft cries sounding. "Soon, Poppet."

"Just... say the word," gasped Daniel, body rippling around him.

Zane's shoulders lifted, pulling Daniel down. "Come on my cock."

Daniel screamed for him, seed spraying over his chest as the tight heat around his cock squeezed him hard. He shot, eyes rolling up as pleasure slid down his spine. Daniel's body milked him; little shivers going through his Poppet, soft moans sounding.

Zane relaxed, eyes closing as the mattress cradled them. Daniel lay on his chest, breath evening out, becoming easy.

He stroked Daniel, slow and steady. "Feel good, Poppet."

"I do, Zane. I do." Daniel placed a kiss on his chest, lips warm and soft.

"Good." He reached out, opened the blinds covering the huge windows, exposing the light show.

"Oh! Zane! Look at that!" Daniel shifted up to kiss him. "Thank you."

He grinned and took another kiss. "You're welcome, Poppet."

Daniel settled back on his chest, watching the lights in the sky, fingers idly stroking his skin.

Zane let his eyes fall closed. Tomorrow he would work. Tonight, he would simply feel.

Daniel is bored

Daniel was bored.
Bored.
Bored.
Bored.

He was stuck in Zane's hotel room on this godforsaken cold planet with no one to play with, nothing to do. He'd been fine until late afternoon when Zane had commlinked him to let him know there was a hold up and Zane would be late.

Daniel was supposed to have supper on his own and entertain himself until Zane returned.

Entertain himself?

He was outraged.

Really and truly.

He picked up the nearest glass object and threw it.

Oh, that was fun.

And Zane had said he should entertain himself.

He found another glass.

Well that had killed a couple of hours.

Of course by the time he was done he'd chaired himself and it took him a half hour to make his way over to the commlink and get housekeeping up to the room and get rid of all the glass.

And even as careful as he'd been, he'd cut his foot.

Blood and everything.

Not that he was squeamish, but this was self-inflicted which was no fun at all.

And now he was bored again.

B.

O.

R.

E.

D.

Bored.

He went through all his clothes, playing dress up and tearing everything off -- nothing was right.

Daniel stood in the middle of ritzy room, put his head back and screamed.

Oh, that was almost as good as the sound of shattering glass.

So he did it again.

"One more outburst, Poppet? And you'll spend tomorrow bound and gagged with your ass too sore to sit on, mark my words." Zane's voice was quiet, sure, firm.

He spun around, glaring at Zane.

He was bored, damn it! Bored!

Zane had brought him here and then left him to his own devices for ages.

"It's your fault."

Zane arched an eyebrow and shrugged out of the heavy coat. "Is it?"

"Is it?" He repeated back, voice rising with his disbelief and outrage. "Is it?" He stamped his foot. "Yes! It is!"

Zane hung the coat up, then sat and pulled off his boots. "Tell me, Poppet. How am I responsible for you acting like a spoiled child?"

"I'm bored. You went away all day!"

He was pouting now. He wasn't a child. And he certainly wasn't spoiled. If he was spoiled, Zane would never have left him alone all by himself with nothing to do for so long.

"I was working. I warned you, Daniel. Some days are long." Zane's voice sounded tired, almost sad as the wide shoulders rolled.

He stamped his foot again and turned his back, blinking back tears. This wasn't his fault. It wasn't.

Zane's heat was suddenly behind him, hands spinning him, mouth crashing down on his and he hadn't even heard Zane move, hadn't been ready, hadn't finished pouting, damn it. He tried pouting into the kiss, truly did, but Zane's mouth was hard and insistent and hot and wet and tasted so good and he melted against Zane with a whimper.

His lover kissed him until he couldn't breathe, then kissed him some more. He unclenched his fists and slid his hands up to those strong shoulders, holding on, clinging, his tantrum and pouting forgotten. Zane held him, hands moving over him, stripping them both down to pure basics -- need and hunger and touch. He wrapped his leg around Zane's hip, trying to get as close as he could.

Then Zane stepped toward the wall, their hips pushing together, Zane hot and hard against him. Those eyes watched him, looked into him, so sure. He hoisted himself up, wrapping his other leg around Zane, crossing his ankles behind Zane's back. There was no one like this man; no one had ever consumed him so completely.

"Mine. Even bratty. Even bored. Mine and I will keep you."

He looked up into Zane's eyes. "No matter what?" he asked. No one ever took him unconditionally. Everyone had conditions. It was the way life worked.

"No matter what, Daniel. You are mine and I love you." No question, no teasing, no bullshit. Just Zane.

He buried his face in Zane's neck, holding on. He would trust; he would believe until the day he pushed Zane too far and then he would find solace in remembering moments like this.

"No. Look at me." Zane pulled back, meeting his eyes. "Tell me, am I lying to you, Daniel? Am I lying when I say no matter what?"

He shook his head. "No." Zane believed it, he could tell that.

"You are mine, Poppet. One day, you'll believe me, wear my collar, be my family."

"I would wear anything you ask me to."

"I want you to wear my collar, Poppet." Zane grinned at him, suddenly. "I want all of you, even when you break twenty glasses and the hotel manager comms me."

"It was twenty-two!" He grinned back up at Zane. "God, that was fun."

"I'm going to have to find things for you to do tomorrow during the day." He got a long kiss. "Planning our collaring ceremony, for a start. Then arranging for our households to join."

"You'll come upstairs. The space is enormous." Zane really meant it, really wanted him to wear Zane's collar. He could almost feel it, settled and close around his neck, reminding him he belonged and Zane wanted him. "You'll have to buy a collar."

"You worry about invitations and organizing and planning. I will worry about finding the perfect collar."

He put his head back, exposing the line of his neck. "Can you see it?" he asked. "I can feel it."

Zane's fingers trailed upon his throat. "Mine."

He moaned, fingers digging into Zane's skin. "Yes, Zane."

Zane's lips followed the path of those fingers. "Yes."

He squeezed tight with his legs, rubbing against Zane's belly as sensation danced through him.

"Are you ready for my cock, Poppet?" Zane was growling, moving against him, teeth scraping his skin.

"Yes, Zane. Please." He'd not spent the entire day in a snit -- he'd masturbated and filled himself with a dildo and it hadn't been enough. So he was ready, he was stretched and slick.

Zane nodded, hands shifting him and tilting his hips, that hot, hard cock insistent as it pressed deep. He cried out, pushing down, opening up to Zane. So big. So hard. So hot. Long ripples went though him, pleasure shaking him.

"Mine." Zane's hips jerked, pushing up into him, stretching him, taking him.

He moaned, so full, so full. "Zane," he whispered, body shaking with his pleasure.

"Yes, Daniel." Zane fucked him steadily, motions sure and firm, leaving room for nothing but heat and need.

He moved with Zane, pushing down into each thrust, crying out every time Zane's cock slid against his gland. They were sliding together, hot and slick, the ice and snow outside no competition.

"Zane, Zane!" He called out to his lover over and over.

"Mine. My Poppet. I would... Daniel!" The thrusts grew wild, Zane slamming into him.

He shouted out, arms, legs, ass squeezing Zane tight as he came. Zane roared, heat filling him, hands bruising his hips.

Daniel buried his face in Zane's neck, just holding on, melted and close. Zane stumbled over to the bed, still buried inside him as they settled. He licked at Zane's skin, murmured happily at the sharp salt taste of it.

A low rumble sounded, Zane's hands sliding over his spine. "Have you eaten, Poppet."

He shook his head. No, he hadn't, not all day.

"No wonder you broke glasses." Zane nuzzled and smiled. "We should dine together, plan your duties for tomorrow, plan our ceremony."

He nuzzled in close, loving the way Zane took care of him. "Yes, Zane."

A soft kiss brushed his temple. "I love you, Poppet."

He looked up into Zane's eyes. "Thank you, Zane."

Zane nodded, lips warm on his own.

Oh, he could stay here in this spot, in this time forever.

Zane promised he would.

It was time to believe and trust.

He held onto Zane and did.

Daniel and Zane in the aftermath of the collaring party

Zane led Daniel to their rooms and straight into the playroom, leaning Daniel over the padded table so the reddened, filled and sensitive ass was in the air. He reached out, scratching it lightly, enjoying the way his poppet jumped, before walking around to remove Daniel's gag. "Well, Poppet, did you enjoy Desmond's collaring party?"

"Y...yes, sir." Daniel's voice was hoarse.

He grabbed some apple juice, brought the straw up to Daniel's lips. "Drink, Poppet."

Daniel's lips closed around the straw, sucking strongly. Zane's free hand stroked through Daniel's hair, petting gently, letting his lover know he was there. Daniel nuzzled into the touch, releasing the straw and making a soft, needy noise.

"There, Poppet. Better?"

"Yes, Sir. Thank you, Sir."

"Good. How do you feel?"

"Exhausted. Loved. You see me."

"Always. Every breath." He stood, unzipping his trousers, hard cock nudging Daniel's lips. "Open, Poppet. I want you."

Daniel whimpered, mouth opening eagerly, pulling him in with fierce suction.

"Yes..." His head slammed back, eyes wide and open, hands in Daniel's hair. So hungry. So fine. His. He growled low in his throat, pushing harder. "Mine, Daniel. My love. My Poppet. My sub. Mine."

Daniel took all he had to give, mouth tight around him, throat open to his thrusts, tongue sliding on his cock. He'd been aching for hours, needing this, needing his Daniel's obedience and care, and he arched, balls tight.

Daniel made a noise, a moan or a purr and the sound vibrated along his flesh.

Zane came with a cry, shooting into Daniel's throat. His Poppet swallowed him down, not missing a drop.

"So good..." He kept petting, touching, loving. "I'm going to leave you filled, Poppet, but you're sleeping with me. Do you want the blindfold off?"

"Thank you, Sir. No, leave it on please, Sir." Daniel nuzzled into the touches, bound body straining toward each one.

Zane lifted Daniel and carried his lover to their bed, setting his poppet down before stripping and curling in close. "You're mine, Daniel. Next month, you'll wear my collar. I'll have it soldered closed and you will wear it always."

"Yes, Zane." A soft ripple went through his Poppet's body. "Yes."

The bound body pushed against him and then Daniel's head turned up toward him. "May I touch you, Zane?"

"Yes, Poppet. Let me feel you." Beautiful man. He reached down and unfastened Daniel's hands, bringing them up to his body.

Daniel whimpered. "Oh, thank you, Sir."

His Poppet's fingers slid over his skin, slowly, gently, touching him reverently. He purred, dropping one kiss after another on Daniel's face, showing his love, his passion, his care. Sweet noises were offered to him, Daniel moving against him, bound body like a rippling wave caressing him. The slender fingers explored more boldly, with more force, fingers tugging at his nipples, counting his ribs, tracing his muscles.

He groaned, smiling against the curve of Daniel's jaw. "You're making me need you, Poppet. I want to bury myself inside you, join us together, feel your heartbeat against my cock."

Daniel froze, moaned. "Oh... As... as you wish, Sir." The slender body moved against him though, that Daniel wanted as well quite obvious.

"You like that, like riding my cock, feeling me spread you wide." He nipped Daniel's jaw, toes curling. "You like the burn, the pressure. The fact that you're mine."

"Yes. Yes, Zane, please." Daniel whimpered, moving hard against him, leather bound cock hot against his belly.

"Yes, Daniel." The words were a growl as he rolled them, taking Daniel's mouth in a bruising kiss. He settled Daniel atop him, fingers pulling the plug free. "Ride me."

Daniel gasped, body bowing as the plug was removed. Trembling fingers wrapped around his prick and guided it to the empty hole. With a cry Daniel sank onto him, his Poppet's mouth open wide.

"Mine." Fuck, it was tight. Hot. Perfect and he couldn't resist thrusting up into that heat, hands wrapping around Daniel's hips and pulling down hard.

Daniel's head went back, soft cries falling each time the slender body came down. Zane dug his heels into the mattress, hips snapping up hard, making sure Daniel felt it, flew with it. His Poppet's cries grew louder, interspersed with desperate panting. Daniel's hands held tight to his forearms.

"So fine, my Daniel. My love." His voice grew to a low cry.

Daniel whimpered. "Please, Zane. Please, let me..."

"Tell me how you feel." No more hiding, not now. His fingers moved to untie the laces around Daniel's cock.

"So full. I feel you everywhere. You make me fly." The words were punctuated by gasps and cries. "I want to come with you. Please, I need to."

"Yes." He freed Daniel's prick, pumping hard. "Come

on my cock."

Daniel shouted his name out, body jerking hard and then going stiff as hot seed sprayed from his Poppet's hard prick. His own orgasm came quickly, cock jerking and pumping into Daniel's body, filling it with heat.

Daniel collapsed down onto him, breathing hard, hands sliding randomly over his skin. He wrapped his arms around Daniel, holding tight, breath slowing. Perfect.

"Thank you, Zane," murmured Daniel, cuddling against him. "Thank you."

"Anything you need, Poppet. Always."

"You," Daniel said softly, tentatively. "I need you, Zane." He could feel the shiver go through his Poppet as Daniel made the admission.

"I'm yours." He held Daniel close, rocking. "And soon you'll wear the collar to prove it to everyone."

Daniel nodded. "My throat aches for the weight of it, Zane. I was so jealous of Connor today. It was like a pain."

"Yours will be finished soon." His fingers traced Daniel's throat. "There are two stones set in your collar. One is a Retil luck stone, the other a Fireruby for passion."

Daniel purred beneath his touch. "It shall be the most beautiful collar there ever was because it is yours, Zane."

"It will be ours and beautiful and I will still see only you, Daniel."

Daniel's hand curled around his chest, holding on to him. "Mine."

Zane nodded, pulling the blankets around them, hand petting Daniel's spine. "Yes. Yours. Always."

Always.

Daniel Plans For His Own Collaring

Daniel moved toward the bar where he was meeting Kestrel to discuss the details of his collaring party.

Zane's seed filled him, held inside by an enormous plug, making him aware of each step that he took. His cock was hard and bound, snug within the leather pants, hinted at by the loose silk blouse he wore.

He knew that he glowed. Knew that he walked with incomparable grace. And soon he would wear the collar that would lay all that at Zane's feet. He purred happily, slinking up to the bar and taking the stool next to Kes. "Hello, old friend."

Kestrel beamed at him, those pretty eyes shining. "Oh, my sweet Daniel! I found the most luscious outfit for your collaring party, dearest! And Moffat's agreed to personally cater the entire thing."

"You're going to stand with me, right Kes?"

He slid his hand on Kestrel's arm, one of his oldest friends, one of the few he'd never pissed off with his brattiness.

"I wouldn't miss it for anything." Kestrel's hand patted him. "He makes you shine, lovely."

Daniel beamed. "I know. I never dreamed... "

Kestrel smiled at him, nodding. "He gives you what you need. Did you know he trained with Mal for cycles before he approached you?"

Daniel gasped softly, his heart thumping hard. "No, I didn't know. No one has ever wanted me, really wanted me for good or ill before." He bit his lip, finding Kestrel's hand and squeezing tight. "I'm scared, Kes."

"Of course you are." Kestrel nodded, held his hand tight. "But that's why you have Zane. Because you can be as scared as you want to and Zane will still be there."

He nodded. It was becoming easier to believe and he wanted to believe, so badly. His beautiful Zane...

"He's something special."

"He is and so are you." Kestrel grinned, hands fluttering. "I love the way his eyes follow you, the way he knows every time you breathe."

A shudder moved through him. "You can see it then? From the outside?"

"Everyone sees, lovely. Zane loves you, wants you. You two... belong together."

Daniel closed his eyes, smiling and put his hand on his chest. "My heart is beating so fast." He took a deep breath and laughed, opening his eyes to grin at Kes. "So is everything in place?"

"I found an outfit for you -- Tralian flamesilk; you'll light the room up. Moffat's dealing with the food. Do you have something you're going to give Zane?"

He shook his head, sudden tears filling his eyes. "I want to, but I don't know what. He deserves something special."

Kestrel peeped and fluttered, fingers dancing over his face. "Now, now. Daniel. Daniel. Jewelry? You... you could get a tattoo? A nipple ring? Uh... You could move you both into your rooms?"

"I would never alter my body except at his behest!" He shook his head and then blushed. "And the move to my rooms is already arranged between us. I just don't know. Everything I think of seems so ordinary."

Kestrel smiled gently. "Daniel. Lovely. You're giving him yourself. There's nothing ordinary there."

"Oh, he already has me!" He closed his eyes again. "He so has me."

"Lucky, lucky Zane." Kes' voice was fond, familiar. Warm.

"Most of the time." He grinned at Kes and wriggled,

gasping a little as the plug shifted.

"No, Poppet. Always." Zane's hands landed on his shoulders. "Good morning, Kestrel."

Kestrel pinked and nodded. "Good morning, Zane-darling!"

Daniel leaned back into Zane's strength, smiling up at his lover. "You finished your business early."

"I did." Zane's eyes were shining, warm. "I had reason to come home."

He beamed, wriggling again, making sensation shoot up his spine as the plug hit his gland. "Me?"

"Always." Zane leaned down, kissed him good and hard. He moaned, opening up to Zane, giving everything.

"Oh. Oh, you're beautiful together. Just beautiful." Zane's eyes never wavered from his, even as Kestrel talked.

Daniel also kept Zane's gaze, peace filling him. He reached up, touching Zane's cheek, smiling at his lover.

Zane's lips left his, just barely. "Kestrel, Daniel's got plans for the rest of the day. He'll have to speak with you later."

He gasped. "Kestrel's helping with the plans for tomorrow's ceremony!"

It was rude.

It was sexy and exciting.

"He is a very, very good friend, isn't he?" Zane's eyes never left his. "I want to watch you swim. Then I'm going to fuck you until you scream and then we're going to see Paul and get matching tattoos."

"Bye, Kes." He melted into Zane with a whimper, giving himself over entirely.

"You both have a wonderful day; I'll take care of everything." Kestrel wandered off, leaving him in Zane's arms.

"Is the swimming important?" he asked, bound cock throbbing.

"Mmm... What do you need?"

"Oh, Zane. I need you. I need you to see me."

He was lifted, drawn into those huge arms, Zane heading toward the elevator without the slightest hesitation. "Always."

Daniel wrapped his legs around Zane's waist, hands sliding over the bald scalp. Zane made him feel so good, made him feel it could always be so.

The lift opened and they headed up, Zane's fingers nudging the plug again and again. His eyes rolled and he jerked against Zane, cock rubbing against the solid belly through his leather pants. He was panting, shaking, need riding him hard.

"So fine. My Poppet." Zane growled the words against his lips.

"Yours. Your Poppet." He whimpered, pushing even closer.

"Mine. Fuck, Daniel. I want you. Want to hear you scream when you come on my cock."

"Yes. Please. Zane. Please." He sawed against Zane's belly, bound cock trapped in his leather pants.

Zane growled and stopped the lift, putting him down and spinning him, tearing his pants down. The plug was yanked from him, leaving him empty, leaving him needing that hard prick.

His cheek pressed against the wall of the lift, ass pushing back toward Zane. "Please," he whispered. "Please."

"Yes. Yes, love." Zane slammed into him, fucking him hard and fast and deep, stealing his breath, his sense. His eyes closed and he just felt, fingers trying to dig into the wall of the lift, sounds pouring from him as Zane's thrusts rattled his bones.

"Mine. Mine. Mine." The words were soft, whispered, Zane singing to him.

"Yes. Oh yes, Zane." He was. Zane's. Zane's to take, Zane's to love, to punish, to need, to fuck.

Zane's hand found his cock, unsnapped the ring and freed him. "Want you to come on my cock, Poppet. Want to hear you."

He whimpered, nodded, words beyond him now. Zane took him hard, pushing in again and again and again, low, perverse promises whispered into his ear. He keened as one of Zane's hands wrapped around his cock, pumping hard in time with the fierce thrusts.

A moment later found him screaming, shouting out Zane's name as he came, body squeezing the thick cock inside him.

"Daniel." Zane growled his name, teeth scraping against his skin.

He shuddered, cock pulsing in Zane's hand as his body shook with expanded pleasure.

Heat filled him, Zane so hungry, so strong behind him. "Love you."

The words pushed at his lips to reply, but he held them back with his breathless gasps. He would offer them to Zane tomorrow at the ceremony. The perfect gift for his lover.

Zane slowly caught his breath, relaxing. "You are a temptation, Poppet."

He wriggled on Zane's cock, gasping at the heat. He wore a plug often, but this heat, this knowing it was his Zane... it made it so much better. "I try," he whispered.

Zane held him, humming. "You are all I want, Daniel."

"I know." He laughed softly, melting back against Zane. "I know."

He did.

Daniel tilted his head back, wanting Zane's kiss. And, as in all things, Zane gave him what he needed.

Daniel and Zane, the Night Before The Collaring

The hustle and bustle of planning for the collaring party was absent tonight, the door locked, just him and Daniel and a quiet meal and no interruptions as they spent the evening together. Tomorrow would be huge, busy, but tonight was theirs.

Zane held Daniel in his lap, petting the flat belly, fingers sliding over the stylized "z" and "d" inked on the pale skin.

Daniel moaned softly, rippling for him, body pushing into his hands.

"Mmm... Poppet. So fine." He nuzzled and licked, addicted to the feel of Daniel's skin against his own.

"For you," murmured Daniel. His Poppet had been so good the last couple of weeks.

"Yes. For me." He smiled, humming low. "Tomorrow you will wear my collar. Tomorrow everyone will see."

Daniel's fingers fluttered at his own throat. "I never thought anyone would really want me enough to ask me to wear their collar."

"I want you. I need you. I want your body next to mine every night, your hands on me every morning." He leaned down, nuzzling and lapping at Daniel's neck.

Daniel whimpered, hands coming up to stroke his head. "Oh, Zane..." Daniel's breath was loud in his ears.

"Yes, Daniel. Every day. We'll be together when we're old, holding each other, playing wicked games together."

"Old? Why, Zane, I'm not planning on getting old. I am going to be young and beautiful forever."

"You will be beautiful forever, my Poppet." Beautiful and happy and his.

Daniel preened for him, eyes shining happily.

"What are you looking most forward to tomorrow?"

He trailed his lips along Daniel's throat, trying to find the best place to leave a mark.

"The look on your face as you put the collar on me."

"I'll be so proud I won't be able to bear it." He nuzzled, feeling Daniel shiver. Ah, there.

"I won't disappoint you, Zane, I swear it."

"No, you won't. I believe in you." He bit down, marking Daniel's fine skin.

Daniel cried out, jerking against him. "Zane!"

He groaned, sucking hard, hips working, rubbing against Daniel's ass. Whimpers and moans filled the air, Daniel's hands reaching back for him, holding on. He wrapped his hands around Daniel's cock, pumping, touching. Loving.

Daniel writhed. "Oh, Zane... Zane."

Yes. Mine. Poppet. He groaned, moving faster, pulling hard.

"Oh. Zane. Please. Inside me."

"Yes. Daniel." He shifted, pushing his loose pants down, cock pushing out. "Yes."

He rolled them, hips shifting, trying to join them. His Poppet's hand wrapped around his prick, guiding it to the tight, sweet hole. He growled, pushing deep, holding them together. "My Daniel!"

Daniel moaned, wriggling on his cock. They moved, his prick deep inside his Poppet, held in tight heat. Daniel's eyes were closed, mouth open on sweet sound after sweet sound. He bit at Daniel's skin, marking, claiming, growling with his pleasure.

"Zane! Please!" Daniel moved on him, pushing into his hand, panting and whimpering, shaking with need.

"Yes. With me, Daniel. Oh. With me." He groaned, hips snapping as he came, filling his poppet with heat.

Daniel's body clamped down around him as his Poppet cried out, seed spilling over his hand. He was held so tightly, Daniel's body white hot and grasping, holding him in.

"Mine..." He wrapped around Daniel, holding close, slowly rocking them down.

Daniel curled into him, slender fingers moving over his skin in sweet, random touches. "Yours, Zane. For always."

"Yes. I'm going to make you happy, Poppet. Going to see you." He was drifting, dozing, warm and sated and comfortable.

"Thank you," whispered Daniel.

"All you need." He licked the dark mark on Daniel's shoulder.

Daniel shivered and pressed closer. "And am I all that you need?"

"All I will ever need, Daniel." He could hear the belief in his voice.

Daniel made a soft sound and pushed harder against him, settling close. "Good."

He nodded, arms holding Daniel close. Yes.

Very good.

Daniel prepares for his collaring

Daniel was fluttering. There really wasn't another word for it.

He was in his rooms, soon to be his and Zane's rooms and he was trying to make his hair work while he waited for Kestrel to come with his outfit. He'd used eyeliner and had to redo it three times. He was on try number four with his hair and it had to be just perfect for Zane and at this rate it just wasn't going to be. Tears prickled at his eyes and he picked up his glass of juice and sent it sailing across the room, giving a little sigh at the sound it made.

Another twenty or thirty or so might calm his nerves.

The knock at the door made him jump and he was still breathless as he went to open it. Maybe Kestrel could fix his hair. Or shave it off for him -- Zane was bald, he wouldn't mind if Daniel was too, would he?

"Oh. Daniel. Love." Kestrel fluttered in, the motion so dramatic it made him feel calmer. "You look stressed. No stress. Come on, let's do your hair and redo your eyes a little and add some glitter. Glitter fixes everything. Do I smell oranges?"

He grinned and wrapped Kes in a hug, feeling better already. "I put essence of oranges in my bathwater this morning."

"It's luscious and just tart enough. I love it." Kestrel kissed him, eyes shining and happy. "Everything is perfect and we have plenty of time. Did you have food yet?"

He shook his head. "I didn't think I could possibly eat. Oh, I'm so glad you're here, Kes. I was getting so nervous." He leaned in and whispered. "I might have smashed my glass of juice against the wall."

"We'll have housekeeping to fix it and no one will ever know." Kes' fingers brushed over his face, his temples.

"It's all going to be perfect, Daniel. You just relax and let me take care of things."

He nodded. "I just want everything to be perfect for Zane. You don't think he's going to change his mind, do you?"

"No. I saw him this morning with Mal. He's glowing, he's so happy." Kestrel gave him a warm smile. "He's loved you forever."

Daniel closed his eyes and took a deep breath. "I still can't believe it sometimes. I keep worrying I'm going to trust it and it's going to fall to pieces. I'm not exactly good all the time."

"Zane doesn't want good all the time. Zane wants you." Kestrel led him to the sofa, then grabbed the brush and cuddled behind him, brushing his hair.

He leaned against Kestrel's warmth. "I figured out what I'm going to give him, Kes."

"Oh? Share!" Kestrel sounded as excited as if the gift were for him. "Oh, your hair's just so soft, Daniel-love."

"I'm going to tell him I love him."

"Oh..." Kestrel stopped brushing, sniffled a little, then hugged him tight. "Oh, Daniel, that's perfect!"

He nodded, excitement thrumming through him, but good now instead shattered and pointless. "It's been true for awhile, but I've been scared to say it."

"Oh, congratulations! It'll be the most amazing collaring ever." The brushing started up again. "Have you decided where things are going to go?"

He preened a little. "It will, won't it? As for Zane's stuff, we'll worry about it next week. His toys are all being moved up into my playrooms today during the ceremony."

"Are you going to share a bedroom?" Kestrel and Jim had just moved in together, turning one playroom into a clothes closet and another into huge vid theatre, complete with loveseats to snuggle on.

"Oh... oh, I just assumed we were -- we've always slept together at Zane's place. Well unless I've earned a time out..." He sighed. "I hope so. I like sleeping with Zane. He's warm and hard in all the right places..."

Kestrel chuckled. "Well, if Zane's anything like Jim, you'll share a bed. It's nice to cuddle close."

He turned slightly and slid his hand along Kestrel's cheek. "Did I tell you how happy I was for you and Jim? You've waited nearly as long as I have for someone to take care of you, to see you."

Kes nuzzled into his touch, eyes lit up, warm as only the mention of Jim's name could make them. "Thank you, Daniel-love. He's so good to me, makes me so happy."

He smiled and kissed Kestrel quickly. "I can tell." Then he laughed and shook his head. "How's my hair?"

"Beautiful, as always. Here, let's fix your makeup." Kestrel fluttered and fussed and futzed and then pronounced him gorgeous.

He spun for Kestrel, feeling light and happy, his nerves dissipated by his friend's presence. "Did you bring my outfit?"

"I did." Kestrel bounced over, held up a pair of gauzy, flowing pants and matching vest made of fire-silks, the reds and oranges and yellows pouring down like a blazing waterfall.

"Oh... Oh, Kestrel, it's stunning!" No one was going to be able to take their eyes off him. And best of all Zane wouldn't either.

His best friend beamed and twirled. "I told you, didn't I? It's perfect!"

He laughed and started pulling off his robe. "I never would have been able to do this without you, Kes. Thank you."

"It's my pleasure, lovely." The silks felt cool and magical against him.

Now that he was ready and dressed, everything perfect, he couldn't wait for the ceremony to start. He wanted everyone to watch him and Zane tie their lives together.

Kestrel dug around in his pocket, then held out a little box. "For you, lovely. I had it made for you."

He opened the box to find an earring with two stones, the color of his and Zane's eyes.

"Oh, Kes..." He wrapped his arms around Kestrel's neck and hung on. "Thank you. So much."

"Congratulations, Daniel. I'm so happy for you."

"Me, too." He slipped the earring on and twirled for Kestrel. "How do I look?"

"Ready to go." Kestrel took his hand. "It's time, lovely. Let's go."

He squeezed Kestrel's hand and took a deep breath. "Yes. I need to see a man about a collar."

Daniel Wears Zane's Collar

Zane wore black -- silk instead of leather, perfectly fit and tailored -- waiting and watching as the room filled with their friends. Malachi was standing with him, Hercules close by. Desmond, Connor, all the regulars were filling the chairs, the little sofas. In his hand was the collar, heavy and fine, the jewels sparkling in the light.

Now he needed his Daniel.

Late, though not late enough yet to worry him. And it would be like his Daniel to come in last, make sure everyone saw his entrance.

Mal grinned over. "You know they're up there fluttering. We should never leave Daniel and Kestrel alone together."

He chuckled, nodded. "I know, but Kestrel makes Daniel feel almost staid."

As if called by his name, Kestrel fluttered in, coming to give him a beaming smile and a hug before standing next to Mal.

A moment later Daniel came in, dressed like a flame and walking with the grace of one as well. The entire room faded, his focus sudden and sharp and complete. His Daniel.

Daniel's eyes met his, shining for him. His Poppet came straight to him.

He held his hands out, their fingers twining. "Beautiful." Daniel just beamed at him, his Poppet glowing.

He looked to Hercules, then to Mal.

Hercules cleared his throat.

"Well today is quite a day, isn't it? Our little Daniel going exclusive, agreeing to wear someone's collar."

Daniel blushed, hiding the lovely face in his arm.

"Mine." He turned Daniel's face up so their eyes met.

"My Daniel. My heart."

"Oh, yes, Zane. Yours." Daniel preened at that and shot Hercules a sassy look.

Hercules chuckled. "It is my pleasure to welcome everyone here to witness Daniel accept Zane's collar."

Zane looked into Daniel's eyes, heart pounding, so happy. "I would join with you, Daniel, with you alone, until time ends."

Daniel nodded. "Yes, Zane."

Kestrel and Mal and Hercules spoke, but Zane didn't hear them, didn't listen. All he knew was the peace in Daniel's eyes. Mal handed him Daniel's collar, nudging him gently, and he held it out for Daniel to see.

Heavy and stiff, it had the appearance of age, of timelessness, the stones in the center glowing, almost singing as they vibrated. Daniel gasped softly, fingers reaching out to stroke the collar, then the lovely eyes turned up to him. "It's beautiful, Zane. I'll wear it with pride."

"Thank you." He placed it around Daniel's neck, clasping it, the click seeming to ring in his ears.

"I'm yours now," Daniel told him. "For always."

"Yes." He smiled, leaned to kiss Daniel, to taste the satisfaction that he heard in that voice.

When their lips broke apart Daniel spoke softly, but clearly. "I love you, Zane."

His heart stopped, eyes fastened onto Daniel's, so honored, so happy, so loved. "Poppet..."

Zane thought his face would split, he was grinning so wide.

Daniel just beamed, glowing. "I love you. I love you. I love you."

"I love you. My Poppet." He drew Daniel to him, taking a deep, hard kiss.

Daniel's mouth opened to him, letting him in as the slender arms wrapped around his middle. He held Daniel's head in his hand, kiss going deeper, harder. Daniel submitted to him completely, whimpering into his mouth. He peripherally heard the cheers and clapping of their friends.

When their lips parted, they were both panting, the world spinning. Daniel's eyes glittered as if he were drunk, body clinging to him.

He cupped Daniel's jaw. "Forever. I swear it."

Daniel nodded. "Yes, Sir."

Hercules chuckled. "Congratulations to you both. I hope you'll both be very happy together. I know it'll be interesting."

He laughed. "With my Poppet? Always."

Daniel blushed and looked up at him. "I try to be good, Zane."

"You are exactly what I need, Poppet."

Happiness was a beautiful look on Daniel.

Heavens willing, he'd keep it there.

Zane and Daniel are Happy

Daniel was flying.

A party had followed the ceremony with all their friends and he'd had maybe a little too much to drink. He giggled as he watched Zane show Kestrel and Jim out. All right. Maybe a lot too much.

But his glass had never been empty and there'd been toasts and now he just couldn't stop giggling.

"Oh, you look fine, Zany-kins."

"Zany-kins?" Zane smiled over at him, chuckling. "You're drunk, Poppet."

He giggled some more. "Maybe. It's that Hercules fellow. He broke out the hard stuff. He thinks I'm not going to be any more trouble to anyone anymore. Because you control me."

Oh, that made him laugh some more.

"Control you? Oh, Poppet, where's the fun in that?" Zane took him into warm arms, held him close.

"I know." He giggled some more and cuddled in. "I guess the joke is on Hercules."

Zane nodded, thumb rubbing his spine. "The collar looks perfect on you."

"I know. Not as good as you look on me though."

A soft chuckle sounded, tickled him. "Don't you mean in you, Poppet?"

He had to think for a moment, figure out what the difference was. "Oh, I don't know, Zany-kins -- I've never seen you in me!"

Zane snorted. "Oh, the Zany-kins thing is so going to stop."

"Oh, spoilsport! Don't you like it? How about Zany-poo? Or Zany-pie."

"I was thinking Lord and Master..." Those dark eyes were dancing, laughing, loving him.

"Oh, I don't think so. I might be wearing your collar but I am not your slave, Zany-kins." He held his head up regally -- which wasn't easy to do when the room was spinning and you were being held in the arms of a very big, very bald man. "I am the royalty here."

"Never a slave, but my Poppet." Zane cupped his jaw, holding him, seeing him.

He beamed up at Zane. "I love you, Zany-kins."

"I love you, Daniel." One hand popped his ass. "Incorrigible beauty."

He shrieked dramatically, wriggling in Zane's arms. They both started laughing, Zane hugging him, holding him, body shaking as they laughed. He looped his arms around Zane's shoulders, pressing kisses onto that laughing mouth.

Zane leaned him down, kissing hard, stealing his breath. He gasped, suddenly so much less drunk, Zane's heat cutting right through the fog.

"Mine." Zane's eyes were so serious, so dark. "Mine."

He nodded, no more giggling. "Yours."

"I love you, Daniel."

He framed Zane's face with his hands, looking into his lover's eyes, making sure Zane knew this was the real thing, not a drunken confession. "Zane. I love you."

Zane made a soft noise, so happy, those eyes wet with tears. "Thank you."

"Oh, shush. You'll be punishing me again in no time, Zany-kins."

"Sooner rather than later, knowing you, Poppet."

He giggled and kissed Zane again. "Love me, Zane, make me fly."

His hands were drawn up, Zane's hands petting him, stroking him. He moaned, arching into the touches. The touches were sure, deep, almost bruising.

He shuddered and whimpered, each touch undeniable. "Oh... Yes, Zane, please."

Zane rumbled, pushed against him with a growling purr.

Oh, he was spinning, flying, but it wasn't from the drink anymore.

"Strip, Daniel. I don't want to tear your clothes."

He was less concerned with his clothes than Zane was, and when his fingers wouldn't work the buttons on his vest, he tore it open. Kestrel would know how to get it fixed.

Zane bent his head, teeth scraping Daniel's skin. He cried out, hands grasping at Zane's shoulders, fingers digging in. Zane tugged his pants off, spreading him wide.

"Yes. Please. Oh, hurry, Zane. I need you." He wasn't above a little begging. Oh, who was he kidding, he wasn't above a lot of begging.

His lover didn't wait, didn't tease, just spread him, cock slamming deep.

"Zane!" He screamed the name, body shuddering.

"Yes. Mine." Zane pushed harder, faster, driving into him.

"Yours." He gasped, fingers reaching up to slide over Zane's collar.

"Yes." Zane stretched him, filled him so deep. "My love. Forever."

"Yours. Yours." Oh, it was so good and he didn't want it to ever end.

"Yes. Mine." Zane arched, pounding into him.

Zane's cock pushing deep and hard inside him, the collar heavy and solid around his neck, these were things that made him fly, made him know he was alive and loved and wanted.

"Love you. Daniel. My Daniel." Zane roared, hand reaching down to work his cock.

He cried out, hands flailing as he fought his need, held on desperately until Zane gave him permission to lose himself utterly in the pleasure.

"Yes. Yes, Poppet. Show me. Show me everything."

He screamed, body on absolute fire, caught between Zane's hand and cock, flying, soaring, coming hard. Zane stilled, heat filled him, the thick cock milked by his body. He shuddered as aftershocks rippled through him, small whimpers coming from deep inside him.

Zane's tongue slid along the edge of his collar.

"Oh!" He shuddered, ass squeezing Zane's cock tight.

"Mmm... mine." Those sharp teeth scraped his skin.

"Yes, Zane." He whimpered. "Yours. Oh, so yours."

"Yes. So mine." Zane purred, nuzzling.

He was purring himself, pushing into each of Zane's touches, reveling in Zane's love and possession of him. The nuzzles turned to long, deep kisses, Zane surrounding him, touching him, holding him.

He wrapped his arms tight around Zane's neck, wriggling on the thick cock.

Those eyes stared into his, so serious, so sure. "You're happy?"

He stilled for a moment and returned Zane's gaze, let himself be open and vulnerable. "Yes, Zane. I have never been happier."

"Good." His cheek was stroked. "My Poppet."

"Yes, Zane. Yours."

He looked up at Zane and wriggled some more. "Gonna prove it again?"

"Until you're feeling it until the day after tomorrow." Zane's laughter was sharp, sweet.

He shivered. "Oh, good."

"Yes, my opinion exactly." Zane shifted, winked. "And then when we're done, I'll take you to the playroom and we'll start playing."

"Oh, you're too good to me, Zany-kins."

"I'm going to beat you, Poppet."

"Oh, goody!" He clapped his hands, laughing.

Zane's hips slammed deep, sliding over his gland. "And I think we'll start now."

"Yes." He hissed the word, shaking at the pleasure that ripped through him.

"Greedy Poppet."

He stopped suddenly and looked straight at Zane. "For you? Always."

"I like that word from your mouth, Daniel."

He preened a little. "You like a lot of things from my mouth, Zane."

"Indeed." Zane pulled out of him, gathered him into those strong arms, heading toward the playroom. "I think someone wants to play."

A shiver of excitement went through him and he pushed, wanting everything Zane could give him. "Always, my Zany-kins."

A sharp slap stung his ass. "I count on it, Poppet."

He giggled and wriggled, excitement sliding along his spine.

Zane pushed the door open, set him on his feet. "Over the table on your belly."

He risked Zane's ire and leaned up to give his lover a quick kiss before rushing over to the table and spreading out on it.

Looking back over his shoulder, he glowed in the look Zane gave him. Loved. Cherished. Seen.

It was all that Daniel had ever wanted.

Daniel and Zane in Public and in Private

Daniel fingered his collar and then let his hand drop, slinking along behind Zane, following his lover down to the main floor. Their first time in public since the collaring. It was dinner time, and the dining room would be at its most crowded.

Time to shine for Zane, put on a show people wouldn't soon forget. Just following that fine ass and that beautiful bald head had him hard. Well. The thick plug that filled him didn't hurt.

Zane was slinking, too, dressed in black leather pants, the laces on the crotch tiny silver chains. The man looked so good, Daniel was tempted to jump him, but he didn't want to disappoint his lover with all these eyes on them.

So he followed meekly.

About half the way there, Zane stopped, turned, and kissed him hard enough it burned. His hands slid up Zane's arms, holding on tight as his head swum. Zane purred, tongue pushing deep, fucking his lips. Everything faded away, the dinners, the anticipation. Everything but Zane's kiss.

"There." Zane pulled back, then wrapped a soft-soft blindfold around his eyes. "Only me, Poppet. No one else matters."

"Yes, sir." He continued to gaze up toward Zane. It didn't matter that he couldn't see, Zane was his total focus.

"My beautiful Daniel." Zane purred, took one more kiss. "Everyone here wishes they were me."

He preened, all but purring. "No one else is."

"No one else ever will be."

A warm hand wrapped around his hip, drawing him along. He walked easily, trusting Zane completely.

He was led up onto one of the dais in the center of the

room, hands drawn down to a chair as he was bent over, petted, displayed. His cock was hard as a rock, his body pushing into the touches.

"Going to take the plug out, Poppet. I have something else for you." Those fingers slid over his hole, petting and stroking.

"Yes, Sir." His voice was even, but his body shook, anticipation and need keeping him on edge.

The plug was eased out, stretching him, moving so slow, so carefully. He moaned, ass squeezing tight for a moment, unwilling to let go of the plug, then with another moan, he gave in to Zane's will.

Zane teased and stretched his hole with the end of the plug, playing. Whimpering and wriggling, he dug his fingers into the chair cushion. Zane lifted him, straightened him, wrists wrapped in soft shackles above his head. Oh, yes. Yes, please, Sir. He stretched, feeling sensual, sexy, glowing for his Zane.

His ass was brought above a chair, a thick, long dildo nudging his hole. "Want to you ride it, Poppet. Want to you ride until I tell you that you can come."

"Yes, sir." His body shuddered, ass spasming. He could do that. He could so do that.

Zane stood behind him, hot and strong, guiding him down.

Daniel shuddered again as the dildo penetrated him, moaning as it seemed to go on and on before he was fully seated on it. His head dropped back, the next moan coming from deep inside him.

"Mmm... my Poppet. How fine you look for me." Zane's hands slid up along his belly.

He purred, pushing into the touches, gasping as that slid the dildo to the side in him.

Zane chuckled. "Feel good?"

"Yes, Sir." Oh, he was breathless, his voice thready, his

need clear.

"Then move, Poppet. Show me how good it is."

"Yes, Sir."

He tried for loud, so everyone could hear how Zane commanded his respect, his will, but it came out just as breathless as before and he moaned, pulling himself up, the dildo sliding and sliding and sliding from his body. When just the tip breached his ass, he started down again, jerking as it pushed past his gland.

Zane's purr was loud, happy. So close.

He gasped again and repeated the movements, shivering with pleasure. Zane's hands moved constantly, pinching here, petting there, driving his passion. His cock was hard, his balls snugged tight against his body as he writhed on the dildo. Each touch from Zane's hands made it that much harder to hold on, his need to come becoming all-consuming.

"You're mine, Daniel. My love. My Poppet, my heart."

"Zane!" He rose and fell harder, wanting to make Zane so proud.

"Yes." A hard hand cupped his balls. "Come for me."

"Zane!" He shouted his lover's name again, body convulsing on Zane's command. Pleasure shot through his entire body as he came, ass squeezing around the dildo inside him.

"Perfect." Zane's voice was proud, low. That sent shivers through him, sweet aftershocks, his cock jerking, spilling a few more drops.

Zane's hand was held to his lips for him to clean off. Moaning, he eagerly licked it clean, tasting himself on Zane's skin.

His hands were released, body lifted carefully off the dildo. He trembled, wanting to cling to Zane, wanting that hard cock inside him. But he was good, he shone for his lover and simply allowed Zane to move him.

Zane moved them, so strong, so fast, the noise and bustle of the main room fading away completely. "Mine."

He wrapped his arms and legs around Zane, sobbing against the warm skin.

Performing used to be the be all and end all for him, he lived for it. Now it didn't matter. It hadn't made a difference, all that mattered was that Zane saw him, that Zane loved him.

"Mine, Poppet." He heard a chain rattle and he was pulled down onto Zane's cock, heat pushing into him.

He cried out, back arching, hands tightening on Zane's shoulders.

"Yes..." That growl was harsh, beautiful, needy.

He squeezed his legs tight, riding that fat, hot cock with all he was.

"Tell me, tell me what you feel, Daniel."

"You. Everywhere. So hot. So good. Oh, Zane. My Zane."

"Yes. Yours." Zane pushed hard, moaning low. "Yours."

"Yours." He repeated the word; it was the only truth that had ever really stuck.

"Yes." Zane groaned. "Close, Poppet. Need you."

"Oh yes, please. Please." He wouldn't come without Zane's word.

"Yes. With me. Now, love. Now."

"Zane!" It was a scream, echoing as his seed pulsed from him.

Heat filled him, Zane's cock throbbing inside him.

He collapsed against Zane, clinging like a limpet again. "I love you."

"Mmm... I love you." Zane sat, still inside him.

He just held on. Nothing else mattered. Not where

they might be or who could see them.

Nothing else ever would.

A Bird in the Hand

A Pretty Bird Is Admired

Gregory, love, did you enjoy your dinner? Excellent. Red is bound and awaiting your will on the fifth floor. Mr. Young? Whatever is the matter? Well, sir, Turtle is a very new boy and Mal did warn you. Perhaps Harley, instead. He's well-trained. Excellent, I'll send him up. Killean? Find Harley and send him to Mr. Young and alert the trainers that Turtle's gone catatonic again."

Kestrel kissed his assistant's cheek and headed toward the bar, greeting and assisting as he went.

"What do you need, Des? I'll contact Hawk for you, he hand makes those interesting little toys. Sir William? How is your meal? Excellent. There is a wonderful dance planned on the fourth floor in an hour. Don't miss it."

He finally made it to the bar and lit on a stool, kicking through his virt-comm unit, messages flashing directly on his eyes. "Edwin, make sure the dancers wear the violet tonight, Sir William's in. Herc, sir? Your supper's being delivered in fifteen minutes in your quarters."

He shoved his hair from his eyes. "Could someone get me a juice, please?"

A glass was placed in front of him. "Mango with a touch of lemon." Jim smiled warmly at him. "Can I order you something from the kitchen, Kestrel?"

"You're a love, Jim. I... Yes. Something light and energizing, please?" He clicked through the communit again. "Kynan? Killean's busy, go work the first floor son, or you'll spend a week with Mal, I swear it."

Oh, he was tired. Ready for a night off. A weekend off.

If Hercules wasn't careful, he'd...

He'd...

Tell Mal.

"Here you go, Sweet Salad. It's got mangos in it. It'll go with your drink."

He looked up and smiled. "Oh, Jim. What would I do without you? Besides starve?"

"Oh, I think you'd manage." Jim gave him another smile.

He smiled over, speared a bit of mango and ate. "Have you been very busy, Jim? Is your staff working out?"

"Still taking care of everyone even on your own time, Kestrel? Who takes care of you?"

He stopped chewing, eyes going wide for a moment, searching Jim's familiar, friendly face. "Takes care of me? I... Why, you do, Jim."

"Me?" Jim chuckled. "I see you for a few minutes a couple times a day."

Kestrel fluttered, hands moving over the plate, over his tunics. "You... You feed me, give me juice. That's care..."

Jim nodded. "It is. But you deserve more than a few stolen moments." The bartender looked at his watch. "I get off in ten minutes. I mean my shift finishes in ten minutes. Would you... Would you like to spend some time with me?"

"Oh." He blinked, heart pounding in his chest as he nodded. "I... I would. Yes. Yes, please. I... Let me check and make sure the boss got his supper and that Turtle's in the infirmary and I'll... " Kestrel grinned. "I'll even turn off the commlink."

Jim put his hand on his heart. "You will. Oh, my." He got a wink and then Jim smiled again. "Thank you, Kestrel. Where should I meet you?"

"Somewhere not on the main floor where people are looking for me." He grinned over. "The gardens?"

"A pretty bird among the foliage -- sounds perfect." He got another smile and then Jim was gone, pouring out a drink for someone else.

Oh.

Oh.

Oh. Oh. Oh.

He fluttered away, forgetting his meal and commed Mal. "Mal. Mal-love. I... I'm meeting someone in the gardens; he said I was pretty."

Mal chuckled. "You are pretty, Kes. Who are you meeting?"

"Jim. Jim the bartender. The nice bartender. The one who..."

"Gets your dinners. Excellent. Go. Play. Laugh. Turtle's fine. Hercules is fine. Go."

He nodded, hair flying wildly. "Yes. Yes, I am. I will, I mean. Oh. Oh, Mal..."

"Relax, Kestrel. Breathe." Mal's voice was sure, dark, pouring through him.

"Right. Breathe. Going to the gardens. Breakfast, love?"

"Of course, Kes. A late one."

He nodded and hurried down the freight elevator, heading toward the garden.

It was closer to fifteen minutes before Jim joined him in the garden with a bottle of rose wine and two glasses.

"Hi."

"Hi." He uncurled from the bench, pushing his hair back again. "The moon orchids are lovely and they smell heavenly."

"Are they?" Jim's eyes were on him.

He nodded, pushing his hair back and exposing one pale, waxy flower caught behind his ear.

"Oh, they are lovely." Jim reached out, fingers sliding over the flower and then his cheek. "I've wanted to do this for so long."

"You... You have?" He gasped, leaning into the touch. It tingled. Tingled. Oh. Oh, my.

"You caught my eyes my first night on the job. I just never had the guts to ask you out." Jim's hand trembled just a little as it continued to stroke his cheek.

"But... Oh, Jim. You've been here for months..." He met Jim's eyes, lips pressing a soft kiss on the pad of Jim's thumb.

Jim's eyes darkened and he took a deep, shaky breath. "You're such a bright, pretty man, Kestrel. I'm just... Jim."

Oh.

Oh, Jim thought he was.

Oh, how lovely.

"You... you are..." His fingers traced over Jim's cheeks, Jim's lips. "There's nothing just about you."

Jim's cheeks heated. "Could I have a kiss, Kestrel?"

"Oh, yes. Yes, I would like to. Love to. Want to very much." He stepped closer, lifting his chin.

Jim's eyes closed slowly as his face drew nearer. Then their mouths were pressed together, Jim's soft moan vibrating his lips.

It was easy as breathing to curl into the strong arms, lips parting to offer Jim a taste. Jim's arms wrapped around him, pulled him close as Jim's tongue slid slowly into his mouth.

Oh.

Sweet.

Rich.

Male.

Tingly.

Oh.

Oh.

He moaned and slid his tongue against Jim's, wanting more.

Kes could feel Jim's prick growing hard as they kissed, the hot bulge like a brand against his lower belly. Kestrel cuddled closer, sliding against that heat. He was trembling, hands stroking restlessly through Jim's short, soft -- oh, very really terribly soft and dark and good on his fingers -- hair.

"You taste better even than I imagined." The words were murmured against his lips, Jim's eyes opening slowly, starting down dazedly at him.

"Your hair is so soft." He licked at Jim's lips, lazy and relaxed against the warm body that held him.

"Yours is beautiful." One of Jim's hands pushed his hair off his face. "I brought wine. Do you want some?"

"I would share it with you." I would drink it from your mouth, lick it from your skin...

"We could share a glass," Jim suggested, smiling and drawing him back to the bench.

He settled, heart fluttering in his chest, hands curling and moving over Jim's thigh, watching as the wine was opened and poured. Oh. Pretty! "I love that color -- almost tan, almost pink, the pretty bubbles..."

Jim chuckled. "Pretty things for a pretty bird."

Then the glass was raised to his lips, pressed against them. It was cool and slick where Jim's mouth had been warm and textured.

He drank, the wine sparkling and fruity and light, flavoring his lips with grape. He licked his lips as the glass was pulled away.

Oh, Jim thought he was pretty! Mal said so, but Mal was... well... Mal and Mal had known him forever and even though they loved each other -- and they did, they did -- it didn't really count. It didn't make him tingle inside.

Jim turned the glass to drink from the same place that he had drunk from. The dark blue eyes stayed on him, making him tingle all the more.

Oh.

Oh.

He licked his lips again, shivering. "How do you do that? Make something so simple make me feel so much?"

"I'm not sure what I did, Kestrel." Jim gave him a soft smile. "But if it makes you feel good, I'll try to do it again."

Kestrel chuckled and scooted closer. "I... it did. You do. I mean, yes. Yes, please."

Jim's arm went around his back, pulling him into the curve of the man's body. "More wine?"

He nodded and took another sip, wetting his lips and leaning close. "More kisses?"

"Oh. Yes."

Jim bent and licked the wine from his lips before sliding their mouths together. He moaned, pressing in and wrapping his arm around Jim's neck. So sweet. Hot. Good.

Jim's hands slid down to his waist, holding and stroking. "Do you... I'd like to make love to you, Kestrel."

"Oh, I'd like that, Jim." He met those pretty eyes, nodding eagerly. "I'd like that very much."

Oh, he hoped Mal meant a really, really, really late breakfast tomorrow.

"We could go back to my room if you like. It isn't very big, but it's private."

"Private is all we need, yes?" He cuddled in, hands moving over Jim's back, his need an ache in his belly.

"Yeah." Jim stood and took his hands, drawing him up. "Are you finished for the night?"

"I am. I am. Take me to bed, Jim? Take me to your bed?"

"Come on."

Jim kept one of his hands and led him back to the staff lift. The doors opened immediately and Jim pulled him into the lift and hit the button for the eighth floor. Then he was pressed up against the back of the elevator, Jim's lips on his.

He moaned, rubbing against Jim, arms wrapping around Jim's neck.

Oh. Oh, so right. He could feel the heat and weight and warmth of Jim's cock, sliding on his belly. Jim's hands slid into his hair, cupping his head and tilting him so the kiss could become deeper.

Oh. Oh. Oh.

He opened wider, whimpering, needing.

Jim's tongue pressed deep, hips pushing against him rhythmically, branding his belly with that heat, even through their clothes. Kestrel was flying, soaring, higher than he'd imagined, falling recklessly into warm arms.

"Oh, sweet heavens!" Jim moaned and grabbed his bottom, raising him to his tippy toes and bringing their cocks together. There were still too many clothes between them, but not enough to slow either of them down.

"Yes... Want... Oh..." His eyes rolled, hips rolling faster, breath coming quick.

The muted noise of the lift arriving at its destination sounded, the whisper of the doors opening, but Jim didn't seem to care, kissing and rubbing against him like he would never stop.

A soft chuckle sounded. “Get a room, you two.”

Kes blinked up, breathing hard. Oh. Oh, Mal. Oh. “Hush, you. You don’t have rooms on this floor.”

Jim’s arms slid away, color high. “Oh. I.” Jim cleared his throat.

“Hello, Jim.” Mal’s grin was evil. “Let’s cancel breakfast, yeah, Kes? I’m headed upstairs for the night. Early supper.”

He nodded, still holding tight to Jim.

“Oh. Oh, are you two. Oh. I didn’t know, I. Oh, don’t cancel your breakfast. I’ll. I didn’t know.”

“Know what?” He blinked up, confused, caught by the movement of Jim’s lips.

Mal chuckled again. “We’re not, Jim. We haven’t been in fifteen years.”

Kestrel frowned. “Fifteen years... You’re going to make him think I’m old, Mal!”

Jim was chuckling softly. “No, Kestrel, he’s making me think you were very, very young when you were lovers with Mal.”

“Oh...” He grinned, snuggling in, just beaming.

“Oh, you’re good.” Mal grinned and eased them out of the lift. “Very good.”

Jim shook his head, arm around Kestrel’s middle. “I just tell it like I see it. I’m not very good at that, what do you call it? Playing games.”

Mal stopped and gave Jim a serious, still look. “He deserves no less than that. He is a delicate one, our Kestrel. Hold him carefully.”

“I would never hurt him.” Jim looked just as serious as Mal.

“Good. Have a good night, Jim, Kestrel.” Then the lift doors slid shut.

“I’m sorry. He’s been my friend for a long time. He

worries."

Jim started them down the hall. "To be honest, I'm happy to see someone looking out for you, Kestrel. You're always so busy making sure everyone else is fine. I worry about you, too."

"I... It's what I do. I take care of things." He leaned against Jim as they walked. "Which one is yours?"

"This one here, near the end of the hall. 812." Jim put his palm on the door and it opened, revealing a small and simply furnished sitting room. "My bedroom's down the hall, past the kitchen and the bathroom. But you probably knew that -- the staff rooms are almost all laid out the same, aren't they?"

"Yes. The managers have suites, but all the others are built the same. Everyone has their own style, though." His suite was frenetic, chaotic, full of baubles and colors and clothes and lights.

Jim's rooms was sparse in comparison to his own, the things that stood out the most being the shelves with books, both in the sitting room and in the bedroom.

"You like to read. What do you read about?" He pressed close, rubbing against Jim almost unconsciously.

"Bartending, history, art, anything I can find in book form instead of on a text reader." Jim pulled him close again, arms wrapping around him. "Now where were we?"

"You were making me fly." He grinned up into pretty blue eyes.

"Yeah? How was I doing that? Like this?" Jim's hands found his ass again, tugging him in close as that hot mouth closed over his, Jim's tongue pressing deep.

Oh.

His world started spinning, hands burying in Jim's hair, fireworks flaring behind his eyes.

Jim walked him backward until the bed hit his legs

and he fell back onto it, Jim following him down, mouth devouring his.

Kestrel stretched, calling out as their bodies rocked together. He tugged at Jim's shirt, needed the heat of skin on skin. Jim helped him, shrugging out of the shirt and tearing his off with impatient fingers when the fastenings proved elusive.

He shrugged out of the remnants, gasping as their skin met, bellies sliding together. "Jim!"

He was pushed onto his back, Jim humping against him, all skin from belly to shoulders, mouth hard on his. He grabbed Jim's ass, tugging them tighter together, wanting skin, but not wanting to stop, not able to stop. Jim didn't seem anymore inclined to stop than he did, moving fast and hard against him, one hand tangling in his hair, the other sliding over the skin of his side and belly.

Kestrel cried out, arching, rutting furiously as he shot, balls aching.

"Oh sweet... sweet." Jim whimpered and moved hard against him and then froze, shuddering above him.

"Yes..." He nodded, fighting to catch his breath. "Sweet..."

Jim fell to the side of him, arms keeping hold of him, keeping him close. "Yes. Very."

His neck was nuzzled, Jim leaving soft, wet kisses on his skin.

"Mmmm..." He stretched, almost purring. So good. So warm.

"I'm sorry," murmured Jim. "It just felt so good, I couldn't wait."

Jim's hands moved to his pants, laughing as those fastenings also eluded his new lover. "Would you like to get naked and take a shower with me?"

He giggled, unfastening the now sticky pants and wriggling out of them, brushing up against Jim as he moved.

"Oh... maybe we'll do more than just wash in the shower..." Jim worked off his own pants, working slowly, stopping often to touch and stroke.

"I like the water. Oh... Oh... Love your hands..." He pushed into those touches, his shaft filling again.

"Oh, look... so smooth. I imagined you'd be smooth... Oh. I mean." Jim colored.

"You imagined me?" He drew Jim's hand down to his bare groin, groaning at the sensation.

Jim moaned softly, fingers stroking his skin, moving around the base of his cock and teasing his balls with so soft touches. "Yeah. When I... you know."

"When you? Oh... Oh, Jim..." He moaned, twisting under the touches.

"Yeah. When I." Jim's mouth moved over his neck, slowly making its way down toward his nipples, all the while the hand at his groin explored, the touch sliding and gentle.

"Oh... Feels so good." His cock was filling again, lifting to try and get Jim's attention. Of course, his nipples were all 'come and get me' too.

"Oh, sweet... sweet. I think we'll save that shower for later..." Jim's hand teased around his cock, touching and almost, but not quite wrapping around it.

"Look at your pretty nipples." Jim breathed on his skin, tongue almost, but not quite touching. "I'm surprised you don't have them pierced or anything. What with all the stuff going on around here."

He whimpered softly, muscles fluttering, toes curling. "Oh... I just never... I hadn't had anyone who wanted... To... with me."

"You mean you don't want to get 'em done unless your partner does too?" Jim's tongue touched his nipple this time, flicking across it.

"Oh..." He tossed his head. "I wouldn't want to get

'em done unless my partner would appreciate them, but sharing would be... Oh... Oh, be nice. I'm good at sharing."

"I've noticed," Jim whispered, wrapping hot lips around his nipple and tugging.

He cried out, pushing into Jim's mouth, heat flaring where Jim's mouth sucked. Jim hummed around his nipple, hand cupping his balls now, holding them warmly as Jim's fingertips teased the skin behind his balls.

He spread wide, hips rocking up and up and up.

"Oh sweet, oh sweet, oh sweet." Jim's finger slid all the way back to his hole, tip going in.

"Oh...In me." Kestrel shifted, pressing toward that touch. "In me..."

Jim's finger disappeared. "What? You want? I need to find..."

Jim shifted away from him, leaning over the edge of the bed and checking the drawer beneath the bed.

"Oh, yes. Please. Please, Jim." He was thrumming, heart pounding, needing so bad.

Jim was back a moment later with a familiar looking gold tube, the club supplied them all with whatever they needed when it came to sex. "Are you sure, Kestrel?"

"Do you want me? You don't have to, if you don't want to..." He needed, but he wouldn't push Jim.

"Oh, I want you. I just don't want to push. I want to so much and don't want you to feel like you have to." Jim framed his face and kissed him softly. "I just want to be with you, Kestrel. Anyway you want."

"Then make love to me?" He smiled up into Jim's eyes, licking at Jim's lips.

"Oh, yeah. Okay, I can do that."

Jim brought their mouths together, moaning into his lips. He wrapped around Jim, arms and legs and heart, just holding on tight. Fingers returned to his balls, slick now, sliding and playing. He giggled and twisted, moving toward and away from that touch.

Jim continued to tease him, lips and tongue sliding against his, the kisses hot, needy, belying the teasing fingers. Oh, those fingers were driving him... Oh. Mad. And crazed. And wow.

Really wow.

He pressed down, moaning and begging with his body.

One of Jim's fingers slid into him and then back out again. Then in, deep, and back out.

"Oh..." His fingers tangled in Jim's hair. "More. More, please."

Two fingers slipped into him, lingering, stretching, before disappearing again.

"Tease..." He laughed, the sound almost desperate.

"Oh. I don't mean to. You just feel good. It's been awhile, since I did this with anyone."

"Yes. Me too. Touch me. Deeper."

Three fingers this time, going deep, sliding against his gland.

He cried out, eyes wide, fingers tangling in the sheets. "Yes!"

Jim did it again, fingers going deep. He couldn't breathe, couldn't think, couldn't do anything but feel.

Over and over Jim's fingers slid into him, stretching him, making him fly. He rode those fingers, gasping and moving and flying and needing and all he knew was Jim and heat and pleasure.

Then the fingers were gone, Jim gasping and moving between his legs. "I can't wait. Need to. Need you."

Kestrel nodded, pulling his legs up and back, spreading himself for Jim.

Yes. Yes, please. Now. Need. Now.

Jim whimpered and pushed against him, pushed into

him. Hot and hard and oh, so good. The pleasure filled him, making him shudder and shake.

Making him fly.

"Oh, sweet heavens...oh, tight. Kestrel." Jim started to move, pulling out and pushing back in, moaning and crying out. He arched up, meeting each thrust, sobbing with sensation.

"Kestrel. Oh. Oh." Jim moved faster and faster, gasping and grunting, half kisses landing on his face.

He nodded, whimpering, clenching hard, hand reaching down to tug his cock.

"Oh! Soon," gasped Jim, movements growing jerky, wild.

Yes. Yes, now. Now, Jim. He couldn't make the words come out. Couldn't, but he nodded, eyes wide open, balls tight.

Jim cried out, face going slack as he slammed in and froze, heat pulsing into Kestrel.

It was the heat deep inside that set him off, made his balls jerk and come spray over his belly.

Jim collapsed onto him, panting and gasping in his ear. Kestrel slumped back, eyes closing, gasping. Oh.

Oh, wow.

Jim whimpered as he slipped out and settled a little less on top of Kestrel, but close. Jim kept them close and touching, breathing the same air.

"Can... can I stay?" He cuddled in, hair tousled and damp, feeling sweaty and messy and wonderful.

"Yes. Yes, please. I'd like that. Very much. Very, very much."

An arm wrapped around his waist. "You still haven't seen the shower."

"I know. And I haven't tasted you either." He grinned and found the perfect spot for him, a nice-Kestrel sized space for him to nestle in.

Jim chuckled and pulled a cover over them without having to let go of him.

"I bet there's lots and lots of stuff we haven't done yet."

"I bet. We'll have to make a checklist." He giggled, hand curling on Jim's chest.

"And when we've gone through everything twice we'll have to make a new one." Jim dropped a kiss on his forehead, voice suddenly serious. "Thank you for agreeing to spend time with me."

He nodded, stroking Jim's skin gently. "Thank you for asking."

"I've been wanting to forever."

Kestrel pinked and held on tight. "I'm so glad you stopped waiting."

"Me, too." Jim squeezed him tight. "Me, too."

He closed his eyes, mind wandering toward sleep. Tomorrow they could play in the shower, spend some time together. Then he'd go find Mal and tell everything.

If Jim had to go to work, that was.

Jim and Kestrel Fly Together

He and Kestrel had spent the morning making love. In bed. In the shower. On the couch in the sitting room. He hadn't thought he'd be able to get it up again, but there'd been another quickie just before they both had to go on shift, too.

Now Jim was only half paying attention to what he was doing. The other half was watching Kes, grinning goofily every time their eyes met. Five more minutes and he was done for the day. He hadn't had a chance to talk to Kestrel, but the man knew what time he finished for the night and he was hoping... for a repeat.

He couldn't see Kestrel anywhere when he finished up his shift, so he left a text message for the man. Just a simple, "Come to my room?" He took the staff elevator up, hoping Kestrel would follow him.

He sniffed and grinned wryly at himself. He had it so bad he thought he could smell Kestrel in the elevator.

Of course, when the lift door slid open Kestrel was there, hands fluttering quietly as the pretty bird waited and worked. Everything about Kestrel was in perpetual motion -- the rainbow colored hair, the gauzy tunics, the long, thin fingers. Even those changeable eyes -- the dat-chips embedded, turning them violet and green and blue and silver by turns

"Oh. Oh, Kestrel. Hi." He grinned and managed to get off the elevator before the doors closed and he wrapped his arms around the pretty bird, nuzzling at Kestrel's lips. "Hi."

The dat-port was clicked off, put away, Kestrel smiling for him, pushing into his arms with a soft, happy little sound. "Hi. Hi. I thought about you all night long. I forgot Herc's name. All I could think about was this. Goofy, huh? But good. Real good."

"Yeah, very good," he murmured, bringing their lips together and taking a long, slow kiss that was just waiting to get all hot and bothered and out of control

"You forgot Herc's name? What did you call him?"

Kestrel blushed a bright red, eyelashes fluttering. "Well... I mean, I was thinking about you and he came up and..."

"Oh my sweet heaven! You didn't call him Jim?" He giggled, nuzzling his sweet Kestrel

"No..." Kestrel giggled quietly and pressed even closer. "I called him 'Jim-love.'"

He gasped and colored. "Oh. Oh, what did he do?"

Kestrel had called Herc Jim-love. Oh. He rubbed them together

"He gave me the Look. You know the one, nostrils flaring, astounded that he's not first and foremost on everyone's mind." Kestrel moaned and scooted closer. "I'm lucky he was in a hurry on his way to a meeting."

"Oh sweet... I'd better be on my best behavior tomorrow."

He giggled and moaned and took Kestrel's mouth, putting an end to their conversation as he pushed Kestrel up against the wall. He wanted this man, desperately.

Kestrel twined around him, almost flowing, soft, sweet trilling sounds vibrating his lips as Kes opened for him, wanted him.

He grabbed Kestrel's ass, pulling them together, rubbing them together. A shiver moved through Kestrel, transferring to him. Kestrel was like a flame, sparking against him. Oh, sweet... they weren't going to make to his room... not the way Kestrel was moving against him, not the way the feelings were making him shiver and shake and push Kestrel into the wall again and again.

Kestrel's hands were squeezing his shoulders, one leg coming up to wrap around his hip. Little happy cries were pushed into his mouth and he could tell that Kestrel was close.

He was too, so he bit at Kestrel's lips. "Gonna come, pretty bird."

Kestrel nodded, cried out, hips jerking.

He drowned his noises in Kestrel's mouth as he came, creaming his pants and not caring for a moment. He kept rocking against Kestrel, the kiss deep and heady.

Kestrel melted against him, moaning low, fingers trembling against his nape

"Oh stars, that was. Oh, Kestrel."

He leaned against Kestrel a moment longer and then stood, arm wrapping around his lover's shoulders. "Come on, pretty bird. Let's get to my place. I wouldn't want to run into the Bossman out here. Or Malachi."

"Mmm... Yeah. Let's go shower and snuggle and play some more." Those eyes shown up at him, so beautiful. So lovely.

"That's the best suggestion I've heard in... forever."

Smiling at Kestrel, he led the way to his room and another night of flying with his pretty bird.

Kestrel and Jim

Kestrel was in love.

Like really and truly, honest to goodnessly.

It was scary and wonderful and stupid and fun and he hoped it never ever, ever stopped.

Of course, he hoped that Jim felt the same way, because if not, then ow. Mal swore it didn't work that way, that the emotion, if it was real, had to go both ways. Of course, Mal couldn't answer how you were supposed to know whether it was real or not, did he? No.

Damn.

Still...

Jim.

Mmmmmmmmm.

He shook his hair out, getting rid of any tangles, and headed to Jim's rooms with a basket of breakfast yummies.

His commlink rang.

"Kestrel." Please, don't let it be something serious. Please. Please.

"Hi Kestrel. It's Jim. The bartender?"

"Jim-love! I'm just on my way to your door with goodies!" He grinned, bouncing just a little.

"Oh! Wow, cool. I was calling to see if you wanted to spend the day. I don't have to work until tomorrow evening."

"Oh? Oh, me either. Me either. Well, tomorrow afternoon, but still. I... I'm here, let me in?" Oh, oh, this heat and fast-beating heart and stuff was... Oh, wow.

The door opened and there was Jim with his commlink in his hand and a huge smile on his face.

"Hi."

"I brought pastries and juice and flowers." He held out the basket, eyes running over Jim's face, down the fine body.

"And best of all you brought yourself." Jim was just beaming at him.

"Oh." He nodded, stepping forward, hungry for a kiss. "I did. I missed you."

"Me too."

Jim seemed to shake himself and pull himself together, taking the basket and dropping it and Jim's commlink onto the floor. Then Kes' hands were taken and he was pulled up against Jim's body.

"Good morning, pretty bird," murmured Jim, mouth closing over his.

His hands fluttered only a second before they settled around Jim's neck, his lips parting eagerly.

Oh.

Oh, good morning.

Jim tugged him in a few steps and closed the door with the hand not on his ass, never breaking the kiss.

Forever.

He could do this forever and ever and maybe even always and oh... His Jim smelled so good.

After a long, long time, Jim broke the kiss to lean their foreheads together. "You taste so good, Kestrel. Makes me never want to stop kissing you."

"Oh. Me either. I mean, me too. I mean... Yes. Yes, it's good." He smiled into those warm eyes and chuckled.

Jim was grinning, eyes shinning. "I'm acting like such a dork. A big, goofy, really happy dork. You want to come in and sit and eat and pretend we're civilized and can keep our hands off each other for a few minutes? Or you want to drop to the floor and fuck?"

"The food will keep just fine."

"Oh good." Jim started kissing him again, hands working to open his shirt. "The floor's not too hard -- I've got carpet."

"Good." He worked Jim's drawstring pants open. "Is there lube close-by?""

"There's none in your basket?" Jim asked, half laughing, half moaning.

"Just... Just juice. That tingles, I bet." He knelt down, nuzzling and licking Jim's heavy cock. "We'll figure something out, Jim-love."

"Oh. We could -- that feels good, Kes -- make our own."

"Uh-huh. Taste good."

He took Jim's cock in, licking at the heavy shaft. Jim moaned, back thumping as he leaned against the wall.

That sound made Kes moan too and they shifted and rocked together, Jim's cock pushing into his throat.

Jim's hands found his hair, stroking through it, fingers trembling.

He purred, head moving a little faster, little tingles sliding down his spine.

"Oh, Kestrel... gonna make me come!"

He pulled back, lapping the end of Jim's cock. "Oh, now. I'm just 'sposed to be lubing."

Jim chuckled huskily and stroked his cheek. "Then you should bend over so I can lube you up, too."

Oh.

Oh!

He nodded, groaning low. "So sexy."

"Me? Nah -- you're the sexy one." Jim knelt and worked on undoing his pants, pushing them off.

He wiggled and shifted, sucking in his belly to help out.

Once he was nude, Jim nudged him onto his back and spread his legs, crawling between them. "I can't wait to taste you."

"Oh... Jim-love. You make me feel... Oh." He spread wide, shifting on the floor.

"That's good, right?" Jim didn't sound like he was worried though.

"Uh-huh. So good."

"Good. I want to... just being with you makes me feel good, Kestrel. I want to return that. You're... a beautiful bird." With that Jim began to nuzzle his balls, tongue sliding back beyond them to lick at his skin.

"Jim!" He drew his knees up, crying out, feeling so sexual, so sensual.

"My pretty bird," murmured Jim.

He was licked and teased, his balls and the base of his cock and the skin between balls and ass. Then Jim's hands spread his ass cheeks wide and that tongue began to play along his crack.

He made soft little sounds, crying out with a mixture of want and pleasure.

"Oh, Kestrel. Oh you taste. Oh."

Jim's tongue pressed right into him, no longer teasing.

Oh, heavens. That. Oh. Oh, sweet. His head lifted up, hips pushing toward the touch.

Jim hummed, pushing that tongue into him over and over again.

"Jim! Jim-love! Need you. Need now. Gonna come." He sobbed, arching up.

Jim stopped and crawled up over him, cock nudging at him.

"Yes." He nodded, bearing down, body stretching for Jim's heat.

"Oh, Kestrel." Jim pushed in all the way and bent to kiss him, tongue sliding into his mouth. He could taste Jim and himself and oh, gods, it was hot. So good.

Jim whimpered and started to push into him over and over again. Kestrel planted his feet on the floor, hips pressing up and up and up.

"Kestrel. Oh. So good. So tight."

Nodding, he rocked into it, whimpering, loving the stretch and burn. Jim gazed down at him, eyes hot.

"Love you." The words just popped out -- just sort of escaped.

Oops.

Jim's eyes went wide, round as his mouth. "Oh. Oh. Kestrel. Oh."

Jim's mouth dropped onto his, kissing him hard. He whimpered, coming as Jim's tongue pushed into his mouth, cock working his body. Jim pushed in a few more times and then cried out, coming, heat pushing into him.

"Oh." He relaxed, holding onto Jim, purring softly. "So good. So good, Jim." He was never letting go.

"Did you say... did you say you loved me?"

He nodded. "Yeah. Yeah, I'm sorry. Mal said I shouldn't tell you, not so early, that I'd scare you away and I'd hate for that to happen but I do and it just plopped out."

"Mal was wrong. He might know about all that whipping crap but he doesn't know about me. I love you, too." Jim looked away and then back at him, fingers sliding through his hair, pushing it back. "I have almost since I first saw you."

"Oh." Oh, heavens. The heat inside him got bigger and bigger, sensation swelling. "Really? Oh. Oh, good. Good."

Jim nodded. "Yeah, good." Jim kissed him again, soft and sweet this time.

"I'm going to have to tell Mal I figured it out." He licked Jim's bottom lip.

"What did you figure out?" Jim asked, nuzzling.

"How to tell it's the real thing."

Jim smiled at him. "You just know."

He nodded. "Yeah. You just know."

Just like he did.

Jim and Kestrel at Work and at Rest

Jim frowned as he watched Kestrel fluttering about the club.

His pretty bird was still doing a million and one things, making everyone happy happy happy, but... that smile was rather forced, the toss of Kes' head coming just a little too often.

Something was wrong.

He served up the last round and told Gerry he was going on break. Then he sidled up to Kestrel, took his lover's arm. "You about due a break, pretty bird?"

Those changing eyes fastened onto him, flat and dull with unhappiness for a second, then warming as Kes nodded. "Yes, yes please."

He weaved in and out of the crowd, leading Kes to the staff elevators. Kes followed quietly, fingers twined with his own, holding on tight.

As soon as they were alone he took Kes into his arms, tilting the pretty face so he could kiss his lover. Kes whimpered and pushed into his arms, moaning and cuddling close. He kissed Kes until the doors opened up on the gardens and drew his lover out to the benches by the flowers.

His lover settled right on his lap, draping over him. "Jim-love..."

"Hey, pretty bird, what's the matter?"

"Big boss and I had words. He's mad at me and I was just trying to help." Kestrel sniffled, the effect actually quite darling.

"Oh, man." He caressed Kes' cheek. "He's a cold bastard. Colder even than your friend Mal."

"Mal...Mal's not..." Kes sniffled harder, tears starting to flow. "He's a good guy. Honest."

"Oh, Kes, I'm sorry, I didn't mean to upset you more."

He wiped Kes' tears away. "Oh, pretty bird, don't cry, don't cry."

Kes nuzzled into his touch. "How do you do that?"

"Do what?" he asked, licking the tear tracks.

"Make everything better?"

He smiled. "Do I do that?"

Those pretty eyes beamed at him through drying tears. "Always."

"Oh." He beamed back, arms circling Kestrel. "Good."

Kestrel cuddled in close. "I love you, Jim. You make me happy."

A little shiver went through him, the sound of that still thrilling. "I love you, too, Kestrel."

"We need a long weekend together, Jim-love. A long, quiet, in bed, naked weekend."

"Oh, Kestrel, that sounds really, really good. Can we go now?"

Kestrel nodded, rubbing against him. "Can you take the time?"

"I've got time coming to me, yeah. You mean it? You really want to do this?" Wow. A vacation. He hadn't taken one in years. Not really anywhere to go or anyone to go with.

Kes nodded again. "Yes. I need some time. Some time to just be your lover."

"Oh, pretty bird, I would like that so much."

"I'll set it up tonight, how long? When can we start?"

"It'll take me at least a day to get someone to replace me, maybe two." Wow. A vacation. They were really going to do this.

"I'll set it up for two days from now, then. Where would you like to go?" Kes was relaxed, warm against him, eyes sparkling.

"What are our options?" The last time he could remember having time off he'd gone to the golf links outside the city.

"Beaches, snow, mountains. We could take a space cruise and watch the stars." Kestrel shrugged. "Anywhere, so long as my commlink stays here."

"To be honest? I don't think we're going to leave our room much, are we, Kes?" What was the point of paying a lot for anything but the hotel if you weren't going to go outside?

Kestrel shook his head. "I just want you. Hells, Jim-love, we can stay here, if you want, so long as we're together, alone."

"We could tell everyone we're leaving and then lock ourselves in."

"Okay. We can use my rooms. I'll get pretty silk sheets and lots of pillows."

"I'll talk to Moffat, get him to cater for us. He'll do it on the quiet." He nuzzled Kes' neck. "We could get a head start on the making love part."

"Mmm... We could. Practice." Kestrel stretched for him, humming softly.

He moaned, Kestrel making him hard and needy just like that.

"Yes. Love. Right here."

"Yes." He lay back awkwardly on the bench, bringing Kestrel down with him, cradling his lover between his legs.

Kestrel's hands slid beneath his head, holding him, loving on him. "Jim-love."

"Yeah, pretty bird. Right here." He echoed Kestrel's words, smiling up his lover, hands sliding beneath the silvery shirt to stroke the small of Kestrel's back.

He could feel Kes' shiver, see those pretty eyes light up for him, sadness forgotten.

"Love you," he whispered, taking Kes' mouth, licking

his way past the sweet lips.

Kes opened for him, moaning, body rubbing against him, cock hard in the hollow of his hips. His hands slid to Kes' ass, cupping them through the velour tights his bright bird wore. He moved them together, pushing his hips to meet Kes' body.

"Oh. Oh, more. Jim. I want you."

"If you undo our pants we can rub together, cock on cock," he murmured, licking Kes' lips, nuzzling the sweet chin.

"Mmm..." Kes grinned, lips chasing his tongue. "I love your cock, your mouth..." One hand slid between them, working open their pants.

He shuddered, sweet shivers going up his spine. "I could come from the things you say, Kes."

"Just the truth. Love when you're in my mouth, making love to me, your kisses..."

Whimpering, he pushed up with his hips, cock meeting Kes' fingers. "Kes... "

"Yes, Jim-love. So hard, so hard for me..."

"Always," he murmured, crying out as Kestrel's cock slid against his own, against his belly like a rod of fire.

Kestrel nuzzled against his throat, soft, rainbow colored hair draped around him as they moved. He kept one hand on Kes' ass, guiding his lover's movements as his other hand slid up to tangle in the beautiful mass of hair. His hips moved, pushing up against Kes, finding a rhythm that would send them both flying. Soft, sweet little sounds filled the air, Kestrel moving with him, wanting him.

"Yes, pretty bird, yes. Fly with me." He was close, shivers going through him as he thrust up against Kes over and over again.

"My Jim. Jim..." Sharp little teeth grazed his neck as Kestrel arched, heat splashing against him.

Gasping, he bucked up, teeth and heat conspiring,

bringing his own pleasure to a peak and his seed shot between them.

Kestrel moaned, lifting that pretty face for a long, sweet kiss. Lazy and sated, his tongue swept in and then tempted Kestrel's back into his own mouth. It sent a shiver through him and he held Kestrel close, wishing they didn't have to go back to work.

Kestrel kissed him as long as possible, moaning as their mouths separated. "Can I come sleep in your bed tonight?"

"Can we make it our bed?" he asked, the words not the simple 'yes, please' he'd intended. He didn't take them back though. "Or make yours ours. You know what I mean."

Kestrel blinked, then beamed at him, hugging him close with a happy cry. "Mine are bigger. All my clothes won't fit in your closet."

He laughed. "Is there room in your closet for my stuff? I promise I haven't very much."

"Jim-love! I have a whole spare room closet! We'll put my older clothes there."

He shifted, the press of the bench cold between his shoulder blades. "Thank you, Kestrel."

Kestrel sat up, bouncing and bright-eyed. "I'll get things arranged, love. Oh, and the vacation and everything and..." He was given a hard, sharp kiss. "I love you!"

Jim grinned, watching happily as Kestrel fluttered and fussed and was the pretty bird he knew and loved. Kestrel stole two more kisses before managing to escape back onto the main floor, hands waving and cheeks flushed, one thing after another being arranged.

He'd like to watch that all night long. Lucky for him, he could.

Touch and Trust

Sampson meets Alain

Sampson liked to play. He was pretty good at it, too. Well, at least by The Elegant Whip's standards he was. The Velvet Glove was a step up from the Whip, though. Well, several steps up. The truth was that the Glove was the premiere BDSM men's club on the colony. If you were into the scene at all, you knew of it. Hell, even if you weren't you'd probably heard of it at the very least.

So for his twenty fourth birthday, Sampson bought himself a year's membership in the club. A level two membership which meant he got a meal every night, a few drinks and access to the playrooms, massage room and pool.

Of course that had taken all his savings, even his rainy day fund had gone into it, but he supposed that was okay -- in the next year he could rebuild the rainy day fund, unless he lost his job as a window cleaner, but at least then he'd still have a daily meal and somewhere to shower and get out of the cold. He giggled a little -- somehow he didn't think that's what the Velvet Glove management had in mind.

Now here he was in his best black pants and red shirt, aware that at six-seven with a shock of light brown curls that he couldn't tame no matter how much he tried, he was going to stand out like a sore thumb. He just hoped he didn't trip or spill a drink on anyone.

Actually a drink sounded like a good idea. He should probably go and have one at the bar; maybe it would help him relax a little. Maybe he should have visited before buying his membership, but that would have cost him fifty creds plus whatever for a drink and then he wouldn't have been able to buy the level two membership and that's the one he wanted. Besides, it wasn't the public areas he was really interested in, now was it?

The violet lighting seemed elegant and intimidating, but he walked right up to the door and flashed his ident card. The lights flashed and the door opened, the doorman glancing at his computer before greeting him. "Welcome, Mr. Scott."

"Oh, thank you. You um, can call me... well Mr. Scott sounds like someone in a, ah formalwear. I'm just um, Sampson. Oh! If you're um, allowed."

"Yes, Sampson, we are. I'll make a note in your file."

"Oh. Um. Cool. Thanks." He nodded and glanced around. The lobby did little to ease the intimidation, purple and gold and ornate and you knew you were walking into a ritzy, upscale place.

"Would you like to make any reservations this evening, Sampson?"

"Reservations? Oh! Um. No. I'll just. Wander." He nodded. Yeah, he'd check the place out, maybe swim a little -- he was less awkward in the water.

"Very well, enjoy your evening, Sampson."

"Thanks."

Oh, now that was nice, made him feel a little more at home, even if it was his first time.

He ducked in through the doors and looked around.

It wasn't early, but it wasn't late yet either and he knew the real crowds showed up after nine and really got into it closer to midnight. At least that's how it worked anywhere else he'd been and it looked like the Glove might be the same. There were people on the dance floor, others at tables eating or drinking or just talking, still others at the bar, but the place wasn't anywhere near packed.

He caught himself ducking his head, and he straightened up, made sure he didn't hunch his shoulders. He was just so much taller than everyone else.

Well everyone looked like they were having a good time, so he slowly made his way toward the bar. He'd have that drink of his and then go check out the playrooms. He might be awkward and clumsy in social situations, but once he had a whip in his hand and found his groove? He did all right for himself.

A brightly colored swirl of energy came zipping across the floor toward him, all laughter and multi-colored hair and dancing eyes. "Sampson! Welcome! I'm Kestrel, Lionel and Brandon are my assistants, they arranged your membership. I'm so glad to meet you in person. How can I help get you settled, lovely?"

"Oh. Hi. Nice to um, meet you, Kestrel. You've ah, heard of me? You guys um, really go all ah, out to make a guy feel welcome. I." He thrust out his hand. "Hi."

"Hello." His hand was taken and squeezed. "And of course we do! We want our guests to feel at home. Now, tell me, what can I do for you? Would you like a tour? A drink? Supper? All of the above?"

"Oh. Yes. Yes, it um, all sounds lovely." And as overwhelming as the place seemed, it was very nice to have someone take his hand and help him out.

"Oh, excellent. Now I'm supervising a collaring party in a quarter-hour, but I know I saw..." Dark eyes lit around the room, then widened. "Oh, yes. I did. Alain? Alain-darling? I need you!"

A sharp-featured man turned, black hair tousled and shining. Thin and graceful, dressed in deep black, Alain headed toward them, finally ending at Kestrel's elbow. "Yes, Kes?"

"Alain, love. This? Is Sampson. He's new and he needs someone who knows everyone and everything and, my beauty, you know everyone. Take care of him tonight?"

Beautiful green eyes looked him up and down, a soft smile covering the thin face. "Oh, of course."

He fought his blush and his initial thoughts that this very pretty man couldn't possibly really want to spend the evening with him and held out his hand. "Hi. Um. I'm Sampson."

"I'm Alain." The man's hand was soft, dry, cool. "It's nice to meet you."

"Oh, yes. It's so um, nice to meet ah, you. It really um, is." He pumped Alain's hand a few times and then let it go a little awkwardly. It didn't help that he didn't want to let it go -- it was a nice hand to hold.

"Have you, um, been a member long?"

"Thirteen years." Alain patted Kestrel's arm. "Go arrange your party, Kestrel. I'll introduce Sampson around and get him fed."

He blinked as the brightly colored Kestrel left and then turned back to Alain. "That's a long, um, time."

"Yes. Harry brought me here a long time ago. Would you like to get a drink?"

"Yes um, please a drink would ah, be nice." He offered his arm to Alain. "Would it be ah, rude to ask who um, Harry is?"

Alain's fingers slid around his bicep. "He was my Master. He passed away last winter."

"Oh, I'm ah, sorry." He petted Alain's finger's awkwardly. How did he always manage to stumble, even if it wasn't a physical thing? He bit his lip, wondering if he should ask about the Master thing and figured he'd already put his foot into it, he might as well insert the other as well. "Master?"

Alain led him to a quiet table, sitting with him. "Yes. Harry was... more than just my top. He was into an all day-everyday situation. He was my Master."

"Wow. That must be um, really hard. That ah, he's dead now -- passed um, away I mean." He pet Alain's hand again. "If you don't want to ah, talk about this you should um, just tell me."

Alain's hand rested in his, rested easy. "Oh, I can talk about it, answer your questions."

"I don't want to um, be nosy... well. I. That's not really um, true, is it? I am being ah, nosy." He grinned at himself. "I like to know what um, makes people ah, tick."

"Yeah? That's a good quality in a top, isn't it?" Alain motioned to a waiter. "What would you like, Sampson?"

"I guess it... oh. A steak? I heard that um, the meat is ah, real here. I'd like a steak um, please." He smiled at the waiter and asked for a salad to go with it and a Glove Special to drink. Then he turned back to Alain. "What about you? What are you um, having?"

"I'd like a fruit salad, please, Michael. No melon. And a glass of white wine." Alain's voice was soft, quiet, almost silken. "And the meat is delicious here."

"Great um, good. Where were um, we? Oh, yes. I guess it is a good um, quality for a top. Being nosy, I ah, mean. That's what pushing a um, sub, is all about, ah, isn't it? Seeing what they're um, made of?" He nodded. That was what it was about. "So have you um, found anyone new? A new top?"

"No. Not yet. I... It's hard to find someone who wants

someone like me -- I mean, most people want someone young, someone to teach, someone who isn't a high-level member, you know?" Alain offered him a sad little smile. "What are you looking for here?"

He petted Alain's hand again, wanting to take that sadness away. Alain brought out the protector in him, all his toppy instincts coming to the fore.

"I joined because um, I wanted to see. I'm a bit of a um, well a clutz to be um, honest, but not in a scene. It's the only ah, place I feel really um... well good, but not exactly that. I don't know if I um, have the right ah, words."

Alain tilted his head. "Well, the world's not really built for you, is it? I mean, you're so wonderfully tall. I bet I would feel clumsy, too."

"Oh. You like that I'm um, so tall? It doesn't make me seem um, freakish to ah, you?"

"Oh, you're quite stunning. No one would ever miss you, lose you in a crowd." Those eyes were bright, shining.

Oh. Oh, he liked that. He smiled at Alain. "And here I was ah, thinking you were the um, stunning one." Oh, smooth. Almost smooth. He felt excited but also easy with Alain.

The pale cheeks pinked and Alain ducked his head in thanks. "I'm glad you think so."

He reached out and gently touched one of the pink cheeks. "I do."

"Oh..." Alain leaned toward his touch, dark eyelashes lowering.

Alain acted like he was starved for the touch. "Have you done a scene um, any scenes at all, since your ah, master died?

"Only public ones when Kes -- Kestrel -- asks. You know, for show. Nothing... real."

Oh. Oh, how sad that such a beautiful and obviously sensual man had not had any real contact since winter. "Would you. I mean I would like to do um, a scene with you ah, tonight. Just the um, two of us." He hoped he wasn't being too forward, but it was just wrong that no one had wanted to work with Alain, even if only for a night. "I mean um, I know we don't um, you know, know each other ah, yet. But I would like to um, start to get to know ah, you."

"Oh." He got a slow smile. "What kind of things do you like? I have my own rooms; we could go, after we eat."

"Oh. Really? Oh. I would, um. Oh, yes, please. That would be um, very nice. I like. Well, I am very good with ah, cat 'o nine tails and um, floggers, whips, canes. My knots are um, clumsy, but I like binding anyway." He looked into Alain's eyes. "For a first scene with someone I had um, just met? I would ask if they um, liked pain and then ah, I would use my hands. I'm um, very good with my ah, hands. I like. I like feeling the um, heat coming up. Feeling what I'm um, doing."

"Oh." Alain nodded, breath coming a little faster. "I have three playrooms, fully equipped."

"Three? Oh. Oh, fully ah, equipped? Oh, that um, sounds good."

Three. Fully equipped. Alain really was a player. Well, he'd said he was. Thirteen years of living as slave to a master. "What... what do you um, like best?"

"I like a slow build up. I like to be made to feel. I like being touched."

"Oh!" he cried out, pained by the thought of someone who liked being touched being without for so long. Of this someone who liked being touched being without for so long. "I can um, do that," he said softly, stroking Alain's cheek again. "I'm so sorry."

Alain whimpered softly. "So gentle..."

Oh, he was going to cry -- he hurt for this man all alone. "It'll be um, all right."

"I will." Those eyes watched him, shining and focused and so bright.

"Good. Good. I can't wait to um, get started."

Alain nodded as their meals appeared -- the steak smelling most heavenly.

"Oh. Thank you, um, Michael, wasn't ah, it?"

"Yes, Sir. I'm Michael, you're welcome." A platter was set in front of him, filled with warm, rich food. Alain's fruit salad was bright, lovely.

Oh, he didn't know how he was going to be able to concentrate on the food with Alain and their scene to look forward to, but now that it was here he couldn't imagine not savoring it.

He took his first bite of the steak. Oh. Oh, it was unbelievably good. He was used to reconstituted food and there was no way this was heat and serve. He allowed himself another bite before forcing himself to put his fork down. The food, like the company, would be best savored slowly.

"Do you have any um, rituals. I mean ah, prior to a scene. Preparation and um, stuff like that."

"I... Harry did. Yes. He liked me cleaned inside, my hair braided and back. Then, before anything, he would bind my cock. Put my collar on." Alain looked down. "How about you, Sampson?"

"I usually um, well. Only have a very light meal. I didn't. Um. We aren't doing anything ah, heavy though. Not tonight. I don't know you well enough um, for that. You don't know um, me." He took a sip of the Glove Special drink, finding it fruity and light. "Do you um, like that? The um, collar and um, stuff?"

He got an almost surprised look. "I don't know. That

sounds silly, doesn't it? But I don't. It was what Harry wanted, what made him happy and that was good."

"Oh." He thought about that for a little bit, took a couple more bites of his heavenly steak. He was going to get spoiled for everyday food. Except. He was allowed one meal a day here so this could be every day food. Wow.

"I believe that um, a dom/sub ah, relationship is a um, partnership. And so ah, both parties' needs should be considered and ah, something worked out." He took another sip of the drink. "Oh! I don't mean your um, Harry was wrong. Just ah, different from me."

Alain nodded. "I was very young when I found Harry. Very scared. I'm... I'm different now. I would like a... a true friend."

He reached out to touch Alain again, fingers drawn to the cool, soft skin. "That sounds like um, a good goal."

Alain leaned toward him. "Your hands feel so fine."

"Yeah? Your skin is ah, so soft and um, warm, but not hot, almost ah, cool."

Alain pinked again, warming under his touch. "Thank you."

"I think, um. Well. I've had enough to ah, eat. What about you?" He was kind of breathless and there were butterflies of excitement in his belly. He wanted to start. Now. Soon. Now.

"I'm finished. Would you come upstairs with me?"

"Yes. I um, will." He stood and held his hand out to Alain.

That cool hand slid right into his, Alain pointed to the lifts. "We're going there. The twenty seventh floor."

He led Alain to the lifts, amazed at the turns that fate took. So far his birthday present to himself? Was looking like the best gift he'd ever gotten.

Alain Gets To Know Sampson

Oh, heaven and saints above, what was he doing? Why was he doing it?

Alain watched the numbers move on the lift, watching Sampson's hand holding his own. He could smell Sampson, feel the heat pouring off the tall body.

He felt awake, aware, alive.

Hungry.

He was hungry.

Alain hadn't been hungry in... too long.

When Kes had asked him to come down, he'd expected a quiet night, a few conversations, maybe a scene with Des, if Des was around. He hadn't expected a tall, puppy-eyed top who wanted to touch him.

Touch him.

Oh, he was a stupid fool, but he hadn't been awake for so long and...

Oh, who was he kidding. He'd known Harry for three minutes before he was kneeling between those thick legs and licking Harry's cock. This was so like him.

Sampson squeezed his hand. "Thank you. For um, inviting me up."

"Thank you for accepting." He looked up (and up and up) and smiled, squeezed back and manfully resisted the urge to snuggle into those arms.

The lift stopped and Sampson squeezed again, smile warm and excited.

"I'm all the way at the end. The blue door." It had been black when Harry was alive. He'd broken it in a bit of a drunken snit. Sort of. So. Now? Blue.

"Oh, nice." Sampson led him to his own home and waited to be let in.

He palmed the lock, leading Sampson into the suite. The whole place had been redone in a wash of blues

-- floors, ceilings, walls, furniture. It was beautiful and soothing and his.

"Come on in. Would you like anything?"

"I'd like um, some water available. For when we ah, start. So if um, either of us gets thirsty we don't have to um, stop. Oh! A safeword. Have you um, got one?"

"Of course. There's a stocked cooler in the playroom." Alain led Sampson to the huge playroom. It had been three rooms once, but they'd had the walls torn down, the atmosphere calm and quiet and empty. "My safeword is china."

He stood at the door, looking in. "I haven't ever brought someone here."

Sampson's hand slid up his back. "Oh. We don't have to, um. If you don't. One of the other playrooms um, might be, um less weird for you?"

He let himself lean back into Sampson's touch. "No. No, I... I want this. I want this with you."

It was the truth, too. There was something in Sampson's hands. Something necessary.

"Oh. Um, good. Yeah, good." Sampson's other hand came up, too, sliding through his hair. "Could I um, kiss you? I don't usually um, not unless it's part of the um, scene, but I ah want to. Kiss you."

He looked up and grinned. "I'd like that. Yes. Yes, please."

"Thank you um, for that. I mean this. Um." Sampson bent, and bent, hand around his back, the other one on his chin, tilting his face up. Sampson's lips were warm and soft, the kiss a touch clumsy.

Oh, there was a heat there, a sweetness and he opened up, lips parting. Sampson's tongue slid in, tasting gently. Alain simply melted, reaching up to feel the wild hair, moaning into their kiss. Sampson seemed content to the let the kiss go on and on, heat building between them. He was getting hard, leaning in to rub against Sampson, see how far he might go.

"Oh. Alain. I want to um, I'm sorry, you invite me for um, a scene and I. Want more than a um. A kiss."

"What do you want?" He moaned, hanging onto Sampson's shoulders.

"I want to um, make love first. And then um, the scene."

"Yes. Yes, please." He met Sampson's eyes, nodding. "Please."

"Um. Where? Here?"

"Come to my bed? We'll do the scene here, later. Make love to me in my bed." He took Sampson's hand, leading down the hall to his private room. The room that had only ever been his.

Sampson looked around very briefly and then turned to him, hands cupping his face, the long fingers stroking his skin, eyes following them, gazing at him. "You're very um, beautiful."

"Thank you." He stepped out of his shoes, stretching into Sampson's touch. "I'm hard for you."

"Oh. Me, too. Well for you, not um, me." Sampson smiled warmly, hand reached down and touching his prick through his pants, but only briefly. "I don't want to um, rush."

"No. I don't either. I want you feel you." Need to be touched. Felt. Please.

"Yes. So sensual." Sampson's long fingers began to work on his buttons, opening his shirt.

He returned the favor, fingers touching the warm, long body, shivering deep inside. Sampson pushed the shirt off his shoulders, fingers trailing over his skin. Alain moaned, shifting under the touches, hair tickling his back.

"So warm. Um... you fell ah, good." Sampson's lips covered his again, the long fingers wandering, taking random paths over his body. He managed to get Sampson's shirt open, fingers sliding up along the long body, searching out Sampson's nipples.

A shiver went through Sampson. "Oh. Can we um, go to the bed? I don't trust my um, knees."

"Yes." He moved to turn the covers back, the blue linen smooth on his fingers.

"Oh. Oh, Alain. What um, your back -- what's um, on it?" Sampson's fingers were back sliding his shirt down the rest of the way. "Oh wow. Oh. Oh."

"My butterfly." He arched, moaning under the touches. "It was done here."

"It's um, amazing. When you move it uh, looks alive." Sampson traced the swirls and circles in the wings, tracing the outline of the tattoo and the patterns within it.

"Oh..." He climbed onto the bed, moaning. "Your hands..."

"They like touching you um, or ah, I do." Sampson climbed onto the bed behind him, hands sliding down to undo his pants while hot kisses were placed along his spine.

He cried out, fingers curling in the sheets. So sensitive there. So good. So... "Good, Sampson. Hot..."

"It's like a um, mountain range on a map," Sampson murmured. "Your spine. Ah, a relief map." Sampson's tongue slid down along each bump.

Alain rippled, rocking, body sliding under Sampson's mouth. Sampson had his pants open and was tugging them down past his hips. He helped, baring himself eagerly, lost in the sensation, in the touching.

"Oh. Oh, so um, beautiful." His cock was outlined by careful fingers, Sampson's mouth working the small of his back, tongue teasing the top of his crack.

"Oh! Oh, I... So good." He jerked, moaning and shuddering and hard.

Really hard.

"You smell um, good. And ah, taste good, too. Alain." Sampson's fingers moved around to spread open his ass, tongue sliding down along his crack until it was teasing his opening.

He was whimpering, eyes wide as he shook. Oh. Oh, so giving. So real. So hot. "Sampson!"

One of Sampson's hands slid back around, checking his prick before returning to keep his ass spread open. Sampson's tongue worked his hole, teasing and licking and all of a sudden pushing into him. Alain's head lifted and he groaned, pushing back against Sampson, hips moving furiously. Oh. Oh, it had been so long. So long. So... Sampson fucked him with quick jabs, tongue as long as the rest of the man and pushing in deep.

"Going to come. Sampson. So good. So deep. Going to come..."

Sampson made a noise, a hum or a moan; all he knew was it sent vibrations along that tongue that was so deep inside him. One of Sampson's hands again slid around to his cock, circling it and pumping firmly.

Oh. Oh, sweet heavens and light. Yes! He felt his orgasm like a jolt of electricity, slamming through him in a wave, ending with heat pulsing from his cock.

As aftershocks shook him, Sampson pushed into him. He was stretched wide and deep before Sampson was pressed up against his ass, the large hands sliding over his back. "Oh, Alain. So um, tight. 's good."

"Oh, Sampson. So full..." He pushed himself upright, into those touches and then against the warm chest.

Sampson's arms came around him, those hands now traveling over his front. Sampson's cheek rested on top of his head, hips moving in long, slow strokes as he was explored. The long fingers slid around his neck and traced his collarbones. They plucked at his nipples and slid over the slim muscles of his belly and down to trace his hips, cup his balls, finger his cock.

Tears slid down his cheeks and he barely noticed, just caught up in the sensations, in being touched. “Oh, feels so good. Your hands, Sampson. Your hands.”

Sampson moaned and moved faster, hands wandering aimlessly now, just touching. He rode Sampson’s prick, flying under the touches, universe humming and vibrating and drawing him higher and higher into pleasure.

“Oh... Oh... Alain. Soon.” Sampson’s thrusts became stronger, filling him over and over.

“Yes. Yes, please. I want to feel you.” His head rolled against Sampson’s shoulder.

Sampson grabbed his hips and fucked him hard, balls slapping against the backs of his thighs. “Oh! Oh! Alain! Oh!”

Sampson jerked into him one last time, cock throbbing as heat pushed deep, deep inside him. The sensation made him moan, his own cock pulsing in response. Sampson moaned, cock sliding out of him. Then he was gently lowered to the bed and turned, pulled against Sampson’s long body.

“Oh, thank you, Alain. That was um, really, really ah, good doesn’t even um, start to cover it.”

He cuddled in, moaning as he was held, surrounded by warmth. “Thank you, Sampson. I... I needed that so.”

Sampson’s hand slid along his arm and his back, petting, touching, stroking. “Good. Good.”

“Yes.” He leaned up and took a slow, quiet kiss. “Yes, Sampson. Good.”

Sampson pulled him in closer. “Can we um, just lie together for um, a bit? Before we ah, do the scene?” Sampson shifted restlessly. “I um, like touching. A lot of ah, subs don’t unless they’re ah, with their um, own special top.”

"Please." He met Sampson's eyes. "Please hold me. I... This feels like magic."

"Maybe it is." Sampson's arms wrapped tight around him, pulling him in close.

"Yes. Maybe it is." He tangled himself in the comfort of Sampson and rested, heart beating easy in his chest.

Sampson and Alain's First Scene

Sampson dozed for awhile, holding Alain, touching the warm, smooth skin with idle sweeps of his hands. Alain's skin just begged for touches. For marks. He was going to use his hands when they did the scene so he could feel the heat come up to the surface.

Alain would look so pretty all marked up, he was sure. And the man was so responsive. Sampson didn't understand why Alain was still on his own. Unless there was some rule he didn't know about how long you had to wait before taking a dead man's sub.

If there was, he didn't want to know about it. He didn't want anyone to tell him he couldn't keep seeing Alain, couldn't keep touching him. Sampson kept waiting to feel restless, to feel the need to go do the scene now, but it didn't come, lying and holding Alain felt natural and easy.

At last he forced himself to untangle his body from Alain's. "Do you still um, want to ah, do the scene?"

Those bright eyes met his, relaxed, happy. "Yes. Of course. What would you like to be addressed as, in the playroom?"

"I'm used to um, Sir, but I'm ah, flexible. I won't have you um, call me master though." He didn't like that at all. A top didn't own his bottom, it was a symbiotic relationship, they belonged to each other. Well, he supposed that was just his philosophy. Still, he didn't want Alain calling him master

"Yes, Sir." Alain nodded and leaned up for another soft kiss. "Is there anything you would like me to prepare?"

"Not this um, time." It would just be him and Alain and his hands.

Alain nodded, pressing close for another heartbeat before sliding from the bed, so beautiful, so still waiting for him.

He got up, towering over Alain, like he tended to do with everyone. Alain didn't make him feel awkward though -- there was a quiet acceptance of his height that was really nice. He took Alain's hand and let Alain lead him back to the playroom.

It was a simple place -- a whirlpool in one corner, an adjustable table in another. There was a low mattress and a series of furniture -- all easily cleaned, easily moved.

Alain brought him to a console in the wall. "This controls the lights, the sounds, the temperature."

"What do you like the um, temperature to be?" he asked, but his fingers were already turning the controls, making it a little warmer so they would both be comfortable naked.

He felt Alain's nod against his arm. "That is good for me. I prefer not to be cold."

"Do you prefer the um, bed or the ah, table?"

"They're both very comfortable. They were made for me. Which would you prefer?" The table was taller, the mattress wider

"The table fits um, my height ah, better." If this were his playroom, he would build the bed up, make it wider, higher so he could stand beside it while touching Alain. It wasn't his room though.

Alain nodded. "Perhaps... Perhaps if you choose to spend more time here, we can order another bed." Those lovely eyes met his, so cautious. "One that suits us better."

Oh.

Oh, yes

"If you still um, want that after the uh, scene." He didn't want to presume that just because the lovemaking had been so good, everything else would be. But he hoped. Oh yes, he hoped very hard.

He got a smile, one that warmed him deep inside. "Yes. Yes, Sir, I believe I will."

Oh. Yes

"China, right?"

"Yes, Sir. China." Alain nodded again, dark hair brushing the pale cheeks

"Okay. Get on the ah, table. On your ah, stomach."

Alain moved gracefully, fingers trailing over another console pad. "This moves and arranges the table, should you wish to do so." Then Alain stretched out on the table, pale and fine.

He went to the table, walking around, looking at how wonderful Alain looked on the dark leather. Reaching out to touch, he gauged what needed to be changed about the table for him to be comfortable. After touching Alain all over from all around the table, he went to the console and made a few adjustments.

He came back and stroked the pretty, pert ass. "Are you um, ready?"

"Yes. Yes, Sir." The pale skin pinked a little, Alain flushing a bit

"I'm going use my um, hands. To ah, make you hot. Um, make you fly." He laid his hands on Alain, dragging them slowly over the smooth skin. Alain stretched for him, moaning softly.

He pressed harder against Alain's skin, warning him and then smacked the pretty bottom. The flesh jumped and pinked for him, the sound loud and arousing as it echoed. The next blow caught the top of Alain's thigh and the one after landed on the sole of Alain's foot. Alain's breath sped, toes curling, muscles shifting and rippling

"Beautiful, Alain. I thought that um, your skin would take ah, my marks."

He hit Alain again and again, palm slapping against

the pale skin, warming it, bringing the blood up to the surface. Alain was shifting and rocking under his touches, swaying with the rhythms of his blows.

He worked Alain until the sweat was pouring off him and his hand was burning and his cock was so hard he hurt. Alain's skin was red and pink and blue, heat and soft sounds pouring out.

Oh. So beautiful.

He wrapped his hand around his prick, crying out at the heat of it and coming over Alain's back. Alain jerked, hissing softly. That dark head fell back and a moan filled the air, body shivering

"You come, too," he murmured, rubbing his spunk into Alain's back.

Alain rippled under his hands, the scent of seed filling the air, a low cry answering his words. He shuddered. Alain was so beautiful, so responsive.

He kept touching, ignoring the burning in his hand in favor of sliding over Alain's warm skin. "Turn over. I want um, to touch ah, you."

"Oh... Yes, Sir." Alain turned carefully, settling gingerly on his marked back.

He frowned. The table wasn't soft enough for Alain's back, but he wanted to touch, needed to touch. Gingerly, he put his arms beneath Alain and carried him over to the mattress

"Oh. Oh, thank you." The slow tears filled Alain's eyes, a quietly overwhelmed, happy look on the thin face. "Your hands, Sir. So fine."

He wiped the tears away with his fingers and started to touch Alain again, the pale skin seemed cool beneath his burning hot palm. "They like um, touching you. I like ah, touching you."

"Thank you." Alain relaxed, purring softly, seeming to drink in his touches.

Such a sensual creature. It broke his heart that Alain had been alone for so long. It was wrong. But he could change that now. Maybe he would have spent all that money on a membership and never use the playrooms downstairs. That was okay though, as long as he could keep seeing the owner of this one

"Thank you, Alain. You um, are truly ah, beautiful. Thank you for um, letting me be a um, part of ah, you."

"My... Ohhh..." His fingers found a sensitive spot in the shallow of Alain's hip and Alain's entire body rippled. "Pleasure."

"So I um, can come ah, back? I mean um, to see, you know -- you?" he asked softly. He was pretty sure he knew the answer would be but he still held his breath

"Do you have to leave?" Alain's eyes opened, catching him. "Can't you stay?"

Oh.

Oh

"I have to uh, work um, in the morning." He wanted to stay though. He really, really did. "I need um, my uniform. And I um, have to be up ah, very early."

"Oh." Alain tilted his head. "What do you do? Is it very important?"

Oh, that was sweet, that Alain might think so. He shook his head. "I wash um, outside windows."

"Do you like it? Because... because there's jobs with Mal and there's a room for you here, maybe." The words were soft, tentative. "If you wanted it until you got staff quarters or even... maybe instead of staff quarters..."

Oh.

Oh.

Oh.

He held Alain really tightly. "Really? You um, think I could get um, a job here? And um, you um, want me to ah, move in. Um. With you?"

"Malachi is always looking for people and..." Those beautiful eyes met his. "I do. I'm lonely and you make me... not."

He couldn't think of anything he'd rather do than to move in with this beautiful man and to be able to do this more often. "Okay. Yes. Um. We should um, check with this um, Malachi first. Because I um, can't afford um, to not have a job." He hoped this Malachi wouldn't mind that he was. Well, tall. And sometimes clumsy

"Of course. Would you like me to contact him?" Alain cuddled in close, purring softly, hand warm on his belly.

He nodded. If he didn't set something up tonight, he'd have to report to work tomorrow and the wait until tomorrow night to find out if he would be able to stay with Alain would be so hard. "Yes, please. I um, want to um, stay with you. Um. Tonight."

"Oh. Oh, good." Alain leaned up, begging a kiss. "I'll find him and arrange a meeting tonight."

"Thank you, Alain." He closed the distance between their mouths, kissing Alain softly.

He hadn't been looking for Alain. Or. Maybe he had been and just hadn't known it. It didn't matter. Alain made him happy. And they felt good together. Like magic.

That was all that mattered.

Sampson Is Hired

Kestrel wandered around Mal's office, touching this and that and this as he waited to sit in on the meeting.

Alain.

Little Alain.

Wanting another live-in.

And not just another live-in, but this young, tall, sweet boy who couldn't be less like Harry if he tried.

Kestrel had been championing for Alain from the time Harry died. He'd been the one who'd gotten the call, Alain screaming and sobbing, Harry cold and still in the tub. It had been -- well, mostly truly icky and three-quarters gross, but still sad.

And then when Alain went through all the grieving.

And boozing.

And wild parties.

And drugs.

And depression and tears and threats and then the still quiet that even Des hadn't been able to penetrate.

And now? All of a sudden? Alain found a new partner.

Boom.

Just like that.

Hell, just like Des, but at least Sampson was a member and not some stranger.

Alain had looked happy, familiar, alive and relaxed and awake when he'd called down, though, and Kestrel thought that had to mean something. Not only that, but the boy wanted to work, wasn't looking to mooch off Alain's money and...

Oh, hell. Kes liked the idea of love at first sight.

It gave him hope.

The door opened and Mal came in with Sampson in

tow. “Kestrel. Sit down and quit fluttering.”

He met his best friend’s eyes and grinned as he sat. “Hello, Sampson.”

“Oh, hi um, Kestrel.” Sampson ducked his head, shoulders hunched slightly in what was no doubt an attempt not to loom over everyone.

Mal looked over, voice firm and sure. “Straighten up, boy. You say you’re a top, look like one. Now, Alain says you’re looking for work. What experience do you have?”

Sampson straightened up; that wild hair had to add a half a foot to the boy’s height.

“I’ve been, um, topping for, ah, five years. Most of my experience is um, at the Elegant Whip. Not on the um, payroll, but ah, they set up um, lists of those who ah, want to top and those who um, sub.”

“That’s a good club. Richocet’s a good man, solid. We’ve worked together before.”

Kestrel nodded in response. “Ric recommended Sampson, Mal. Called him...” He looked at his datapad. “A solid, confident top in scene. Thoughtful, sensitive. Don’t let the slouch fool you.”

Sampson pinked a little. “Everyone’s just so ah, short.”

Mal actually chuckled, the stern face relaxing a touch. “So tell us, what do you like? What are you into?”

“I’m ah, very good with um, hitting implements. Flogger, hand and uh, cat ‘o nine tails are my um, best tools.”

“Oh? Mal’s a whipmaster! You can share tips!” He bounced, clapping his hands happily.

“Kes.” Mal’s voice cut across the room and he settled.

“Oh, I’m sure I’m not um, a master. I um, don’t have that um, kind of um, experience. Oh.” Sampson looked chagrined. "Did I just um, talk myself out of a ah, job?"

"Not as quickly as you would have had you lied." Mal was going to hire the boy. Kes could tell. Mal always got that glint in his eye when he thought someone had potential.

"There wouldn't be any uh, point of um, lying. The first time I um, worked a scene you'd ah, know. I like um, what I do. And I'm uh, pretty good at ah, it. Not a ah, master though." Sampson's face screwed up. "I ah, don't like that um, word."

Kestrel tilted his head, curious. "Why not?"

"Because um, subs aren't ah, slaves. They're um, partners with the dom."

Mal leaned back, steepling his fingers. "You do understand the relationship Alain and Harold had, don't you?"

Kes nodded. "Harry was Alain's master in every sense of the word. Alain had no money, no possessions. Harry ordered his clothing, his food, everything."

"I don't ah, work like that."

Mal nodded. "Alain's older now, more confident, but you'll have to understand that he might be reluctant to express his opinion in daily life. It's his habit."

"Alain loved Harry. Very much. But..." Kes shrugged. "Their relationship had issues."

Sampson frowned. "I don't mean to be um, rude. But what does this um, have to ah, do with the um, job?"

"The job?" Mal shook his head and smiled. "Nothing at all. You can start tomorrow. Five hundred credits a month, free room and board and your membership fee will be refunded as you're now an employee."

Sampson gasped. "What do you um, I have to do ah, for that kind of um, benefits?"

"You'll work three nights and two days -- two days in the training room working with the new subs. Two nights on the floor answering questions, doing shows, demonstrations. One night you'll do private parties, private requests."

"Will I be um, expected to have ah, sex?"

"That's completely up to you. You'll be asked to complete a form outlining your limits that paying customers can access."

Kes grinned at Mal. "It's almost like your entrance form, Sampson. In fact, if you want, you can simply modify those answers."

"Oh, good um, all right. So, it won't um, affect my ah, position if I don't want to um, have sex with the ah, paying customers?"

"Not at all. I don't have sex with the customers. Neither do many of your coworkers."

Kestrel nodded. "And the ones that do usually have a small set of personal customers that they will... indulge with."

"Okay. Um. Where do I um, sign?"

Mal handed over a communit. "Here. And welcome aboard."

Kestrel bounced, clapping. "Welcome!"

Sampson grinned at him and smiled at Mal and ducked his head. "Thank you. Um. Yeah, thank you very ah, much."

"Remember, Sampson, head up." Mal stood. "All right, meet me in here tomorrow afternoon and we'll get started. I need to get back out on the floor."

"All right." Sampson nodded and held out his hand to Mal. "Um. Thank you."

Mal shook Sampson's hand, then turned to leave. "Don't nag him, Kes. The man's had a long day."

Kestrel blushed and grinned up at Sampson. "I wouldn't."

"Oh, Kestrel has been um, wonderful. He um, introduced me to ah, Alain." Sampson said Alain's name softly, almost reverently.

Kestrel stood and took Sampson's hand. "Do you have any questions I can answer?"

"Um... I don't, ah, know." Sampson squeezed his hand.

"About the Club? About..." He looked up. "Alain?"

"Alain..." Sampson smiled goofily. "Did I, um, say thank you? For um, introducing us."

Oh, the boy was as lost as Alain.

Utterly besotted.

How perfectly lovely!

"You did, but you should do it again. Come, let's go up and give your Alain the good news."

"Oh, yes. Um. Thank you." Sampson offered his arm.

He took that long arm and they headed toward the lifts. Oh, such fun. So many happy men.

So much love.

Sampson and Alain begin anew together

Kestrel was called away before they got back to Alain's rooms on the twenty seventh floor. Sampson hadn't ever seen anyone so busy or so full of bounce and life. He knocked tentatively on the door. It was really late, or rather really early -- nearly three am -- but he'd told Kestrel he didn't need his own rooms.

He still couldn't quite believe that in one night his world had turned around like this, but Alain was like gift from out of the sky and he wasn't about to turn it away.

He waited a moment and knocked again, even more softly this time. He could always just hunker down against the wall and doze for a few hours -- he'd had worse nights.

The door opened, Alain's beautiful green eyes blinking up at him, hair wet and curling around the thin shoulders. "Sorry. I was in the shower. Tomorrow morning, we'll change the palmlock so you can get in."

"If you're ah, still sure." He reached out, touching Alain's cheek. Such a lovely man.

Alain nuzzled right into his palm, a soft little sigh sounding. "I'm sure. Come home, Sampson. It's late."

"Oh. Um. Okay. Good, I mean, um... Oh. Thank you." He slid his arm around Alain's shoulders as he went in, loving to be close to this wonderful man.

"Would you like..." Alain's eyes glanced up at him. "Would you like to sleep with me, to share a bed? Or do you want to spend the night in your own room?"

"Oh. I would love um, to sleep with ah, you." He nodded. He really would. A lot.

"Oh, good. I had the sheets changed." Alain led him down the hall. "Are you sleepy? Hungry?"

"I'm a bit um, wired ah, actually. But I ah, want to

um, hold you."

Alain nodded and drew him into the peaceful room, hands slowly undressing him. "I'd love that."

"You'll let me um, touch? Your ah, skin is so um, soft."

A soft moan sounded, Alain nodding and pinking. "Please. I... Your hands. Your hands make me feel so good."

His shirt was removed, then his pants opened, Alain's cheek smooth on his belly.

"Oh!" He gasped, hands dropping to Alain's shoulders, pushing Alain's robe off thin shoulders and moaning softly as his hands slid along warm skin.

"I... um... feels good."

"Yes." Alain let the robe fall away, pushing his pants off. "Bed? Should we go to bed?"

"Um. Yeah. Yeah, I ah, let's go to um, bed."

Sampson wrapped his hands around Alain's shoulders and helped him stand, bending down to take a soft kiss. Alain's lips parted easily, the kiss light and sweet, those soft as silk hands sliding around his shoulders.

He walked Alain back toward the bed, keeping the kisses light while he was still trying to get them safely to the bed. It would be so easy to get lost in the kisses and the way Alain's skin felt under his fingertips.

They slid into the sheets, still sharing those soft kisses. Alain reached out and dimmed the lights, snuggling right into his arms with a happy little sound.

"Oh. Alain. You feel so um, good and um, warm." He slid his hands down along Alain's spine. It was like a path to the smooth, round, hot buttocks.

Alain's sounds were soft, warm, the slender body almost dancing against him. He moaned, licking at Alain's lips and then deepening the kiss. Alain gave a soft sob, hands digging into his hair and holding him close.

"Oh. Alain? Are you um, okay?"

"Oh, yes. Yes. It's just so good and I'm awake, you know? Awake for the first time in so long..."

"You've been um, sleeping?"

Those green eyes met his, so serious. "My heart has."

"Oh. Oh!" He smiled, heart full, belly so warm. "I woke your, um heart up?"

Alain nodded. "Yes. Yes, you did."

"Oh. Oh, Alain..." He stroked Alain's chest and put his hand flat over Alain's heart.

Alain's heart was pounding, those eyes fastened onto him. "Tell me you don't think I'm stupid, please?"

"If you're stupid, then I'm stupid, too, Alain."

"Oh. Oh, I can live with that. I can." He got a smile, wide and wondering and completely bare of that sorrow.

"Me, too."

He kissed Alain again, hand stroking the skin over Alain's heart, moaning softly. Alain pressed against him, legs tangling with his.

Sampson explored Alain slowly, fingers memorizing the curves and angles the soft skin covered. Alain's lips trailed over his skin, tongue sliding down his throat, over his collarbone. He moaned and took in one stuttering breath after another. This was... really, really good and he still couldn't quite believe it was happening. Well, except the warm body plastered to his was real enough.

He looked down at Alain's back, fingers tracing the lines of the beautiful butterfly inked there.

Alain shivered, gasping against his nipple. "Sampson..."

"It's so ah, beautiful. You're um, so beautiful."

"It feels so good. I feel so good." Those lips wrapped around his nipple, suction making him gasp.

"Me, too," he moaned, breathless, body moving against Alain's in time with the sucks.

Silken hands wrapped around his cock, pulling gently, fingers stroking.

"Alain!" Oh. He rocked into that touch, his own hands fumbling around to find Alain's cock so he could return the favor.

They found a rhythm, sliding and sucking and pulling and rocking together, creating a circle of pleasure and sensation.

"Oh, this is um, so good. Alain. Ah. Good."

Alain groaned, face lifting for a kiss. "Yes. Yes, so good."

Leaning in, he took Alain's mouth, the kiss hard and needy, reflecting the way their bodies were working together, searching for that high. Alain groaned, shuddering, hands squeezing as heat splashed over his fingers.

"Oh!" He cried out, his own pleasure slamming through him and making his hips snap hard against Alain as he sprayed into Alain's hand. Alain moaned, hand moving slowly, drawing out his pleasure.

"Alain. Oh. That was um. Yes, wonderful."

Alain nodded, settling close. "Yes. Yes, it was."

He wrapped his arms around Alain and settled his chin on the top of Alain's head. Oh, he could sleep now, long and hard and comfortable.

A soft blanket fell around him -- no, around them -- and Alain relaxed, soft snores starting almost immediately.

Oh. Oh, how did he get so lucky?

He held Alain close, his own eyes closing as he drifted off to sleep.

Sampson and Alain

Alain woke from a dream of Harry -- a familiar one where he was searching the club, searching for his master, for his lover, for his Harry. He had a thousand things to tell about -- days and days and days of sorrow and mistakes and new people and new lessons and Kestrel's help and Sampson's hands and the blue walls and Des and and and...

And he couldn't find Harry.

Still.

Damn it.

He gave up searching only moments before he woke. It was a shame, really. Harry might have liked Sampson.

Alain woke up wrapped around a warm body, almost clinging.

Sampson's hands, large and thin and warm, slid along his back, Sampson making some sleepy soothing noise.

Oh.

Oh, yes.

So much nicer than dreaming.

Alain cuddled in, hands exploring Sampson's belly, stroking and petting gently, careful not to disturb anything. Sampson's murmur was soft, happy. He drifted, sometimes asleep, sometimes not, just listening to Sampson's heartbeat.

"Your skin is so soft," Sampson murmured. "Like flower petals. Or a butterfly's wings."

He purred softly, pleased all through. He worked hard to keep his skin perfect, desirable, markable. "It aches for your touch."

"Mine specifically? Already?"

"I..." He blushed dark, hid his face in Sampson's chest. How fickle and flighty and impossibly naive he must sound. "You must think I'm silly."

"No. No, I um, think it's ah, great. I... um. Well my hands ah, ache to um, touch."

Sampson squeezed him. "I mean um, you specifically."

"Oh." He relaxed and grinned, pushing even closer. "Okay. Good."

"You think, um, other people are um, gonna ah, censure us?"

"Us? No. But you'll get lots of warnings, I'm sure." Alain sighed, hand petting Sampson's hip. "Lots of people are... mad at me." Maybe even furious.

"At you?" Sampson sounded disbelieving. "Why would anyone be mad at you?"

"Because after Harry died, I did some really bad, really stupid things. Lots of people wouldn't mind if I left the club, but Kes -- Kestrel -- helped me."

"Yeah, but, um, Harry died and you were, ah, left all alone and nobody, um, touched you. Of course you did stupid things -- you, ah, just wanted someone to um, touch you!" Sampson's arms tightened, held him close.

He nodded, eyes filling with tears. "Yes. Yes, that's it exactly."

"Oh, don't um, don't cry. Ah, please. You aren't ah, alone anymore."

"I'm sorry. I just..." He blinked quickly, clearing his eyes. "I don't mean to make you uncomfortable. It just feels so overwhelming, having someone understand me."

"I just don't want you to um, be sad." The long fingers wiped his cheeks. "You don't have to um, be sad anymore."

"Okay." He nuzzled into the touch, already distracted.

"You're so, um, sensual." Sampson chuckled. "We're never um, gonna make it, ah, to another um, scene. You keep, um, distracting, ah, me."

"I imagine we'll find our way back to the playroom, eventually." He grinned, nuzzling Sampson's chin.

"Will all this, um, beautiful skin just, ah, waiting for my, um hands to ah, mark them, I'm um, sure, too."

"Oh, yes." He shivered, hips shifting of their own accord, pushing toward Sampson.

"Can I, um, taste you?"

"Oh... Oh, yes, please." He nodded, rubbing against Sampson, wanton and ready.

"Cool." Sampson kissed him and then turned him onto his back, slowly kissing his way down.

He shuddered, thighs parting. "Hot."

"You, um, are." Sampson sucked at his nipples and licked a circle around his navel.

He peeped, toes curling. "Oh!"

That wicked tongue dipped into his navel and then nuzzled down toward one hip. "I um, love your skin."

"Thank you. Oh, you feel good, Sampson." He shifted, purring softly.

"You taste um, good. Really good." Sampson nuzzled his cock and licked the tip. "Really, um, good."

A soft groan escaped him, toes curling with the jolt of pleasure that shot through him.

Sampson took in the tip of his cock, sucking softly, tongue flicking across the very top. He whimpered, hips jerking restlessly, hands opening and closing again and again. Sampson hummed around his prick, mouth going slowly down on him.

He stretched out, vibrating with pleasure. "Sampson."

Sampson's hands were sliding over his skin, soft and gentle, as if reading him with the long fingers. He was lost to sensation, twisting and arching, babbling softly with pleasure. Then Sampson took him all the way in then let him out and then took him deep again, headed bobbing slowly. He arched, muscles ripping, balls drawing up tight.

Long fingers slid beneath him, grabbing his ass and sliding into his crack as the suction increased. Alain spread wide, crying out a warning scant seconds before he came, prick throbbing in Sampson's lips.

Sampson drank him down, sucking softly, gently.

He settled into the sheets, eyes dropping closed. "Oh. Oh, Sampson."

"Mmm... I love the way you um, taste. And the way, ah, you feel. So good, Alain." Sampson continued to lick at his skin.

Alain purred, hands reaching down to tangle into Sampson's hair. Sampson nuzzled into his touch, slowly kissing his way up. Every touch was pure warmth, sweet and right and easing his soul.

Sampson gazed down at him and brought their mouths together, kissing him, sharing the taste of his own come with him. He moaned, opening wide, tongue sliding deep into Sampson's lips. The long body more than amply covered his, keeping him warm, cocooned within Sampson's heat and aura. He took a moment just to revel in it -- the warmth, the pressure, the pleasure, the feeling.

Long-fingered hands cupped his face, thumbs stroking his cheeks. Sampson was so sensual, always touching. He pushed into that touch, moaning softly, almost shaking with pleasure.

"So sensual," murmured Sampson. "So, um, lovely." Sampson's cock was like a brand against him, sliding over his skin as Sampson slowly moved.

Alain reached down, hand wrapping around Sampson's cock. "How... What would you like? How can I please you?"

"Whatever you want." Sampson kissed him softly, eyes shinning down at him.

"Make love to me?" He reached up, stroking the wild, bright hair.

"Oh. Yes. Um, yes, please." Sampson nodded and smiled, looking pleased and eager.

The oil was close and he slicked his fingers easily, wrapping them around Sampson's cock and spreading the smooth oil, groaning at the heat.

Sampson groaned, eyes rolling, hips pushing into his hand. "Alain! Oh."

"So hot, Sampson. So hard." His thumb rubbed across the tip of Sampson's cock, pressing against the slit.

A squeaking gasp was his reply and shaking fingers dipped into the oil and then pressed against him. He spread, taking the touch easily, moaning with the sensation.

Two of Sampson's fingers pushed right into him, long and warm, finding his gland and stroking across it. "So, ah, hot."

"Your hands..." His body reacted immediately, eager for more sensation, more feeling.

"They're big." Sampson chuckled, and gave him a quick, hard kiss. "You feel so ah, good, everywhere, Alain."

"Love your touch." He gasped, pumping Sampson's cock in time with the movements of those long fingers inside him.

"Love, um, touching you." Sampson kept playing his gland, fingers scissoring and stretching and making him need again.

"Good!" He arched, heels digging into the mattress.

"Oh, I can't, um. Need to be, ah, inside you, um, now." Sampson's fingers slid away as if they were loath to go, the long body settling between his legs.

He drew his knees up, spreading wide, exposing himself completely.

"Oh, Alain.... so um, pretty and uh, needy."

Sampson's prick was so hot and slick as it pushed into him. Last night had been overwhelming and wild, but this morning, the sensations were clear, fierce, intense and right deep inside him.

Sampson stopped once he was all the way in, seated deep, deep inside. "Oh. So um, hot. Tight. Good. Um. Alain."

He wrapped his legs around Sampson's waist, nodding, encouraging. Sampson started moving, motions quick and needy as the long cock pulled almost all the way out before sliding back in again and again.

"So deep..." One hand fell to his belly, pressing down, trying to feel Sampson moving inside him.

"Feels... um, good."

Sampson kept moving, hands braced on either side of his head, the long, deep strokes sliding past his gland and beyond. He nodded, leaning up to nuzzle Sampson's throat, shoulder, hips meeting each thrust. His new lover moaned at his touches, driving the thrusts harder, faster. Oh, it felt good. Fine. Hot. Necessary.

"Touch yourself," whispered Sampson.

He whimpered, hand sliding down immediately to stroke and pump and rub, his body clenching around Sampson's prick.

"Oh! Yes." Sampson's breath was coming faster and faster, matching the thrusts of those thin hips.

He could hear his breath whistling out of him, thin and quick, wanting so bad.

"Soon, Alain."

"Yes. Yes, Sampson." He arched, eyes closing as he flew.

Sampson cried out, jerking hard into him, filling him with heat. His own orgasm followed, a flush of warmth spreading throughout him. Sampson lay on top of him again, still inside him, weight held off him with one hand. The other was busy touching him again, sliding gently along his side. He rested his cheek in the curve of Sampson's shoulder, purring softly.

"Oh, Alain. I, um... Um... Alain, I think, I um, love you." The words were soft, but sure despite the pauses, whispered into his ear.

"So soon?" He closed his eyes, snuggling in.

"I've just, ah, never, um, felt anything so, um, right. What else would it, ah, be?"

Alain smiled and shrugged -- he wasn't sure. Could be love, could be lust. Could be raw need. "I don't know what else it could be. We'll just go with love and see if that works for us."

"I'm um, sorry," Sampson murmured, pulling out of him and shifting. "I didn't um, mean to make you, ah, uncomfortable."

"Sampson?" He reached out, loath to lose the contact. "Please. I've been alone so long and you're the only one beside Harry who ever made me feel so much. I just... I want to be sure."

Sampson's arms came back around him. "You don't have to um, say it ah, back. I just... I don't want you to um, be uncomfortable if I ah, say it. Or, um, think it. I just... Um. This feels like, ah, um, perfect to ah, me."

"Oh, good." He leaned up for a kiss. "Because nothing's felt so right in forever."

"Yeah? Um. Good. I'm, ah, glad." Sampson kissed him softly, tongue teasing its way into his mouth. He met the kiss, moaning happily, arms wrapping around Sampson's neck.

Sampson pressed against him, hands sliding over him again as the kiss went on and on, leaving them both rather breathless.

"We're going to have to have food delivered in

here..."

Sampson chuckled. "I was just, ah, thinking I was um, hungry for more than ah, you."

He laughed, holding on tight as the chuckles echoed through the room. "What would you like and I'll have it ordered."

"I don't, um, know. I usually, ah, have, um, nutrition bars."

He wrinkled his nose. "How about fruit and bread and cheese? It'll be bright and yummy."

"Oh, that um, sounds really, ah, good." Sampson nodded, eyes a little wide.

"Cool. I like fruit and cheese." He reached up, stroking Sampson's cheek. "You'll have to tell me everything you like, so you'll feel at home."

"I've never, um, eaten out very much. Mostly, ah, just nutribars and, ah, the workers' cafeterias. I um, really like, ah, pancakes. And um, real meat."

"Mmm... pancakes. Yummy." He grinned. "I could have blueberry ones brought up."

"Oh! With that um, sticky, ah, sweet stuff?"

"Syrup? Of course. Caffe or tea?" He sat up and reached for a commlink, tapping in their order.

"Oh, um... would it, um, be too, ah, greedy if I, ah, asked for um, synthmilk?"

"Are you allergic to the real stuff? I can get that."

Sampson just looked at him. "Real? Oh. Oh, wow. Um. Oh, wow."

"I'll take that as a yes." He ordered some milk and some juices to be delivered.

"I didn't um, think they, ah, made real ah, milk anymore."

"Well, the cattle are rare, but Hercules keeps us supplied. He's a good man."

"Wow. I, um, I'm not sure I, uh, can, um, afford, ah,

this kind of, um, thing."

"You're on salary, yeah? I mean, even if not, I can order what I want, but you get to eat -- free." Herc was good to his people, very good.

"Oh. Yeah, I am. But, uh, I didn't know that um, meant real, ah food. I thought they would, um, hand out, ah, nutrition bars and um, supplement drinks."

"No. Hercules doesn't work that way." He grinned, ordering a few random snacks and items.

"Wow. Cool. Um. I think I'm, um, going to like, ah, working here."

"I hope so." He twined their fingers together. "I hope you like more than just working here."

"Oh. Oh, you know I, um, like you more, um, than pretty much, ah, anything. Don't, um, you? Because I um, do." Sampson nodded, hand squeezing his.

"Yeah." He chuckled, wiggling closer. "Yes. I do, too."

"Cool."

Sampson held him close. "You're um, happy? I'm happy and I um, want you to, ah, be happy, too."

Alain nodded. "I think so, yeah. I feel... awake and alive."

"Good. Okay. Um. Yeah. This is, um, good." Sampson's hands stroked his spine, tracing the butterfly from memory now.

"Mmm... Yeah. You want to get a shower?" He shivered, scooting closer.

"Is it, um, big enough for, ah two?" Sampson didn't seem in any hurry to let go of him.

"It is. There's a bench and everything. Detachable head. Interesting toys..." Harry loved playing in the water.

"Oh." Sampson laughed. "Oh, that sounds, um, fun."

"There's a lot about living here that's fun. I hope we can share them. Together."

"I um, like the, ah, sound of that, um Alain. I like the um, sound of it, ah, a lot."

Sampson's First Night As an Employee of The Glove

Sampson's first night of work had been... interesting. The better part of the evening had been spent following Mal around, finding out where everything was kept and how things worked. The club had everything anyone could possibly think to want and more besides. It was as amazing as it was intimidating and he kept reminding himself that he was an employee here now, he had no reason to be intimidated. Except perhaps by Mal, whose admonition to stop slouching had become a mantra.

Mal was extremely intimidating without even opening his mouth. The man had a presence that everyone could feel -- he'd watched as every time they came into a room, everyone immediately looked to Mal and the respect and awe there was palpable.

By the end of the evening spent with Mal, he'd found himself standing just a little taller, with a little more pride -- he never once felt too tall or overbearing with Mal.

He'd spent the last couple of hours of his shift teaching a man how to use a cat 'o nine tails most effectively.

Most beginners made the same mistake and whipped too hard, bloodying the skin immediately which shortened the session dramatically. The trick was to have a delicate touch, to make the tails an extension of your hand, like nine fingers. Of course, if you touched the skin too lightly, it was more of a caress than a blow.

It took time and practice and a willingness to try it until you got it right to become good at the tails, let alone an expert at them. The top he'd been working with was patient though, as were the half dozen subs in training they'd gone through.

The top, who'd looked skeptical when Mal had first

introduced them, booked an appointment for next week and gave him a very large gratuity. Which he'd handed over to Mal, believing it to be the club's fee.

He'd been floored when Mal had tossed the credchip back to him and informed him that the staff were entitled to keep any tips they got, but not to expect them as they were not in any way expected of the guests.

He made his way up to Alain's rooms, rubbing his right arm. It had been a rather long work out. He only just kept himself from knocking on the door. This was his home now, too.

Who would have believed that he would find himself in the most luxurious suites in one of the most exclusive clubs in New Angeles? Oh, he'd heard the whispers and the rumors. Only five people had suites on this floor and there had been many who'd wondered how an employee came to have his palmprint open one of them.

He let himself in, calling Alain's name softly. He didn't want to wake his new lover, but he longed to touch the beautiful, soft skin again, to look into those warm eyes that made him feel so good.

"Alain?"

"In the bathroom, love." There was a soft chuckle, then a splash.

His heart started beating faster and he made his way to the bathroom. Oh, he was lost, just lost.

Alain was lounging, neck-deep in bubbles, a bit of fruit juice by the tub. He got a smile, warm and true and happy, one thin leg appearing from the froth. "How was your first night?"

"It was um, different. But ah good." He sat on the edge of the tub, fingers sliding over Alain's leg. "Did you, um, have a good, ah, evening?"

"I missed you. I had an appointment with Hawk to do a show, but..." He shrugged. "I didn't know how you felt."

"Oh." He blinked. "What kind of, um, show?"

"Hawk does whippings, some, but he's mostly about penetration -- fisting, plugs, that sort of stuff." Alain stretched under his touch. "I sometimes act as a warm body."

"Do you, um, like it?"

"Do I like what?"

"Being a, um... warm body?"

Alain pinked and shook his head after a long pause. "No. No, I don't."

"Oh. Then don't um, do it." He slid his hand up Alain's leg into the water, teasing the soft skin, so silky in the soft water.

"Would... would you want me to?" Alain spread easily.

"Not with um, anyone, ah else. But I would, um, be proud to ah, show you , um, off."

"Oh." Alain gave him a smile -- all pleasure and happiness. "I would be at my best for you."

"We need to um, get to, ah, know each other properly first. I mean, um, in , ah scenes." He leaned in. "Can I um, come in with ah, you."

Alain reached up for him, eyes shining. "Yes. Yes, please." The scent was soft, musk and a hint of flowers, the bubbles thick.

He took his clothes off eagerly and slipped into the water. Oh, it was hot and silky and his legs tangled with Alain's.

Alain purred and snuggled close, hands pouring water over his chest. The long fingers slid over his skin, so warm, so soft. "Hi."

"Hi." He leaned in, kissing the lovely lips.

Alain tasted tart and sweet and bright, lips opening easily for him. He moaned softly, hands sliding over

Alain's skin. So soft. He had never felt any man so soft.

"Mmm..." Alain pushed up against him, rubbing, cock slowly filling against his thigh.

"Oh. You make me um, so hard. Make me, um, want." His slid his hands around to Alain's back, tracing the lines of the butterfly he now knew by heart.

"Good. I want you. I was touching my skin, getting hard, waiting for you."

"Oh." Oh, Alain said the most amazing things.

Alain's soft black hair floated in the tub, tickling his belly. He giggled, taking Alain's mouth in a happy kiss. Alain fed him a sweet sound, leg wrapping around his waist. He moaned, hands sliding to Alain's ass, cupping the round cheeks and squeezing. Alain felt so good against him, the oiled water increasing that. Alain shivered and pushed back into his touch, a sweet sound vibrating between them.

One of his fingers teased Alain's hole, sliding along it, pushing in just a little as he sucked gently on Alain's tongue.

Alain's eyes -- so bright, so clear -- stared at him, pleasure sharp in them.

Always so open to him, even though they'd just met. Alain's need to be touched and cared for sang to him, he still could not believe he was the first to respond to the sad beauty. In fact it incensed him that Alain had been left to his own devices the way he had, left to wander and linger and need. It made him growl, his hands growing hard on Alain's skin.

A needy sound was pressed from Alain, those lips swollen and parted. "Oh... Please..."

It snapped him back to where he was and he pulled Alain tight against him, rocking their hips together. "What do you, um, need?"

"You." Alain rubbed against him, panting softly. "You

make me feel so alive."

"And you've been, um, asleep for, ah, so long." The oily water made their skin slide easily together and he held tighter to Alain, pulled them harder together, his hips moving. "Oh, you feel so, um, good. So good."

"Yes. Yes, Sampson. So good." Alain's fingers tightened on his shoulders as their motions grew rockier.

He took Alain's mouth again, licking the kiss-swollen lips and dipping his tongue inside. Alain cried out, lips fastening around his tongue and pulling. It was as if Alain was pulling on his cock, making his balls ache with each tug to his tongue.

Whimpering, he rubbed them together harder. The water splashed around them, Alain jerking and shuddering, then going still, come spraying between them.

Oh! He held on tight to Alain as his own orgasm hit him, the water unbelievably wonderful against his skin.

Alain cuddled in, purring softly. "Oh, Sampson. I...I'm so glad you're home."

"Home. Yes. Um. Me, too."

He wrapped his arms around Alain, fingers softly stroking. Touching Alain was like breathing -- necessary and done without thinking. It was impossible. So new, so soon, so much. But impossible or not, he loved and was loved. He was home.

Sampson and Alain After Work

Alain dozed, the water automatically being exchanged with warm, fresh, clear liquid. Sampson's heart beat under his ear and he felt at one with the universe.

Finally he nuzzled against Sampson, purring softly. "How was your first day at work? Was Mal good to you?"

"Hmm? Oh. Yes. I um, mostly followed him, ah, around. Learned the ropes, he ah, called it. Then I, um, started, um, teaching someone how to, ah, use a cat." Sampson's hands still moved on him, never seeming to tire. "Mal um, put me down as, ah, a free, um, top, who ah, won't have, um, sex with the uh, clients."

He swallowed, looking into Sampson's eyes. "Oh? Really? That's good." That meant that making love? Was theirs.

Sampson nodded, smiling down at him. "I don't want to um, do that with, ah, anyone else. You're um, special."

He blushed hot, reaching up to tug Sampson down for a long kiss. "So are you. So special."

"I'm glad you um, think so." Sampson's cheeks were pink, clashing with the wild red curls on his head.

"I do. Really. Would you like some food? What do you like to do after work?" He stroked through the amazing curls, smiling at the texture.

"This was, um, nice. Relaxing. And yeah, I'm, um, quite hungry now. And um, kind of wanting to, ah, play." Sampson's blush got darker. "Working evenings, I'll probably, um, sleep during the, ah, day. Do you, um, mind adjusting your, ah, schedule to, ah, match mine?"

"I don't. I'm a notorious night owl. What would you like to eat? Something downstairs or up here?" Oh, and let's play. Now. So hurry and eat. Please.

That sweet blush got darker still. "Ah, um, a protein shake will, um, do me. Light and um, quick."

He nodded, shivering with anticipation. "What flavor? I have cafe, chocolate, berry, vanilla, and mint."

"Wow. I, um, I've never had, ah, anything but, um, cafe and um, funny tasting chocolate, um, before. I um, will try the ah, mint."

Sampson kissed him and stood, bringing him up. "But you, um, tell me where the, ah, cold unit, ah, is. You aren't my, um servant and I um, can get it, ah, myself."

He handed over a towel, blushing, but nodded. Right. Right.

"Come on, I'll show you where it all is and where you can make orders to have brought up."

"Thank you, ah, Alain. Maybe um, sometimes, I'll ah, serve you."

"Oh. I... You don't have to do that. I..." He blushed darker, blinking up at Sampson. "I'm going to take a little while to get used to this -- to being with someone who is my partner."

Sampson kissed him softly, holding him close. "Is it, um, okay? I don't think I can, um, treat you like, um, a slave, but I could, um, try if you needed, ah, that."

"No. No, I want this. It's a matter of habit." He found a grin for Sampson. "I can just make us a better habit."

"Oh, good." Sampson kissed him again, looking happy. "Let me, um, get my, ah, drink. I really, um, want to play."

They wandered into the kitchen, Sampson drinking while Alain showed him the whole set up, the whole works. "You can order anything and they leave it in the little cabinet outside that you can access here. That way, you don't have to leave the rooms."

Sampson giggled. "So you can, um, stay naked and no

one, um knows."

He grinned and nodded. "Especially after a long session -- you know, when your skin can't bear fabric?"

"Oh, do you, um, like that?"

"What part?"

"Long, um, sessions that, ah, leave you too sensitive to, ah, wear clothes." Sampson was blushing, but he was grinning, too, eyes bright.

He bit his lip, balls and nipples going tight. "Yeah. Yeah."

Oh, yeah.

Sampson's smile got bigger. "I was, um, teaching someone the ah, cat today. So I'm, um, all warmed, ah, up."

He shivered again. "I'm all relaxed. Ready."

Real ready.

"Okay. You go to the um, playroom. I'll get my um, cat from my, um bags."

Oh. Oh, yes. He was covered in goosebumps, shivering as he turned the heat up a little and adjusted the new bed he'd had delivered today -- one that addressed Sampson's height.

Sampson was not far behind him, looking as eager as he felt, giving him such a warm, happy smile. He offered Sampson a smile of his own. Oh, this was so different, so easy and warm and simple.

"Would you like, um, to stand or lie down and um, bound or, ah, stay still by, um, your will alone?"

"What do you like, Sir? I prefer to be bound, if I stand."

"For the cat I, um, prefer um, standing and bound. It, um, stretches you, ah, out more that, um way."

Sampson looked around, still unfamiliar with the playroom. "I assume you've, um, got that, ah, built in?"

He nodded, pulling out his step stool and climbing up to open the panels on the wall. "Do you want rope or leather or cuffs or chains?"

"Are the um, cuffs lined?"

"We have silk lined and fur lined and unlined." He pulled the rack of items out, showing them all off.

"Wow. Anything I, um, want. The silk, um lined ones. The only, um, marks on your, um, body should, ah, be mine."

He bit his bottom lip, stifling his low moan, and nodded, pulling them down. "They tighten here. Do you want ankle restraints also?"

"Yes, I do."

Sampson let him pull them out and then stepped forward and put him into the cuffs, hands so gentle on his skin. "I want to, um, hear your ah, noises."

He stretched out, nodding and letting his sigh escape as he tested the restraints. "Yes. Yes, Sir."

Sampson tightened the arms a little, stretching him a bit more. "Are you, um, comfortable?"

He nodded, relaxing into the cuffs. "Yes. Yes, I'm good, sir. Thank you."

"Do you need, um, any time to, ah, get ready?"

"No. No, I'm ready. I'm here." If he was any more ready he'd be begging for it like one of Mal's worker bee trainees.

"I'm ready, um, too."

The cat 'o nine tails slid over the skin of his shoulders and down along his left side, across his buttocks and between his legs. His fingers tightened and he shivered, forcing himself to breathe slowly, steadily.

He could hear Sampson's breathing as well: even, calm breaths.

The leather tails left his body and the soft whisper of them through the air was his only warning before they landed on his back. His breath left him, the sensation sure and sweet, leaving a burn behind.

Again and again the tails fell across his back, his shoulders, his ass and thighs. The whip landed with various strengths, now almost whisper soft, now hard enough he was sure his skin must have split. His head fell back, hair protecting his skin, making it itch, driving him wild as he gasped.

The next time the cat 'o nine tails fell two of the tails licked between his legs, kissing his balls. He cried out, thigh muscles going hard as stone, balls trying to draw up inside his body.

The next lick also managed to touch his balls, whisper soft but there.

Oh, fuck. Fuck, he'd known Sampson was good, but this? This was...

Oh, sweet fuck.

The whipping continued until he was burning from neck on down to ankles, time having fallen away leaving only the touch of the tails on his skin. He was flying, a constant low moan pushed from him. Alain stopped waiting for the next blow, stopped anticipating, simply was.

He hadn't even realized the whip had stopped falling until Sampson's voice sounded at his ear, soft and whispery. "I'm finished."

He couldn't form words, throat just working, lips parted.

A straw was placed at his lips. "Just a few, um, drops to, ah, start with."

He sucked the juice in, moaning at the cold and bright and sweet, muscles shaking.

The juice disappeared and Sampson's hands slid over his ankles, warm as they removed the cuffs. "Can you, um, stand?" Sampson asked, hands on his wrist.

"Yes, Sir." He nodded, then swayed, leaning against the wall.

His wrists were unbound and Sampson helped him turn, helped him walk over to the bed, holding onto his hands.

"Thank... thank you, Sir." He held onto Sampson's hands, slowly coming down.

"It was my, um, pleasure, Alain."

Sampson laid him down on his stomach and touched the thermostat, turning the heat up a little before sliding onto the big bed with him. His hair was brushed from his back and from his face, Sampson leaning in to kiss him softly.

He moaned into the kiss, slow tears leaking from his eyes as he relaxed. Sampson's mouth slid from his, kissing his nose and his eyes, tongue stopping to lick away his tears. One of the big hands wrapped around his own, fingers sliding along his palm.

"Please stay with me." He was floating down, holding onto his lover.

"Always, Alain."

He nodded, sleep sliding up to get him, his body unwilling to move.

Always.

He was good at always.

Sampson and Alain Get Ready to Go Out

Sampson's first few days of work went well. His first few days with Alain were amazing.

He'd taken some teasing for moving in with Alain who was older and had a bit of a reputation since his former master had died. He didn't like it. People talking about them and getting it wrong.

So he decided he and Alain needed to go out so people could see them, could see that they cared about each other and he wasn't Alain's master, that they had a symbiotic relationship. That Alain wasn't using him and he wasn't using Alain.

And then the rumors could move on to the next new thing.

"Alain?" He called for his lover as he got home from working a half day. "How do you um, feel about ah, dancing?"

"Hmm?" Alain looked up from a mat on the floor, his lover stretching, dressed in a tight bodysuit that hid nothing. "I love dancing."

"Then ah, let's go for um, dinner and ah, dancing this evening."

He was tall and awkward on the dance floor, but he loved moving to the music and he thought maybe he would be distracted enough by Alain, he'd forget to be self-conscious about it.

And he had the perfect idea to make it a little more fun, a little exciting.

"Okay. I'd like that." Alain rolled up and stretched, wiggling a little. "How was your day?"

Sampson watched Alain move for a moment, distracted by the slender body. "Oh, um, not ah, bad."

He opened his arms. "Half days are um, apparently, ah, for, um, cleaning and uh, ordering and ah, filing."

Alain pushed into his arms with a happy little sound, those beautiful eyes smiling up at him. "Ick. Cleaning."

"It's not so um, bad. Gave me, um, ideas."

He leaned down and kissed Alain, moaning softly at the taste. Oh, Alain tasted good. Alain rubbed against him, opening easily, tongue sliding against his, meeting him halfway.

Just like that his cock started to get hard. Wow, he really did have it bad.

"Let's go to, um, the ah, bathroom. I have um, an idea."

Alain nodded, following him, fingers twining with his own.

"I thought that um, we'd, ah, go out before um, doing anything."

Alain looked up at him, surprised. "Oh. Okay. I can do that."

One hand brushed against his cock. He whimpered softly. Well... they didn't have to wait.

"Mmm... You want." Alain stopped, knelt before him, mouth hot through his pants. "Please, love. Let me?"

He nodded, hand sliding through Alain's hair. "Yes."

Alain purred for him, those clever fingers unlacing his pants and freeing his cock easily, lips sliding down the shaft. Moaning, he spread his legs slightly for balance and then he just watched as Alain made him feel so good.

Alain's head bobbed slowly, lips and tongue hot on him, so hungry, so eager. So beautiful and giving. Sampson still couldn't believe no one had wanted this lovely man. Alain was moaning, mouth working upon him, his cock sliding deep into the tight throat. Alain's hair brushed his pants legs, making a soft swishing sound.

So sexy.

"Feels good," he whispered, moaning as Alain's tongue did something amazing around the head of his cock.

Alain kissed the tip of his cock, nodding. "Love you." Then he was taken back in deep.

"Oh! Love you, ah, too."

Whimpering, he started moving his hips, trying hard not to lose control -- he didn't want to hurt Alain. Alain's eyes met his, throat relaxed, hands urging him to move, to press deeper.

"Oh." He gasped softly and slid his hands around Alain's skull, holding it lightly as he moved his hips, giving Alain everything.

Alain took him, open and easy and wanton. Pleasure went up and down his spine, settled heavily in his balls and made him moan and cry out.

"Close, Alain."

Alain moaned, swallowing hard, fingers hot on his balls.

"Alain!" He shouted out, nearly falling as he came hard.

Alain kept him upright, kept him steady, tongue pulling aftershocks from his body.

"Oh, Alain, you um, make me ah, feel so um, good."

"That's what I do, love. I want to make you feel good."

"Thank you." He stroked Alain's cheek. "Come on. It's, um, my turn to, ah, make you um feel good."

"Mmm..." His hand was nuzzled and then Alain stood, following him, cuddled into his side.

"I want to um, try something."

He found a tube of lube. "Oh. I um, need a dildo. Something not too, ah, big, but you have to um, know it's ah, there."

"A dildo or a plug, sir?" Alain's voice was low, husky.

"Oh, a plug." He nodded. "That would, um, work better." He smiled shyly. "You're going to ah, wear it while we um, go dancing."

"Oh..." Alain shivered, eyes shining up at him. "Y... yes, Sir."

Oh, he liked putting that look in Alain's eyes.

Alain scooted off, returning with two plugs, one heavy and one smaller with a controller. "I wasn't sure which you'd want."

He took the one with the controller, checking it out. Oh, this would be fun. But not while he was trying not to step on Alain's feet.

"This one we'll use um, another, ah, time."

Alain nodded happily, pushing into his arms. "We're going to play."

He wrapped his arms around Alain, giggling softly. "Yeah." He bent and kissed Alain, tasting himself in Alain's mouth.

"Mmm..." Alain pressed close, purring, hands sliding up his arms.

He slid his hands along Alain's body, looking for away to get the sexy outfit off. Or at least open.

Alain brought his fingers to a hidden zipper, under his arm.

"Oh, I never would have um, found it." He slid the zipper down and helped Alain get out of the suit, fingers lingering on the warm skin. Alain hummed, wriggling against him, cock bobbing and full.

"So soft. Um. I just want to ah, touch you um, all the time."

"I love your hands, Sampson, love your touch." Alain was glowing, moving for him.

"Oh, you look, um, perfect." He stroked Alain's cheek. "Bend um, over the sink."

"Yes, Sir." Alain bent deep, thin thighs parted, ass flushed a sweet rose.

Oh, so obedient. So beautiful.

He slicked up his fingers and slid one into Alain's body. Alain purred, entire body rippling, taking him in. He pushed another finger in, slowly working Alain, stretching Alain as he bent and kissed Alain's back.

"Oh... Oh, love..." Alain started moving, fucking on his fingers.

"You're not, um, allowed to ah, come. Do you need ah, something?" He wanted Alain to wear this glow while they ate, while they danced.

"Oh. Oh, please. I... You make me need so much, your hands."

He reached over and opened the cabinet, finding a simple cockring there. Reaching around, he found Alain's cock, hot and hard and leaking. Alain went up on his toes, hips jerking, ass clenching around his fingers.

"Shh. Shh. Don't, um, come." He slipped the ring around Alain's cock, snapping it closed. "It's not too, um, tight?"

"No. No. God. Sampson." Alain's hips were moving, the sweet lips parted, eyes shining. "Oh, you make my body sing."

"You look so um, beautiful." He added another finger, watching as Alain pulled them in, moved on them.

"Yours. Oh..." Alain flushed, body begging, sheened with sweat, so excited.

He pulled his fingers away and bent to kiss the sweet hole. Alain's cry was sweet, needy. All for him. Sampson licked and kissed again and then took the plug, slicking it up before bringing it to Alain's hole. "Open, um, for me."

Alain's thighs parted, the slender body pressing back, slowing spreading.

"Oh, Alain... Oh." He watched as Alain's body slowly took in the heavy plug, opening to his desire.

"Sampson... Oh... Filling me. Oh..." The cries were

sharp, hungry, Alain panting.

"So beautiful," he murmured, one hand stroking Alain's back, the other continuing to feed the plug into Alain's body.

"Yours. Love." Alain's body shuddered, finally snapping around the base of the plug.

"Yes, um, mine."

Oh, yes, his. So beautiful and all his.

He twisted the plug.

"Sampson!" Alain jerked, hips pushing back into his touch.

Oh, perfect. Beautiful and responsive and perfect.

"Come dancing ah, with me." Suddenly he wanted to show Alain off, not to prove anything to anyone, but because Alan glowed, was beautiful and everyone should see something like him once in their life.

"Yes. Yes, Sampson." Alain stood, cock full and dark, proud, curving toward the flat belly.

He petted it gently. "I love you."

"Oh. Love you. What should... Oh, love, your hands... What should I wear?"

"Um... something ah, tight like what you were um, wearing before." Me.

Alain nodded, eyes fastened onto his, desire almost palpable. He stroked Alain's belly, wanting almost more than anything to stay in and mark Alain, make him truly sing and then send him soaring to the skies.

But he wanted this too. "I'll change and um, meet you at the uh, door in, um ten minutes?"

"Yes. Yes, Sampson." His lover moved like a dream, so careful, so graceful filled.

He watched until Alain's door closed before going to his own room. Wow. He had to be the luckiest guy ever.

Sampson and Alain Go Dancing

He was wearing black, the material clinging to him like a second skin, his hair down and loose, invisible against the material. He'd painted his eyes for Sampson, the black paint and silver glitter making his eyes huge.

Aware of every step he took, he moved down the hall toward the door, eyes lifting to meet Sampson's. "I'm ready, love."

Sampson's soft gasp was his reward, green eyes dark beneath the explosion of red curls. "You're so beautiful."

Alain smiled, spinning so slowly, body thrumming. "Yours."

Moaning softly, Sampson held out his hand. "We should um, go. Before I ah, change my um, mind." Sampson was wearing a dark green silk shirt over dark grey pants, looking as elegant as Alain had ever seen him.

He nodded, hand settling on Sampson's belly, so warm, so soft. "Yes, love. You look so handsome. Come let me show you off."

Sampson giggled. "I thought I was um, showing ah, you off."

He chuckled. "No one wants to see me, love. You're eye-catching."

Sampson gave him a disbelieving look. "I look like um, a dork. You look like ah, beautiful."

"You look like my lover, my Sampson." He pressed close, shuddering with sensation. "You make me need."

Sampson's arms came around him, hands on his ass. "I love you."

His lover bent, bringing their mouths together in a soft, but deep kiss. Alain cried out, ass pushing instinctively into Sampson's touch, needing. The long fingers teased his crack, touched the plug, jostling it gently. He shuddered, body rubbing against Sampson's, more aroused, excited than he could remember in years.

One of Sampson's hands came around to slide along his cock, his hard flesh outlined in the black material. "Everyone will, um, see," Sampson murmured, voice husky.

"Does that please you?"

Sampson nodded. "Yeah. They'll, um, see you and ah, know that you ah, want, um, me." Sampson's hands slid over his body. "I um, do this to ah, you."

"Yes. You do. I need. You make me need." He reached up, stroking Sampson's hair.

Sampson hunched down, giving him easier access. His lover was smiling at him, looking happy.

"Mmm... you'll dance with me? Touch me?"

"Yes. That's the um, idea." Sampson kissed him again and then took his hand and led him to the lift.

Every step made his balls throb, his entire focus on his body and Sampson's will. Sampson held his hand in the lift, looking down at him now and then and smiling, looking so happy, eyes shinning. There was a bulge in Sampson's pants that his lover made no move to hide.

The bass from the music was pounding as the lift door opened, vibrating through him, making him gasp and shiver. Sampson stroked his cheek and then they were moving out into the main floor of the club, Sampson slowly winding them through the crowd toward the dance floor.

He watched Sampson walk, moaning softly as the plug shifted, jostled. Sampson turned at the sound, hearing him even with the music pounding loudly, or maybe Sampson just knew, already so attuned to him.

Alain felt his cheeks heat, cock throbbing. "Sampson."

That earned him that sweet smile. "Come um, dance?"

"Yes, love." He reached up, arms wrapping around Sampson's shoulders. "Yes."

Sampson's arms looped loosely around his back and they started to move together. Every motion, heated him, made his muscles liquid.

"You're amazing," Sampson murmured, smiling down at him, those eyes looking nowhere but at him.

"I'm yours." He blinked up, entranced. "You make me so hard, Sampson."

"Feelings, ah, mutual." Sampson drew him closer, drew him against the long body and he could feel his lover's hard cock against his belly.

"Oh..." He rippled against Sampson. "Are you going to take me, love? Later?"

"Yes." One of Sampson's hands started to slide down his back. He groaned, looking up into Sampson's eyes, need filling him.

"I love um, the way you ah, move. So um, hot."

"Oh. Oh, good." He hummed, rubbing a little faster, a little harder.

Long fingers pressed against his ass, moving the plug.

"Sampson!" He gasped, going up on his toes.

Sampson grinned at him and kissed him quickly, pulling him deeper into the dance floor. The lights were swirling, his head was swimming and he just went with it, hips jerking. They moved together to the music, eyes on each other, bodies rubbing. There was a ball of heat in his belly, heavy and hot and filling him. Sampson's eyes got darker and darker, a wet spot growing in the front of his lover's pants.

Oh, he felt awake, alive, sensation buzzing through him.

"Have you, um, danced enough?" Sampson asked him

suddenly.

He nodded, breath coming quick and shallow.

"Me, too." Sampson grabbed his hand and dragged him back toward the lift.

Every step drew a soft cry from him, his control shattered by Sampson's need. Sampson moved faster, the long legs covering the ground quickly.

The lift doors open, Desmond and his new boy stepping out. Sampson pushed past them onto the lift and he thought he heard Desmond's soft chuckles, but then Sampson pushed him up against the back of the elevator, kissing him hard. He cried out, cock rubbing against Sampson's thigh.

Sampson slammed his palm against the control panel and the doors slid closed. Then his clothes were being torn, Sampson's hands shaking as they slid over his skin.

"Please. Sampson. Please. I need." His head bumped into the wall, sparks filling his sight.

"I know. Um. I ah, know."

Sampson turned him, pulling the scraps of his clothes from his body, pushing his naked body against the back wall. He spread wide, a low keening filling the lift…

"Oh, God, oh, Alain. Oh."

Sampson's fingers fumbled at his ass, jostling the plug hard before getting a grip on the base and pulling it out. He pushed his hips back, begging body and voice and soul. Empty and needing, he could feel his body trying to adjust to the loss of the plug.

He wasn't empty for long, Sampson's cock pushing into his body, hot and hard.

"Yes!" He arched, screaming with his pleasure. Never had he lost control like this, riding his lover in abandon, sounds pouring from him.

Sampson's hands were hard on his hips, pulling him back onto the long cock over and over again. Low sounds of want and need came from Sampson, joining his. The world spun faster and faster, the sound of their bodies slapping together the finest music. One of Sampson's hands slid around and tugged the cockring off, freeing his prick.

He clenched around Sampson's cock, come pouring from him, his scream echoing.

"Alain!" His name filled the lift as heat filled him deep inside.

He slumped, panting, breath coming hard. Sampson's arms wrapped around his chest and his lover turned them both, leaning against the wall and holding him close.

He pressed close, cuddling, holding. "Sampson. I... Oh..."

Sampson bent and kissed him softly. "I love you." Then he was lifted into Sampson's arms.

He buried his face in Sampson's neck, breath slowing, letting Sampson take him wherever he needed to go.

Two Men for Two Twins

Introducing Rivan and Kytan

Rivan let himself in and tossed his gym bag into the alcove, knowing one of the club's boys would deal with it when they came through later in the day.

He was hot and sweaty and pumped up, having spent a couple of hours in the weight room, working himself hard. The sweet burn in his muscles left him with a rush of endorphins and he was in a good mood, horny.

It was time to find Kytan and let off a little steam before showering and seeing where the day would take him.

"Brother-mine, where have you gotten to?"

Kytan's rumbling purr answered him, his golden-haired brother curled in the center of one of the huge beds, a real paper book in the square hands.

Rivan sat heavily on the bed, letting his weight bounce his brother, disturb Kytan.

Honey brown eyes that matched his perfectly glanced up. "You're sweaty."

"I know. And in a moment you'll be sweaty, too." He reached out running a finger along Kytan's breastbone.

A low chuckle sounded, the book carefully set aside

before he was given Kytan's full focus. "And do you intend to make me sweat, Van?"

"Oh, yes. But I'll rub off on you either way and you'll wear the salty kiss of my skin." He leaned down and placed a soft, chaste kiss on Kytan's lips. "Tell me, brother, does your book hold a candle to reality?"

"Never." One hand slid over the back of his neck, pulling him in for a deep, sure kiss, Kytan's tongue pushing into his lips, opening him.

He moaned, not holding a thing back from his twin. Others came and went, but Kytan was his for always and he would not hide.

Their bodies moved together, Kytan's skin warm and smooth, oddly soft for such a muscled man. He rubbed, painting Kytan with his sweat and then licking it off.

Kytan's heavy cock slid against his thigh, against his hip, the need between them familiar and comfortable, eternal. He rolled them so they were side by side, bodies moving as one toward their pleasure. Their legs tangled, fingers pulling and pushing, stroking here and petting there, Kytan's rumbles growing deep and rich as the scent of their need blossomed.

All days needed to start this way, shared and hot, fragrant with desire and, soon, satiation.

Kytan brought their mouths together, one huge hand wrapping around their cocks, tugging with a sure, confident rhythm. His own hands found their nipples, teasing first Kytan's and then his own. He flicked and pinched and tugged, making them both gasp.

Kytan's motions sped, hand growing tighter, harder.

"Brother!" He cried out, hands sliding up to hold his Ky's shoulders.

"Van! With me." Ky's hips rolled, thumb pushing against his slit.

"Yes!" He brought their lips together again, their

tongues tangling as he came, heat pouring over his brother's hand.

Kytan's body answered his call, seed spraying between them, a low roar sounding. The kiss softened, their bodies still moving together.

Ky's eyes were warm, fond, smiling at him. "Good workout, Van?"

"Yes, Ky. As always."

He brought his brother's hand up and licked their mixed come from the thick fingers.

Kytan's tongue slid against his own, playing. "I have an appointment this afternoon with Malachi and the doctor. They have someone to introduce me to."

He hummed. "A sub? How wonderful!" It had been just him and Ky for some time now, they both needed someone new to exert their will over. "And hand-picked. I'm quite jealous."

"I'm not sure you shouldn't pity me. The rumor is the sub's quite broken and requires intense, constant attention." Ky petted his cheek. "Shall I inquire for a match for you, Van?"

"I would pity you, brother, if I didn't know how much you enjoy a challenge." He nuzzled into the touch a moment, considering Ky's question and then shook his head. "I have a... feeling."

"Mmm... delicious." Kytan trusted his instincts, his hunches, believing in him when no one else would.

He smiled. "I knew today would be special for us both. Well..." he rubbed against Ky. "More special than usual."

Their soft laughter melded and joined, golden hair sliding against dark. "Shall we keep this room as our own, Van? Our sanctuary?"

"Yes, Ky. But I will not hide our relationship."

"No. They will accept our will, brother. Your own and

mine."

"Yes."

He kissed Ky again, tongue sliding into familiar warmth. "I love you, Ky."

"As I love you. Shall we shower? Ready to meet our pets?"

He nodded, licking against at Ky's lips before sliding from the bed. He watched as Ky moved, his lover's skin now as slick with sweat as his own.

Perfect.

He was ready for what else fate would bring him this day.

Rivan Finds His Jewel

Rivan wandered, letting his feet find their own way.

He and Ky had showered, then breakfasted, feeding each other bits and bites of their favorites. A lovely morning. A good day indeed.

He found himself leaving the club, smiling up into unexpected sunshine. It had been raining for weeks on end.

"Why pay for the Glove boys? We're a quarter the price and twice as tight!" The little crowd of whores and panhandlers that gathered outside the Club were congregated, working while they could. Eventually, the security trucks would nab who they could and send the others running.

They were a grubby, slutty bunch -- all sparkle and glitter and paint to cover the hollows left from using Risque or Bear or any of the other street drugs. One caught his eye, thin and pale, different colored eyes glittering with whatever the boy was using.

The boy's hair was short-short, dark roots visible under the white bleach-job, and the makeup was over-done, but the lines of the boy's face were lovely, intriguing. His interest was noticed. "You looking for a quickie, man? There's a quiet alley around the corner..."

He grinned. "A quickie the best you can do?"

One dark eyebrow went up. "A quickie's the standard. How much are you looking spend?"

"Money's no object," Rivan murmured, looking the boy up and down. He'd look pretty good cleaned up.

"Money's always the object." The kid motioned over toward the side of the building. "You want to talk, though, we gotta go over there. The guy at the door will get pissed."

"How would you like to shock the guy at the door?"

He nodded toward the club. "Come on in and have a bite with me while we discuss our transaction?"

"They won't let me in." Those fascinating eyes shot toward the door. "You gotta pay big creds to get in and shit."

"They'll let you in with me." He inclined his head. "Come."

The boy vibrated -- literally, physically vibrated, interesting -- and then nodded. "Okay. Sure. So we can talk terms."

"Exactly."

He led the way back in, hand sliding to the boy's back as they went in. The doorman didn't even blink an eye, as Rivan knew he wouldn't.

"Whoa..." The sound was impressed, surprised, a flicker of emotion ghosting over the pale face before disappearing into affected boredom.

He bit back his smile, continuing to lead the boy into the dining salon. He nodded at Reg, the maitre d' and chose a table that afforded them a good view. He held the lad's chair for him.

"Thanks." The lad sat carefully, eyes flicking here and there. "So, what all do you have in mind?"

He sat across the table from his guest and held out his hand. "First things first, I'm Rivan."

"Hey." His hand was taken and quickly shaken, the lad's skin almost feverish, the drugs heating the lad's blood. "Jewel. Pleased and shit."

"Would you like me to order for you, Jewel?"

"Order? Okay. I'm not fucking for food though. I'm not hungry enough for that."

"Of course not -- the food is in return for negotiating with me indoors instead of in the alley." There was something fascinating about Jewel, starting with the strange eyes, on to the screw you attitude.

"Oh. Oh, wicked. Okay. Yeah. I... I'll eat anything." The shabby lace jacket was smoothed, pulled around the slim frame. "Pretty cool place."

"It suits me well. I live upstairs."

He smiled at Gabrielle and ordered stir fried chicken with salads, a soda for Jewel and an ale for himself.

"Oh." Jewel arched that eyebrow again. "Then why are you interested in trolling for ass outside? They got pros in here. You knew that, right?"

He laughed, absolutely delighted. "I'm not looking for a pro. I'm looking for something different."

"Different. Okay. But... " Jewel shrugged. "I got one asshole, just like everybody else."

He tried to look disappointed. "Really? Are you sure?"

"Unless the last guy who threatened to drill me a new one was right. Yeah." Jewel chuckled, shook his head, and almost grinned.

"Well Jewel, I know all the boys here and they're lovely boys, I've played with a lot of them. But I need someone full time. Someone without outside distractions who will devote themselves to me and my will." He wondered if it would make Jewel bolt, but he didn't believe in subs being brought in against their will. They had to know what they were getting into.

"Oh. That's nice. Uh... good luck?"

He grinned. No running away at the words. Excellent. "The pay's good, the quarters and food unparalleled."

"Sounds like somebody's got a good job waiting on him, yeah?" Jewel shifted, sliding a tiny autoinjector out of one pocket and into the pale flesh in a movement almost too fast to see.

Rivan raised an eyebrow. "You're not interested then? You'd rather live out on the street, selling your ass to anyone with a few creds and staying hopped up on whatever it is you're taking?"

Those eyes went wide for a heartbeat. "Hey. I came in here to talk about a fuck. Everybody knows the big man owns this place don't hire street users, only hires clean boys that are into chains and following rules and shit. I'm not clean and I don't do rules."

"I'm not the big man -- I can hire who I want. You could be clean and I think it would be no end of fun teaching you to lean the rules, to follow them." He smiled, running his tongue along his teeth. "It would be even more fun when you break them."

"What? You all offer rehab?" Jewel snorted, eyes going glittery again. "You look fucking hungry."

"I am hungry, Jewel. Hungry for a proper sub of my own. And it's not rehab so much as changing your environment and making the drug unavailable."

"I told you, I'm not proper. I'm a street rat. Been on the streets since m'Da was shot. Been using since the first trick I turned." Slender fingers fluttered over ruffles, twitching and nervous.

"By proper sub, I meant fulltime. Mine. Not a house sub." He shook his head, laughing at himself, he suspected Jewel only understood one thing. "How much for your services for the day, Jewel?"

"The whole day?" Jewel tilted his head. "Hundred creds."

"Done." Jewel was selling himself cheap.

"Cool." The slender body was swaying to the piped in music, fingers tapping unconsciously. "What now? We still gonna eat?"

"Yes. And then I would like to watch you dance. After that I think a shower, a trip to the leathershop for some clean clothes."

"The leather shop? I like dancing. I'll dance for you."

"I imagine as long as I keep paying, you'll keep doing

whatever I want," he noted sardonically.

"Maybe. I got limits."

"That's good to know. Perhaps you'd like to choose a word to say if we reach them, something to let me know to back off?"

"Stop won't work?" The food came and he heard Jewel's stomach trying to tear itself out of the thin body to get to the goods.

He shrugged casually and picked up his fork. "That's boring though, and stop could come up in casual conversation and you'll confuse me."

"Oh." Jewel picked a bite of tomato from the salad nibbling. "But if I said stop... I guess it could sort of be confusing..."

"Yes, exactly." He nodded and speared a piece of chicken and some rice, eating slowly.

Jewel ate only a bite or two, the drugs making the boy restless and edgy. "It's good."

"Yes, the best are hired to keep club members happy."

Jewel nodded. "The people coming in and out look happy, yeah?"

"We are." He speared another piece of chicken and held it out to Jewel. "You never did pick that word."

"I... Chicken, I guess. Chicken will work." Jewel plucked the chicken off his fork, stripping it into tiny bites.

He watched the little white teeth behind the brightly painted lips. "Chicken. I like it."

Jewel looked around, refusing to look away from anyone, including Mal and Desmond, who wandered by, deep in discussion.

"Are you done?" he asked when it appeared Jewel wouldn't be eating anymore.

"Sure." Jewel pushed away from the table, doing that

vibrating thing again. "What now?"

"I'd like to watch you dance." Watch you move. I'd like to watch you do it naked.

"Where?" Jewel was completely draped in faded black -- head to toe -- layers ghosting over the lines of the thin body.

"There's a dance floor," he told Jewel, nodding toward the back of the club. "You'll need to lose a couple of layers."

"Lose?" He got a quick frown. "Is there a place I can put them? I mean, it's my costume, yeah?"

"Take it all off but the pants and I'll have them cleaned. You can pick them up again on your way out tomorrow." He wouldn't risk bringing vermin into his home. Ky would never forgive him.

"I... Okay. Sure. Is there a place I can wash my hands? Change?" Those quick hands started shifting things -- injectors, pill cases, a little sharp knife.

"You don't need to wash your hands." He held out his own. "I can hold your stuff and you can leave your clothes on the chair. The waiter will take them to the laundry."

"I..." Two injectors and a pill case were slid into the waistband of the pants, the little knife and other paraphernalia handed over. "It's all I got, yeah? Don't lose it."

He pocketed the items, watching Jewel. "I can afford to replace anything I lose."

Jewel was skinny, pale, but he had tight, wiry muscles. There was a ring in one surprisingly dark nipple, a red bite mark on one shoulder, a crudely inked diamond on the flat belly.

Heat flared in Rivan's belly. Such pretty skin. A beautiful canvas.

Jewel moved toward the dance floor, hips swaying to the beat, hands sliding over his skin. Oh, he moved like a dream. And he looked like one. There'd been a few moments while they were eating that Rivan had wondered if he had the right boy, but now... oh yes.

Jewel moved onto the dance floor, entire body flowing to the music, uninhibited, sensual. Rivan moved to a closer table, sitting with his legs well-spread to give his growing prick room. He couldn't wait for Ky to see Jewel move.

The music sped, Jewel's motions matching the speed, hands sliding over the pale skin, the boy making love to himself. Untutored, unconscious, luscious beauty.

Rivan's hand dropped to the front of his pants, rubbing at the sight.

Jewel's body slowly sheened with sweat, the pale skin shining, waistband going dark. He could imagine Jewel's back covered in stripes, the diamond tattoo worked into something a little more elaborate that would move with Jewel's body. Rivan was breathing hard, as if he were the one dancing.

Jewel's hips began to roll, moving as if he was being taken by a ghost lover, thin thighs parted. Rivan swallowed hard. Oh, what a seduction. The motions continued as long as the music did, fading away as the song changed.

He got up and walked slowly toward Jewel, not making any attempt to hide his arousal.

Jewel danced toward him. "You like to watch."

"I do when what I'm looking at looks as good as you."

"I like to dance." Jewel's eyes glittered at him. "How do you want me?"

"On your knees for a start. Use your mouth to undo my pants."

"Here? Security won't come?"

"We could go to the stage over there if you prefer,"

he murmured, nodding to where the stage sat, currently empty and unlit.

"Okay. Yeah." Jewel took his hand, led him over into the shadows, kneeling before him, lips freeing his cock.

He hummed, hand sliding through the short hair. "Show me what you've got, Jewel."

Jewel's lips wrapped around his cock, taking him deep, suction strong and sure, designed to make him come, make him need. He started to pump his hips, pushing slowly. Well practiced, Jewel took all of him, never gagging, just accepting him.

"Look at me, Jewel," he murmured.

Those mismatched eyes blinked up at him.

"Yes." He came, fingers tangled in Jewel's short hair.

Jewel swallowed, taking him in, drinking him down, eyes closing. Aftershocks rocked him as Jewel's throat closed around him. Oh, lovely, talented boy.

Jewel leaned back, his cock sliding free, clean and shining.

"Not bad. Not bad at all."

"Thanks. Guy's gotta have job security and all." Jewel winked and stood, stretching up tall.

Rivan watched the slender belly, eyes slowly rising to meet Jewel's. "I think you'll manage somehow. Now shall we go see Mouse and get you some clean pants? And then that shower."

"Pants? Mouse? Man, this place? Is something else."

"Yes. Yes, it is." He tucked himself back into his pants.

It was going to be an interesting twenty four hours.

Kytan Finds His Dove

Kytan met the Doctor and Malachi in the med office, wrinkling his nose at the scent of antiseptic. He was quite excited -- they'd played at the club quite extensively and he and Malachi had many conversations regarding his particular interests and this was the first match Mal had offered him.

He nodded to his friends, as well as the pale, retiring little thing the Doctor had claimed. "Good afternoon, gentlemen. How does the day find you?"

Trip got up and shook his hand. "Good, good. I'm glad you came."

"I hope I will be, too. Malachi says you have someone for me?"

Trip nodded. "I do. A colleague of mine referred a psychiatric patient to me."

He arched an eyebrow. A psychiatric patient? Intriguing. "And my name came up because?"

Malachi chuckled. "Because you're a controlling man, Kytan, and you and your twin are the most stubborn men alive."

"Oh. Well. Yes."

The doctor chuckled. "Hinton cuts himself to deal with his issues. But it isn't helping and he's escalating the behavior. He needs someone to control him. Someone to recognize what he needs and give it to him, in a safe environment. His last cutting session found him in the hospital with dangerous blood loss."

"Is he dangerous? Is he here willingly?" He relaxed into a chair, curious, but unwilling to endanger himself or his brother.

"He agreed to give this a try and he's only dangerous to himself and even that -- he's not trying to kill himself, just deal with the pain inside." Trip turned to his companion. "Ghost has spent a little bit of time with him. Is he dangerous, Ghost?"

Ghost's eyes went wide and the boy shook his head. "He's hurting, scared, but not scary."

"What's he running from?"

"Pain. Lots of pain." Ghost paled, face going still and blank, eyes closing. "He's very sad, I think."

Trip looked intently over at Ghost for a moment and the boy seemed to ease.

The doctor opened a file folder. "There was an accident. The father pushed him to safety and then he watched his parents burn to death, trapped in their transport. There's plenty of people that would have driven insane -- the boy has a core of steel, he just doesn't know it."

Oh. He nodded, hearing Van's soft chuckle in his head, accusing him of always searching for a challenge. "Is he aware that he will be required to submit to me totally, to relinquish his control?"

"He has been informed, yes. He didn't seem to care one way or the other. I think he realizes he's not going to survive on his own and at this point just wants to stop hurting emotionally." The doctor flipped through his file. "Physically he's fine, but if the cutting progresses as it has been, he's going to go too far and kill himself."

Kytan looked over at Malachi, admiring the still, fine form. It was a shame the man was a top, such control would be addictive to break. "Well, Mal? Is it a good match?"

Mal nodded. "I wouldn't have contacted you if not."

"Well, Kytan? How about it? Shall I bring him out? There need not be any commitments made immediately. Spend some time together. Get to know each other. This boy needs you and from what I understand, you will get what you need as well from the match." Trip looked at him expectantly.

"Yes. I imagine I should meet him." Not that it mattered, he had already made his decision. Still, there was a protocol to follow.

"Ghost, would you bring him from the other room, please?" Trip turned back to him. "He seemed to be more comfortable with Ghost than Mal or myself."

"Ghost does seem to have made a connection with him." He watched as Ghost headed out the door. "What does he cut himself with? Is there a ritual about it?"

Trip went through his file again. "Whatever he can get his hands on while he was in ward -- including the bedsprings. He's bright enough, anyway. The doctor never could get the lad to tell him about the ritual, though he suspects there is one."

Kytan looked over at Mal. "Have my supplies in the training room delivered to our quarters. I will want to start his training immediately."

"Mind made up already?" Trip was grinning.

"Planning in advance." He winked, slowly.

Trip chuckled, looking up as Ghost brought in a slender, pale lad with dark curls falling around his face and large grey eyes.

Oh, surprisingly lovely. Kytan took a long look, admiring. Very lovely.

The lad looked around from the Doc to Mal to him and crossed his arms which were covered in long sleeves.

Trip smiled at the lad. "Come Hinton. We've found someone to take you on. Someone who will help you deal with your pain. Hinton this is Kytan, one of our residents. Kytan -- Hinton."

Kytan stood, held out a hand, eyes fastened onto the boys. "Hinton."

Hinton hesitated a moment and then held out a hand. "Ky... Kytan, right?"

"Yes. Kytan." He took Hinton's hand in his and held

it, feeling its warmth.

Hinton looked up at him, the grey eyes sad, troubled.

"Do you know why you're here?" He kept Hinton's hand in his own.

Hinton nodded. "Because I cut myself."

"But why here in this place? What do you hope to find?"

"Peace."

Interesting. "Do you believe you can find it?"

Hinton shrugged. "I don't know."

So little spark, so little passion... He looked over at the doctor. "Has he been medicated?"

"Yes. A mild sedative. Apparently he wouldn't settle the last time he was caught cutting, kept trying to tear the newskin off." The doctor took out a hypo. "I can counter it if you wish."

"Not here." He shook his head. "How long until it wears off on its own?"

"Within the hour."

"That will give us time to be settled." He nodded, satisfied. "Have his belongings delivered to me and his records, but his palmprint only to enter our quarters, not leave." He could feel the heavy warmth of anticipation, of learning a new series of challenges.

"Good, good," murmured Trip. "Well matched, Mal."

Hinton's hand remained in his own, the lad pliant enough with the drugs in his system.

"Come, Hinton. It is time to go home." He met Malachi's eyes. "I need my things, Mal. Is it arranged?"

Malachi nodded, eyes unreadable. "Kerr and Andy should be delivering them as we speak, Kytan."

"Excellent."

"All right. I'll let Hinton's records show that you and he have agreed to work together. I hope you can help him find what he needs." Trip typed away and then closed the file. "Good luck to both of you."

"It is not a matter of luck, but determination and skill. Good day, my friends." He pulled gently, leading Hinton down the hall toward their home. As he reached the lift, he commed Van. "Van, love, we have a new addition to our household. Hinton."

His brother's laughter was sweet and soft. "Indeed, then we have two. I'll be bringing Jewel by as soon as he is clean and clothed." Van chuckled. "Well, mine doesn't know it yet."

"Oh, congratulations. I will take the green room for Hinton, leaving the blue room for you and we can share the larger playroom, yes?" He smiled at his brother, enjoying the excitement in the honey-brown eyes.

"Yes, my brother. It is a good day for us. I will see you later -- I have to attend to my new charge."

"Indeed." He closed the comm, offering Hinton a smile. "That was my brother, Rivan. He will share a suite with us."

"Okay." The grey eyes looked up at him with a little more interest. "Are you lovers?"

"We are. Does that offend you?"

Hinton shook his head. "It must be good to have someone to love."

"It is." The lift opened onto the twenty-seventh floor and he moved to the fourth suite. "Please. Come in. This will be your new home."

He could see signs that housekeeping had been in, taken Van's laundry and delivered his goods. Excellent.

"Home? I thought I wasn't allowed to leave? Like at the hospital."

"I would ask that you not leave without me, Hinton. In fact, I imagine much about your life will seem changed after today." In truth, Hinton would need only to obey his will, he would accept nothing less.

"Can you really help me?" Hinton asked him. "Can you really make the pain tolerable? Dr. Veil said it would, but he said the drugs would and they don't, they just trap me with it."

"I will not lie and promise you relief, but those that know both of us, believe it to be so and you must also. No more drugs, Hinton. We will explore alternative paths to healing." Poor lad, such pain. Kytan saw many, many hours spent together with Bowie and Katashi as well, once the initial training phase had passed.

"The only time the pain doesn't seem so bad in my head is when I cut myself. The color of the blood makes everything go away."

"Then we will find other pathways for the pain to escape. Come, Hinton, let us begin." He let Hinton down the hallway to the pale green doorway, opening it to a soothing, peaceful room, filled with soft, rounded shapes. He had designed this room for comfort, for long-term scenes, for relaxation. It would suit well.

Hinton looked around, fingers scratching at his arm.

He walked over to the cabinet, tapping in the combination to unlock them. "Strip, please, and bring me your clothing."

Hinton did as he asked, pulling off the long sleeved shirt and the hospital style pants. The lad toed off his runners and brought it all to him.

"Thank you." He placed them all upon a clear shelf in the cabinet, removing thick fur-lined, fingerless mitts that locked securely at wrist and forearm. "Hold out your hands, please."

Hinton obediently held out his hands, fingers curling slightly before straightening again.

He carefully placed the mitts over Hinton's fingers, fastening them securely, denying the lad the use of his hands altogether. “There, Hinton. No matter the temptation, the will be no cutting unless I choose to allow it.”

Hinton nodded and looked up at him, a tear falling along one cheek.

Kytan reached out, catching the tear on one finger before pulling out a soft, warm blanket and cocooning Hinton within it. “Come now. We will rest and sit and wait for the drugs to let loose of your soul. All will be well, Hinton.”

“I just don’t want to hurt anymore,” Hinton told him softly, head resting against his chest.

He settled them both upon an overstuffed divan, holding Hinton close. “I can understand that, sweet Dove. Together we will find your path to peace.”

“Thank you.”

Hinton lay lax against him, quiet and still until the drugs started to wear off. Then there were soft twitches, sighs and more than once Hinton rubbed his arms with the gloves.

“We will keep the gloves on, Dove. Until your fingers lose the desire to tear your skin. I will be your hands.”

“The tearing distracts me, Kytan, keeps my head quiet.”

“What is your head saying, when it is loud?”

“Fire. Everything is on fire and I can hear them screaming.” Hinton started to rock slowly against him.

He purred softly, hands petting as he nodded. “You saw a terrible thing, your heart must be crying.”

“Yes. I can’t make it go away. Not by myself. That’s why I... cut. It feels so good -- makes everything go quiet for a bit.”

“You are no longer by yourself.” He kept touching, fingers sliding over thin scars. “You live under my eye now, Dove.”

“You’ll make it go away, Kytan?” Hinton asked, shivering.

"I will be, at least for the beginning of our journey, the center of your life. Not your pain, not your noise." He wrapped Hinton tighter in the blankets, keeping them close.

"I like the sound of that, Kytan," Hinton whispered, rocking against him.

"Good." He did not offer Hinton a choice, a safe-word. He simply held and watched, purring as Hinton's body rid itself of the sedative.

Rivan introduces Jewel to a new world

It had been the weirdest day in the history of days. First Dean had thrown him out of the flat for letting Pool fuck him -- honestly, a quick fuck for four hits! Who could blame him? And he'd have shared.

One.

Then the transport driver'd caught him sneaking a ride and tossed him three airblocks short and...

Well...

Then there was Rivan.

Wow.

One hundred creds.

Food.

Music.

Fucking pants.

Now? Rivan said they were going to have a shower.

With water.

The boys were never going to believe this.

He looked up and grinned as the lift zoomed. "You're way up high."

Rivan gave him that soft smile again. "The owner lives in the penthouse. We're the next floor down. As high as you can get."

"We?" He ran his hands over the tight, warm leather pants, fingers sliding over the autoinjector, to make sure it was there. "You live with someone?"

"My twin, Kytan. And it seems, he has a new pet himself."

"A pet? They let you have real pets? Cool." He didn't have any brothers or sisters, at least none he'd ever met.

Rivan smiled again, a twist in the corner like he was trying not to laugh. "Indeed, they do."

"Cool." He thought about taking another quarter hit. He liked it that way best, lots of little bursts, always buzzing.

"You'll brush your teeth when we get to the bathroom. And put cream on your face to get rid of the makeup. Then we'll shower together. I can't wait to kiss you."

Rivan's hand settled in the small of his back, fingers stroking his skin.

"Get rid of the makeup? But... " He reached up to his lips. It was part of the costume, part of the deal.

One of Rivan's eyebrows went up. "Are you saying that will cost me extra?"

"No. I just..." He shrugged. "I kinda lost all my stuff this morning and I gotta make this last." He lifted his chin. "One day I'm gonna get permanent stuff inked on."

Rivan's free hand went under his chin, the man contemplating his face. "I can see that. Black to line your eyes, ruby to keep your lips dark. You don't need much more than that on your face. But here," Rivan's fingers slid over his belly, "you would look lovely with a curving design. It would have to be done by someone with considerably more talent that the artist who did your diamond."

His belly jumped and he was shocked to feel his cock throb, trying to fill. Man, he didn't. Not usually. The Risque kept him from... Wow.

"It was done one night in the secure cells."

"Well perhaps we can negotiate more time together in return for some work by the club's artist. Paul does magnificent work."

Rivan's fingers lingered on his belly, sliding over his abs.

"Maybe." He felt himself flush, skin getting hot and tingly. He stepped away, fingers sliding into his waistband to grab the injector.

Rivan's hand grabbed his wrist and pulled his hand

up, holding it firmly. "I think I'm paying enough to warrant honest reactions from you, Jewel."

He blinked up, tugging at Rivan's hand, breath coming faster. "You didn't say nothing about not using."

Rivan shrugged, hand holding his wrist easily. "I didn't realize it would be an issue. I'll give you another hundred creds."

Oh.

Oh, gods.

"How long?"

"Until after we've fucked."

Oh. Okay. They'd get naked in the shower and fuck. Okay. Okay. He could do it. A hundred creds would get him set for almost a week. Almost. "Okay. Okay. I can do that."

"Good. We can negotiate from there." Rivan never let go of his wrist, just tugged him along as the lift doors opened.

"I said I wouldn't... Man, there's a lot of hall for not very many doors..." He'd never seen anything so... huge.

"There are five apartments on this floor. Usually there are fifteen to thirty on a floor this size."

The hold on his wrist changed, Rivan's hand sliding down to hold his, their fingers twined.

"Wow." The carpet was so soft he couldn't hear their footsteps.

"What?" Rivan asked, looking around.

"Nothing. It's just... quiet." And clean.

And not broken.

Or crawling with things.

"Ah. Well the rooms are all more or less sound proofed."

They stopped in front of one of the doors, Rivan opening it with his hand on the palmplate. "I'll show you around after we've dealt with getting clean."

"It's not like I'm muddy."

Rivan laughed. "Indulge me, Jewel."

"Okay." Like he was going to argue about having a real water shower. "I had a real water shower once, last summer. Me and Bryce sneaked into a hotel and took one."

Rivan stopped and looked at him, one hand sliding along his cheek. "I forget sometimes, that not everyone lives as Ky and I do."

Grinning like a boy, Rivan all but ran down a hallway and into the biggest bathroom Jewel had ever seen. There was a huge tub in the center of the room and a shower stall big enough for a half dozen taking up one entire wall. There were mirrors and sinks and vanities, chairs and benches. The room was easily bigger than the apartment he'd shared with Dean.

"Oh. Oh, wow. Wow. Rivan. Wow." He laughed, clapping as his voice echoed.

Rivan chuckled. "You like it."

"It's... huge and wonderful and who wouldn't like it?" He looked at the tub, fingers sliding on the sides.

"It's one of my favorite places." Rivan went to the shower, sliding the glass door aside. "The back is a mirror, special glass that doesn't fog up. So we can watch ourselves."

"Cool." He peeked in, looking at the controls, looking at the containers of soaps and stuff. Wicked yummy. "Where should I put my stuff?"

Rivan was already stripping, tossing his clothes at one of the benches. "If you stick your new pants on one of the vanities, housekeeping won't take them to laundry. They'll bring the rest of your stuff up later today, I'm sure."

"Okay." He wriggled out of his pants, lying his stuff in between the folds, the temptation to give himself a hit held at bay only by the promise of a day's wages for holding off a few more minutes.

Rivan turned the water on -- four spouts all angled toward the middle of the shower. The man held a hand out to him, inviting him in.

"Did you want me to wash my face first?" For a hundred creds? He could buy new.

"Oh, yes. There should be some cream you can use on the blue vanity."

"Okay..." He wandered over, looking at the bottles and jar, finally finding a thick cream in a lapis jar. He scrubbed his face steadily, layers of paint making the cream grey. He finally rinsed off, wincing as he saw himself in the mirror -- a skinny, pale, weird-eyed kid with a gee-I-need-a-hit tic.

Ew.

Rivan appeared in the mirror behind him, body bronze and ripped. "Do you know what I see, Jewel?"

"Huh?" He looked up, short hair rubbing on Rivan's chest.

"I see a study in opposites. We're stunning together." Rivan smiled, hands sliding around his hips. "Come on. Let's get you wet. Clean. Fucked."

"Okay." He nodded, enjoying the heat of Rivan behind him.

Rivan snagged a toothbrush and tooth gel, leading him into the shower with its multi-head spray. He watched, stunned, as the water poured out, warm and clean. He cupped his hands, watching the clear water fill them. Rivan gave him an indulgent smile and then began to wash him. The man started with his hair, working a softly scented soap into it.

"Oh..." He shivered, pleasure tickling. "What do you want me to do?"

Rivan handed him the toothbrush. That tickled him

and he started giggling, hands trembling as he squeezed the gel over the brush and started cleaning his teeth. Rivan smiled at him, rinsing the soap from his hair and beginning to soap up the rest of him with stuff out of another bottle. This soap smelled good, like Rivan, and the touches were less business like, Rivan's fingers sliding sensuously over his skin.

The temptation to close his eyes and just feel was huge and he fought it. Creds weren't worth dying over and what if this guy was a murderer and picked up whores to strangle in this big bathroom?

That would suck.

Jewel kept his eyes open.

Rivan's eyes were on his hands, following them as they slid over Jewel's skin. The heat in the stall seemed to ratchet up. His cock started to fill, slowly but surely taking in interest in the proceedings. Rivan's cock was also interested. Very interested.

Fingers slid across his nipples and tickled his ribs. Rivan touched his ass, pushed lightly against his opening as soap was spread down his crack. His balls were cupped, cradled in one large hand and then his prick was stroked, the way slick and smooth with soap.

Jewel moaned and his eyes did close for a second. Oh, no fucking ever felt like this.

Rivan bent, washing his legs as thoroughly as the rest of him and then he was pushed again into the spray. Jewel let himself enjoy it for a minute -- hot and water and good smells and clean.

Rivan stood and took the toothbrush from his fingers. "I'm going to kiss you now."

"Okay. Okay." He nodded, suddenly worried, heart pounding furiously.

Rivan's mouth covered his, hot and wet, tongue sliding between his lips. His lips parted, unsure whether Rivan wanted him to stand there or kiss back or what.

"Respond," murmured Rivan, licking at his lips. "Show me what you want, let me know when I do something you enjoy."

"I... Okay." This was different. Scary... Well, not scary, but unsettling, unnerving. Unprofessional.

Then Rivan was kissing him again, the man's hard cock sliding along his belly. He reached out, fingers circling Rivan's cock, starting to stroke it. That he understood.

Rivan's hand found his and took it, placed it on the man's belly instead. "We have all the time in the world. Or at least most of the next twenty four hours, Jewel. Take your time. Explore."

"You don't want me to make you come?" His hands were curious, sliding over the wet, slick skin, rubbing.

"Eventually, Jewel. But I'm not in a rush." Rivan's hands were returning the favor, sliding over his skin, teasing his nipples and his neck.

"Oh." He arched a little, teeth sinking into his bottom lip. "I... Okay."

"Relax, Jewel, enjoy yourself." The words were murmured, Rivan's eyes closing. Rivan's hands slid over him, mapping him almost.

"I... This is so different." He stroked Rivan's belly, moving slowly upward, eyes falling closed.

"It's good, Jewel. This is what life can be like when you go beyond a quickie."

Rivan's mouth slid to his shoulder, tongue tracing the bite mark there, teeth teasing the flesh next to it, threatening.

His cock jerked and he gasped, breath coming faster. When the guy yesterday had bit him, he hadn't even cared, but this... "I... "

"Yes, Jewel?" Rivan's fingers found his ass again,

teased along the crease.

"I don't... It's not supposed to be so much. It's a job." He wasn't supposed to get hard, he was supposed to get high and get fucking and then get high again.

"Just feel, Jewel. You can worry about it tomorrow."

"Oh..." His fingers found Rivan's nipples, sliding over them, making them hard.

Rivan moaned. "That's it, Jewel." Two fingers pushed against his hole, not in, just against.

Jewel gasped, body shivering, their bellies rubbing.

Rivan's mouth returned to his, the kiss more urgent now as Rivan's cock slid against his belly, hotter than the water that pounded against them, making his skin so sensitive to each touch of Rivan's fingers.

He kissed back, moaning low, arching into Rivan's heat. Rivan's fingers teased harder against his hole, the tip of one pushing in before dancing away again. He shivered, body going tight and melted in turns, feeling as if he were spinning out of control.

Rivan's mouth slid across his jaw and down his neck, returning again to lick at the bite mark on his shoulder. "No one else will mark you without my permission," murmured Rivan as two fingers pushed into him.

His eyes went wide, the water splashing into them, confusing him, unnerving him as his body took those fingers deep.

Rivan's mouth continued down, lips wrapping around his nipple and tugging.

Oh, gods. He was going to come. He was and Rivan hadn't yet -- well, he had, earlier, on the dance floor, but not in here and oh...

He gasped, crying out low as he shot, balls emptying themselves.

Rivan purred, moving to kiss his other nipple before bringing their mouths together again. The fingers inside him kept moving, stretching him. He held on, gasping, hips riding those fingers, lips open to the touches. The kisses were deep, the fingers inside him finding his gland and sliding across it.

"Oh... Oh... Please, again." He whispered the words into Rivan's mouth, completely lost in sensation.

"This?" Rivan's fingers slid past his gland again and then again, sensation sparking through him.

"Yes." He nodded, blinking up into Rivan's brown eyes. "Yes."

"Yes," murmured Rivan, working his gland until his cock hardened again.

He just held on, shaking now, almost frightened at the pleasure, at the sheer amount of feeling.

Rivan's fingers finally slid out of him, large hand cupping his buttocks, raising him off the ground. "Put your legs around my waist, Jewel."

He nodded, wrapping his legs around the trim waist, strong muscles holding him easily. "You're holding me..."

"I am." Rivan shifted him, heat pressing against him. "Let me in, Jewel."

"Okay. Yes." He pushed down, surprising himself as he moaned, pleasure and heat coursing through him.

Rivan's moan echoed his. "Hot. Good."

He nodded, leaning back into the spray, gasping, stretching. A shudder went through Rivan, but the hold on him never faltered. Then Rivan began to move him, hands pulling him up off the long hard cock and then bringing him back down again.

Oh, gods. This was why people paid for it. This was why.

"Pump yourself. I want to feel you come around me."

Again? So soon? His mind insisted he couldn't, but his

hand was wrapped around his cock, tugging hard, pulling in time with Rivan's strokes.

"That's it, oh, you're close, I can feel it."

Rivan's mouth slammed against his, kissing him hard as he was pulled down onto the large cock. He cried out, clenching tight, body rippling and milking Rivan's cock as he came, entire world greying out.

He came back to, cradled in Rivan's arms, the warm water still falling against his skin, soft purrs sliding on his skin as Rivan drank from his neck and shoulders.

Jewel blinked slowly, settling back into his body reluctantly. He reached out, stroked the dark hair, fingers sliding over the wet mass. Rivan nuzzled into his touch, tongue still busy licking the water from his skin.

He chuckled as Rivan found a ticklish spot, body tightening around the flesh still buried deep. Rivan's breath caught, another soft moan sounding. Jewel repeated the motion, the knowledge that he affected Rivan heady.

"Oh, Jewel, clever boy."

He laughed again, unreasonably pleased at the praise.

Rivan purred and pushed him up against the wall of the shower, beginning to thrust again, cock sliding out and in.

"You can, again?" He laughed, reaching up for a showerhead, body relaxed and open, warm.

"Clean living and a sweet, pliant body. Does wonders for the libido." Rivan winked at him, pushing in again, prick sliding across his gland. The spark that touch sent through him wasn't enough to make him hard, but it was good and he wanted to feel it again.

Rivan kept moving, fucking him with long, slow strokes, each one passing across his gland as Rivan nuzzled and licked his neck, his shoulders, his face.

Oh, it felt good. Quiet almost, a rich, deep sensation that filled him. It went on and on -- it looked like Rivan could do this for fucking ever.

"Rivan..." His breath came in deep gasps, matched by Rivan's thrusts.

"How do you feel, Jewel?"

"I... Big. Deep. I feel here." He shrugged, unable to find the words that meant anything.

Rivan seemed happy with his answer though, a deep purr sounding. "Good."

One hand came up and slid across one of his nipples. "Do you want to come again, Jewel?"

"I don't think I can." He stretched under the touch, body rippling.

"Are you sure?" Rivan asked, fingers closing around his nipple to tug.

"Mmm..." His toes curled and he nodded, gasping a little.

"Quite sure?" Rivan's fingers slid across his skin, finding the barbell in his other nipple and twisting it.

"Oh!" He arched, body twisting, unsure whether to push toward the touch or pull away.

Rivan purred, the speed of his thrusts increasing, each one sparking sensation along Jewel's spine. His barbell was twisted again, Rivan's mouth working his neck, sucking hard enough to leave a mark.

All the sensations melded together, hot and real and good and he let himself feel, let himself come again, the sensation leaving him with empty, aching balls, feeling wrung out and shaken.

Rivan's heat filled him, a shout echoing in the large bathroom.

His hands slowly slid from the showerhead, body relaxing into Rivan's arms, eyes closing.

Rivan's cock slid out of his body and they stood in the shower a moment or two longer, the water cleaning the come from them. Then Rivan carried him out and he was wrapped in a warm, unbelievably soft towel.

He was running on autopilot, eyelids heavy, limbs seeming weighted down from a mixture of pleasure and the effect of his last hit wearing off.

They were moving again and he forced his eyes open, watching as they moved into another room, this one a bedroom done in soothing blues. Rivan put him down on the bed and curled up around him. "A nap and then dinner."

"Oh..." The bed was... "So warm and soft." Jewel cuddled into Rivan's heat, luxuriating in the sensations, eyes already closed again.

"This could all be yours Jewel; dream of that."

His? No. No, he belonged...

Before the thought could complete, Jewel was sound asleep, dreaming.

Hinton begins to Learn What it Means to be With Kytan

Hinton rocked slowly against Kytan's solid warmth. The drugs were receding, no longer forcing him to be trapped inside his head with the pain, but that meant the pain was growing sharp and heavy and, nice as rocking against Kytan was, he needed something just as sharp and heavy to distract him from it.

His hands were trapped though, all rubbing his arms did was gently stroke the soft gloves over his skin.

He used to be able to go months between cutting, then weeks and then it became daily and it was just as easy to rip at his arms with his fingernails. They didn't like that though and he was put into a straightjacket and then drugged when he started screaming and bashing himself against the padded walls, desperate for something to take the pain away.

He shook his head, whimpering softly. "Kytan... please."

"Yes, Dove?" Solid, steady, unmoving, there was something implacable about that touch, those eyes.

"It's everywhere. I need something to make it go away, please."

Kytan's hands started running over his skin, fingers pressing hard enough to burn. "You need only to focus on me, Dove."

He whimpered again. "Okay."

His mitted hands were drawn up over his head, gently fastened to heavy hooks. "There is nothing to do but feel, Dove. I will not make you face this alone."

"Promise, Kytan?" he asked, stretched out, body straining toward Kytan's hands.

"You have my word, Dove." His ankles were bound, body stretched.

He watched Kytan, trying to make the stretching be enough, along with the sight of his new... keeper? "What are you?" he asked softly.

"I am..." Kytan tilted his head, then smiled. "Your focus."

"Oh." He smiled back. "Okay." He kept his eyes on Kytan, trying to ignore the sharp pain that was building, burning inside him.

Those hands kept moving, kept pushing deep into his muscles. He groaned, the massage working long-tense muscles.

"There you go. Accept it. There's nowhere to go and I'm here."

"My focus," he murmured. He couldn't help wishing it was more, but it was something and Kytan had promised he wouldn't be alone.

"Yes." The fingers pushed harder, deeper, leaving dull aches behind them.

The aches sank into the sharpness, not alleviating it, but breaking it up, so there was something else there.

"Tell me, Dove. Tell me about your life, about the things that please you." The hair beneath his stretched arms was tugged, slowly pulled, drawing his focus. He hissed as the sharp scattered in the face of this, letting him think for a moment. "Limes. The way the taste explodes in my mouth."

"Mmm... I will remember that." Another slow tug kept him focused. "What else?"

"The cutting. The color of the blood is like magic and the pain... nothing's so sharp as that, not even the fire and the memories."

"How about sex? Music?" Those fingers trailed along his inner arms, the touch maddening.

"Industrial like Rasputin's Monks. And I've never had sex."

"Never? Why not?"

"I've never really wanted to. The doctors said is was a side effect of the drugs and when I'm not on them... well the last few years have been rough, before then I wasn't interested." He frowned suddenly. "It's not a problem is it? Nobody asked, nobody said it was important."

"Not at all." Warm brown eyes looked at him, sure and firm. "I simply wanted to know."

"Oh, okay. Good." He managed a smile for Kytan.

He got an answering smile, his cheek stroked. "Do you like the water?"

"Sometimes."

"I will bind you sometimes and sit with you in the water, let it surround you, let you float."

He shivered. "Sometimes I think about different ways of dying. And I think drowning would be like burning, only quiet."

"I will not let you drown. I will let you float." His body was carefully wrapped in layer after layer of soft material, almost as if he was being swaddled.

"What are you doing?" he asked, twitching just a little. How did Kytan expect something so soft to fight the sharp inside him?

"Letting the material hold you." That voice was as calm as ever. "You must learn to accept your pain, Dove. There is a huge power in bondage, in peace."

Tears started to fall, he didn't understand. It was like the straightjacket. Nicer, but still holding him, keeping him trapped with the pain.

Lips brushed his cheeks and Kytan's hands stroked through his hair. "Let it out, Dove. I will be here with you after the pain has gone."

He couldn't move at all, couldn't run, could only stay still and cry as the pain filled him, overwhelmed him. Kytan remained with him, sometimes turning him, lowering his arms, drying his eyes. Finally a straw was offered to him, the bright cold splash of sweet and ice and lime surprising him.

He sniffed hard, almost hiccupped, realizing that it was quiet inside him, only the sharp, sour lime filling his belly.

"Welcome back, Dove." A cool rag washed his face, another drink offered.

He sucked on the straw eagerly, gasping as the cold, tart liquid filled his mouth.

His eyes felt puffy, swollen from crying and he had a headache, but the pain was faded, caged. It would be back, it always came back, but for the first time in months it was caged instead of it caging him.

A simple white patch was placed on his neck, Kytan's fingers so gentle, soothing. "A simple analgesic for the headache. Nothing strong. Would you like anything?"

"No, I... I'm good." He smiled at Kytan. "I'm good."

"Excellent." His hair was brushed back from his face, that cool cloth moving again. "You are doing beautifully."

"But I didn't do anything but cry." He didn't understand Kytan at all, but things had eased; as long as he had that, he didn't need to understand.

"Yet, here you are. Awake, at ease. Whole."

"Yeah. Thank you."

"You're welcome." Kytan gave him a smile. "Come, it's time to shift you, I don't want you to get stiff."

His legs were loosened, then bent and bound so that he was in a fetal position, mitted hands settled before him, cheek on a soft pillow.

He felt so rested, good. "What now?"

"Now? We watch something easy on the vid. We relax. We talk and learn about each other. Then we sleep."

"Oh." He thought about it for a moment and then

smiled. “I think I can do that today.”

Kytan’s hand stroked his cheek. “Excellent. We will share our evening. Together.”

With that, the vid came on, some mindless comedy playing, Kytan resting behind him, every now and again offering him a sip of juice.

Hinton relaxed, enjoying the quiet company, the quiet in his head.

He could get used to this. And right this moment, that didn’t seem too scary.

Rivan with his Jewel

Rivan dozed lightly, not really sleeping. Mostly he just listened to Jewel breathe, watched the boy sleep. He'd wondered, just a little, if he'd made a mistake, but once they'd made love -- pardon him, fucked -- he'd known his instincts had not failed him.

Now all he had to do was convince Jewel.

He didn't think it would be that hard -- he just had to adjust his thinking and keep the lad off-guard, appeal to Jewel's baser nature. There would be time for softness and emotion soon enough.

Jewel woke slowly, blinking awake as if it were hard, painful work. "Fuck. Fuck, need a hit..." The shit those kids took was powerful -- allowing them to stay awake for hours, offering energy and excitement while sapping their appetites, their natural drives, their ability to feel.

Breaking Jewel of the habit would be one of the first things they did together. He was pretty sure Doc had something that could make it easier, but he wasn't planning on going that route. They would learn a lot about each other going through it without outside help.

He slid his hand along Jewel's belly. "A hit of me?"

"Hmm?" Jewel blinked up, moving into the touch for a heartbeat before shaking his head as if to clear it. "Man, I'm all fucking fuzzy. Where's my shit?"

"In the bathroom. Don't worry, it's safe. You can get it later." He wrapped his hand lightly around Jewel's hip and nibbled at the lad's neck, licking the mark he'd left.

"You can't be horny again..." Jewel laughed and shivered, head tilting before pulling away, goosebumps rising. "Tingles."

"I'm always horny." He licked Jewel's ear. "I feed my appetites as often as possible. With sex. With food. With music. With laughter."

"Yeah?" Jewel gasped and laughed again, mismatched eyes closing. "You're something else. Different."

"Thank you." And he meant it. He didn't want to be just like everyone else and he certainly didn't want to be like all the faceless people Jewel had fucked for money.

"You're welcome." Jewel took a deep breath. "Did I sleep long?"

He shrugged. "A while. There's no clock in here. Don't worry; we have all the time in the world." He went back to stroking Jewel's belly, the whipcord thin muscles fascinating his fingers.

"Mmm..." Jewel hummed, relaxing for only a minute before tensing again. "I can't stay longer than a day, though. I'll lose my spot outside, yeah? Them's the rules. If you leave your spot for a day you end up on the sidewalk and I'm short. No one sees you when you're short."

"I see you, Jewel."

He licked Jewel's ear again, hand sliding down to fondle Jewel's balls. "I have a proposition for you."

Jewel's legs parted, the motion instinctive, addictive. "A proposition?"

"Mmmhmmm." He rolled the soft balls. "Have you ever considered going exclusive?"

"Ex... exclusive? Just one person? No. No, I mean, I got them that'll come back for more, but..." Jewel shrugged, sacs wrinkling under his touch, so delicate.

"How much do you suppose something like that would go for? Room, board, what else?"

"I don't know. Uh... Makeup. Clothes. Stuff. The Risque itself takes damned near all I make from the corner." Jewel's eyes were closed, body relaxed, face dreamy.

"Clothes and makeup, food and a place to sleep would be provided. Give me a figure, Jewel, I want to make you an offer." One you can't refuse. He stroked Jewel's inner thighs, the skin so soft.

"I... I don't know. I can't think when you're touching me and I need my stuff. It's been too long. I can't think. I need a hit." Jewel shivered, pretty ass instinctively rubbing against him.

"All right, let's just do this first." He kept touching, fingers sliding over Jewel's skin, searching out places that made the shivers increase, rubbing his cock against that sweet ass.

So sensitive, so responsive, sensation unhindered by drugs -- Jewel moved for him, gasping and twisting, turning. He slid his cock between Jewel's legs, moving in and out. He wrapped one hand around Jewel's prick, the other playing from nipple to nipple, over the sweet belly.

"I... Why me? Why are you... Oh, I..." Jewel was shivering, fingers twisting in the sheets.

"Because you respond so beautifully." He kept moving, kept touching, letting the sensations take them both.

Jewel cried out, hips rolling against him, seed spraying over his hand. Oh, so lovely, so responsive. Just what he wanted.

He pumped his own hips a few more times, coming.

Jewel rested in his arms, relaxing for a long moment before sliding free. "Bathroom? Gotta piss."

"I'll show you."

He got up and grabbed two robes from the closet, holding one open for Jewel.

Jewel blinked at him and slid into the robe, snuggling into its warmth. "Thanks."

He wrapped it closed, hands sliding along Jewel before he backed off again. "This way. The blue room will be yours if you stay. It has its own sitting room, a small playroom and bathroom which you're about to see."

"A...another bathroom? Man. How... how many are there?" Jewel was shivering, following him.

"One in this suite, one in the green suite, one off my

and Ky's room, one for guests and the palace." He grinned at Jewel. "That's...five."

"Oh. Where's my pants? I can't just walk around without them." Jewel washed his face, his hands, doing his business quickly, tremors visible through the robe.

"Of course you can, Jewel. This is a private suite -- clothing optional." He moved in close, hand sliding along Jewel's back.

"Oh. Okay. Man. I need a hit, okay? I usually do a quarter hit an hour, sometimes two. Where's my fucking pants?" Those mismatched eyes were scared, panicked, needy.

He stroked Jewel's face. "I want you to quit. So it's just you and me, feeling and real."

"I can't. I need it. I gotta. I can't quit."

"You don't need it."

Jewel nodded. "You don't know. I do. Where's my stuff?"

"Where you left it." He slid his hand along Jewel's belly. "How much for you to stay?"

"I... a hundred creds a day. I don't remember where the other room is, please..."

"Done." He held out his hand to seal the deal.

Jewel took his hand, looking confused, wide-eyed. "My stuff?"

"You're quitting."

"I never said I would. I know I didn't."

"No, I don't believe you said you would, but you are."

"No." Jewel was sheened with sweat, adrenaline coursing through the thin body.

"I'm not paying you a hundred cred a day to do Risque. I'm paying you to be here, to feel, to be real." He slid his hands over Jewel's shoulders. "I'll help you, but you are quitting. Starting now."

Jewel shook his head, eyes wide, unbelieving. “I can’t. Please. I want to go home.”

He wrapped Jewel in a warm hug. “Shh, shh. You are home, Jewel.”

“I...” Tears started falling, tinged a pale violet from the drugs. “I can’t quit. I can’t be real.”

“You already are.” He stroked Jewel’s back.

“Please. Just let me have my stuff. I’ll dance for you again, anything. Please. It itches.”

“Imagine how the dancing will be without the junk. Oh, we’re going to have such fun together you and I, exploring the limits of our bodies. But for that you need to be clean.”

“I can’t.” So scared, so frightened, like a quivering animal against him.

“You can, Jewel. We can. I won’t leave you alone, I’ll help.” He slipped the robe from Jewel’s shoulders, slid off his own, pulling the slender body against him.

“Please.” Jewel shook and sobbed against him. “I’m a whore. A whore. I’ll lose my spot and be ugly and...”

“Oh, sweet Jewel. You could never be ugly. Never.” He slid his hands up and down along Jewel’s back. “You don’t need your spot anymore. You live here now.”

“I itch.” Jewel’s voice was hoarse, muffled. “Let me have a little bit. Go off it easy?”

“Tell me where you itch, and I’ll scratch.” Oh, the begging was going to be hard to ignore.

“Inside. It’s all too big, too much.” Jewel pulled away from him, scrambling for the door.

He followed, wrapping his arms around Jewel, holding him tight. “There’s nowhere to go, Jewel.”

“No...” A low, desperate, broken sound left Jewel’s mouth before the lad went limp, head hanging down. He picked Jewel up, carrying Jewel back to his bed. Jewel didn’t fight him, seemed quiet, tiny tremors still moving through the pale body.

He wrapped himself around Jewel, petting and touching, giving the sweet body something else to focus on.

"Why me? Why did you pick me?" More of the pale purple tears escaped, Jewel's eyelids heavy.

"Your eyes."

"They don't match."

"I know. Still, they're beautiful."

"I'm scared. I'm not sure... I don't think I..."

"You leave the thinking to me." He kissed Jewel's forehead, fingers stroking warm skin.

"You don't know me." Jewel's eyes closed, body relaxing, at least for the moment.

"No, but I will. You'll tell me and show me. And you'll learn me. It's very exciting, Jewel. The beginning of something new."

"And when I'm not new anymore?" Jewel sniffled, suddenly so young. "I'd rather just get thrown out to the corner now than to be... used to this. Used to no rats biting at you at night and being warm."

"When you're not new anymore? Oh, Jewel, that's when the real fun and excitement begins." He purred softly, imagining how they would push each other.

"Fun?" Jewel was shivering and sweating lightly, fingers pressed flat against him.

"Kissing. Touching. Showering. Making love. Pushing boundaries." He chuckled softly, nuzzling Jewel. "Of course I'm sure it'll sound better once you're clean."

"I'm scared." The pale face lifted for him.

"I know." He kissed Jewel softly. "But I won't let you fall."

"Gonna lose my place on the corner..." Jewel murmured, beginning to sink toward sleep again.

"Don't need it, Jewel, you've got a place in the sky now."

He pet Jewel softly, encouraging the sleep.

Finally the thin body relaxed, attempting to heal itself, free itself from the grip of the Risque.

He held Jewel as the lad slept. He would do so for as long as Jewel needed him to.

Kytan and Rivan Talk

Hinton was asleep, face peaceful, body relaxing in its bondage. Kytan curled up in a soft, comfortable chair and commed his Van. It had been quite the eventful day.

It took a moment, but his brother's face finally appeared on the small screen. "My Ky," murmured Rivan softly.

"Van." He smiled and settled in. "Is this a good time, love? We haven't talked all day."

"Yes, brother, my Jewel is asleep. I miss you. Did you have a good day? How is your boy?"

"Sleeping." He smiled, shrugged. "He is very broken, Van, but full of a sweet hope. He cannot be trusted alone, though. He will harm himself."

Van chuckled. "It seems we have again proven to be brothers. My boy is also broken and not to be trusted. Risque. He's lousy with it, but is quitting cold turkey. It's going to be interesting."

He laughed, fingers stroking the lines of Van's face on the screen. "Risque? You have picked a tough battle, beloved. He is lovely, your new boy? My sweet dove has lovely grey eyes, such hidden strength..."

"He thinks himself ugly and nothing but a whore, but I will teach him to love himself." Van blushed. "As I already do. I know what you will say, but oh, my brother, his eyes are two different colors and like his name -- jewels. His skin is pale, his need... exquisite."

He purred, hand sliding down to stroke his hardening cock. "Mine is untried, I do not even know if he wishes to be touched, loved, but his tears are sweet."

"He will wish to be touched, my brother. No one could know you and not fall in love." Van's eyes softened, the rich voice growing husky. "I love you, Ky."

"Oh, I love you, my Van..." He slid his fingers along his prick, moaning softly. "I want you to meet him, to see my little dove's strength and beauty."

Van purred. "And I want you to meet my jewel. Soon, yes?" Van licked his lips, eyes meeting his through the screen. "Are you touching yourself, brother?"

"Mmm..." He nodded, thighs sprawling, need pouring into him.

"Oh, Kytan..." Van moaned, the honey eyes growing dark, his twin's breath catching. "Our hands are so alike, but your touch on my flesh is so much more than my own."

"One day, beloved, we will curl together with our boys, all together, loving and needing each other." He moaned, tongue wetting his lips.

"Yes, Ky, it is my dream as well." Van's words were little more than husky whispers and he imagined he could hear the slap of Van's hand stroking flesh.

"Tell me, brother, tell me what you will teach your sweet broken one." He looked over to the lovely boy bound and sleeping in peace, hand moving faster.

"I will teach him to love himself, brother. And to love the pleasure and pain he finds at my hands. I will teach him to yearn for my touch, to seek his limits, to be pushed past them." Van's voice slid over his skin like a caress, he could almost feel the warmth of his brother's breath. "I will teach him to love me, to love you, to embrace us within his body and his heart. Ky!"

He arched, seed splashing over his fingers, the look of pleasure on his brother's face too great a beauty to resist.

"I love you, my brother," murmured Van.

"Mmm... I love you, Van. It will be a few days, I imagine, before we have time for one another. Enjoy your pet."

"Thank you, brother. Enjoy yours as well and know that I await our pleasure together with anticipation."

The commvid went dark, the afterimage of his brother slowly fading.

He cleaned himself up, then moved to curl against his sweet dove, one arm wrapping around Hinton's waist, letting the soft, sweet breaths lull him to sleep.

Hinton wakes in Kytan's arms

Hinton woke slowly, keeping his eyes closed as he always did. There were days when he had no desire to face the world and would not open them at all.

Today, like many days, he was bound, immobile. But the rough material of a straight jacket was missing; instead he was bound in softness, from head to toe. He was warm and could feel soft breaths against his neck and the sharp, burning pain of his memories were muted, there, threatening, but manageable.

Oh yes, Kytan. His focus.

He opened his eyes slowly, blinking at the soft, soothing green of the room. He'd hardly seen it last night, all his focus had been on the pain and then on Kytan.

Hinton liked the room.

He liked his focus more.

A soft, gentle kiss brushed his jaw, one hand warm on his belly. "Good morning, sweet dove."

"Oh. Good morning... Kytan? Or should I call you my focus?" They'd explained how things worked to him before they'd brought him here, but a lot of the details were lost in the drugs.

Still, he distinctly remembered titles being important.

"Either is fine, my Dove. Follow your heart. Would you like to relieve yourself? Shower perhaps?"

As soon as Kytan mentioned it, he needed to piss desperately. "Oh, yes, please."

Kytan moved, unwrapping him quickly and helping him stand. His hands were kept in the mitts, but the rest of him was released and he was led to a simple bathroom right in the suite. "You can sit and piss or I can hold you and aim. Your hands will stay in the mitts."

"Oh." He turned to sit when he realized suddenly that

he wanted those warm hands on him again and he cared little for why or how, just that they were. "Could you help me, please?"

"Of course." Kytan stood behind him, solid and hot and strong, one hand holding his cock gently, as if it were the easiest thing in the world.

It might have been awkward, a little hard to go if he hadn't needed to so badly.

"Thank you," he murmured once his bladder was empty.

He rested against Kytan's warmth, loath to leave that warmth. "How am I going to shower with the mitts on?"

"There is a hook we will fasten the mitts to, so they stay dry." His cock was still held, cradled in one big hand. "Then I will wash you. Things will be different for you, Dove, but just remember to focus upon my will and we will find peace."

Hinton nodded. "It's been good so far. I haven't woken with the pain this quiet in..." Tears filled his eyes suddenly. "I can't remember the last..."

"The last time matters not at all, Dove. Only now. Here. With me." Those hands turned him, led him to a shower were his hand were fastened above his head. "Now, let us get clean and then we can break our fast. What is your favorite food?"

The water started up, warm and good, spraying him from all sides. Kytan removed one long, metal thing that was attached to a hose, unscrewing it and screwing on a showerhead, using it to wet his hair.

He closed his eyes, enjoying the feeling of the water against his body, of Kytan's hands sliding on him. "Most food doesn't taste like much, does it? I like limes. And the taste of my blood."

A citrus scented shampoo was worked into his hair.

"We will have fruit and nuts and toast and eggs. Good food to help your body."

"Whatever you want, Kytan." He would do anything for this peace, for even now, as the sharp points of pain tried to poke him, Kytan's fingers on his head seemed to dull them.

"Yes, Dove." Those fingers rubbed and cleaned, then fresh water poured over him. Next a loofah was covered in soap, his body scrubbed.

With his eyes closed it was like he was floating in the warm sensations. He moaned softly, surprised when his penis jerked as Kytan washed it.

"Would you like to come, Hinton?" His balls were washed, then behind, one gentle finger sliding just inside his body.

He moaned as his cock filled at the touches. "I... yes?"

Kytan stood close to him, the finger inside his body moving slowly, one hand surrounding his cock. A soft, pleased purr sounded, Kytan watching him.

"Oh, Kytan... I can feel you." He moaned again, enjoying the touches, finding pleasure in them.

"Yes. See? We will fill ourselves with pleasure, with peace." A soft kiss brushed his forehead.

He nodded, shivering as the pleasure grew, becoming bigger, too big to keep inside him.

"Relax and breathe, my sweet dove. Let the pleasure fill you. I will keep you safe." Kytan's thumb pressed into the tip of his cock.

"Kytan!" He cried out as the touch made the pleasure explode. He'd never felt anything like it. If he hadn't been held up by his hands he would have fallen. As it was he sagged against Kytan, whimpering softly.

"Beautiful." Kytan's hands cleaned him, supported him, and soon the water stopped falling, his hands unhooked, a soft towel surrounding him.

"That was... nice." He smiled slowly at Kytan, feeling like he was floating.

"Yes. Pleasure heals." Kytan smiled at him, leaning down to take a soft, slow kiss that did nothing to dissipate the floating.

Hinton put his arms around Kytan's neck, holding on. Kytan's hands held him, so gentle, so warm, cradling him against the warm body, so safe, so close.

He rested against Kytan, wishing he could stay in this soft, peaceful place forever.

Jewel Begins to Believe

He hurt.
Itched.
Ached.

Needed.

Now.

Jewel cracked his eyes. Rivan was sleeping.

Sleeping.

Snoring.

Good.

His stuff was not in here, but out there and he needed to move.

Slide.

Slip.

Out of the bed.

Onto the floor.

Through to the sitting room and...

No.

No.

He pressed the lock again and again, tears sliding down his cheeks.

Large hands slid around him and settled on his belly, pulling him back against warm, solid skin.

"Unlock the door." He didn't want to relax, but he was cold and Rivan was warm and eased the aches in his bones.

"As you wish." Rivan's mouth slid along his shoulder, lips soft and warm as Rivan leaned forward and pressed his hand to the palmlock.

He bolted as the door slid open, hurtling down the hall, looking for something he recognized. Rivan followed him, not hurrying, but not letting him get too far ahead either. He searched, pushing at the doors, sobbing when he finally found the big bathroom, eyes searching for his pants, the drugs hidden inside.

His pants weren't there, the place had been cleaned.

And now Rivan was standing in the doorway, golden eyes soft with sympathy.

"No. No, those... Those things were mine. I paid for them. I..." He sank to his knees, sobbing, so tired. "They were mine."

"Your belongings are in your suite, Jewel. The Risque, however, was destroyed. You will be credited the street value if it's the money you're worried about."

No. No, not all of it. There was three days worth, almost four. No one would just destroy it. No one. "It's not about the money. It's been almost a whole day."

"Yes and you're doing beautifully. Sleeping, feeling. We'll work through this, Jewel. I won't leave you to do it on your own."

He shook his head, stomach clenching as he cried and he crawled to the toilet, dry-heaving, nothing in him to come up. Nothing in him at all.

Rivan crouched next to him, hand on his back, stroking, soothing.

Jewel finally stopped, eyes closing, head on his forearms. "I'm going to die."

"Oh, I hope not, little love. I've only just found you."

"I ache. It hurts. Please." His body rumbled, eating at itself.

Rivan sat and pulled him back into the warm body. Large, sure hands slid over his skin, caressing him, warming him.

He should fight.

He should.

Hit Rivan and scream.

But he was so tired...

So scared.

So empty.

Rivan began to sing, soft and low and slow, the big hands moving over his skin in time. He leaned against Rivan, breathing in time to the music, resting. He hadn't been held in so long.

One song flowed into another, Rivan's voice wrapping around him, cocooning him. He might have dozed, might not have. He wasn't sure. He didn't care. He simply rested, hiding in the peace of Rivan's voice. At length the singing stopped, only Rivan's breathing remaining.

"Are you hungry?" Rivan asked softly.

Jewel almost didn't answer, unwilling to cope with reality. "I don't know."

"Fair enough. I, however, am hungry. So I will eat and you can watch, or join me." Rivan stood, bringing him up, still cradled in the strong arms.

He closed his eyes again, the room spinning. "Risque users aren't hungry. We don't do hungry."

"You aren't a Risque user, little love."

Rivan carried him back into the corridor and to a kitchen where he was gently placed in a chair. He pulled his legs up under his chin, refusing to look, to see how normal, how much like the vid-feeds this all was.

Rivan pushed a button and music filled the room, soft and sweet like Rivan's singing.

In short order Rivan sat across from him with a bowl of ice cream with berries and granola on top. A spoon was silently placed in front of him. Two large glasses of water were set down and then Rivan sat and began to eat.

He took a long drink of the water, moaning at its sweetness. "It's sweet."

Rivan looked startled and took a sip of the drink, frowned. "It's just water."

He shook his head. "No. Water tastes more... chemically. Bitter. This is sweet."

Rivan shrugged. “This is how water tastes here.”

“Oh.” He was going to cry again and he didn’t even know why.

Well, he did too know why. His friends were all outside and made up and dressed up and high and laughing and he was naked in a chair needing a hit and drinking weird water.

“Would you like to see how ice cream and berries taste here?” Rivan asked him, offering him a spoonful.

“Are they nasty?” He sniffed, wrinkling his nose. Medicine came in spoons. Icky stuff came in spoons. His tongue flicked out, sliding along the cream, eyes going wide. “Oh!”

Rivan chuckled, eyes warm, twinkling. “Some more? You could sit in my lap and I could feed you.”

He tilted his head and thought, then nodded. He was cold, uncomfortable, unhappy and Rivan was warm.

“There are wonderful chairs in the sitting room. I’ll bring the ice cream, you bring one of the glasses of water.” Rivan smiled.

Rivan got up and led him through to the room across the hall. It was decorated in dark greens with bright, bloody red accents. And there were indeed many huge, soft looking chairs. Rivan sat in one, ice-cream set on a small table next to the chair, arms open for him.

He only spilled a little of the weird water, feeling a little overwhelmed as he stood there. “Y...yesterday morning I woke up because a rat bit me and my friend Mickey killed it to eat.”

A shudder went through Rivan. “You don’t live there anymore, Jewel. Your life isn’t like that anymore.” Rivan patted his own knees. “Come sit.”

Jewel nodded, sitting on Rivan’s lap, the warmth so good, seeping through him. He seemed to fit perfectly in Rivan’s lap, their skin sliding warmly together. Rivan scooped up a spoonful of ice cream and held it to his lips.

He opened, shivering at the taste, at the sensation, the explosion of flavor in his mouth.

"Good?" Rivan asked, taking the next spoonful for himself.

It was easy to nod, relax, curl into Rivan's chest, toes sliding on the soft cushions.

Rivan fed him several more spoonfuls of the ice cream and berries and then bent, bringing their lips together. Rivan's lips were cold, tart and sweet, flavored with the cream. Jewel opened to the kiss, tears escaping his eyelashes and sliding down his cheeks.

Rivan's tongue was hot, licking at the inside of his mouth before Rivan sat back, fingers brushing his tears away. "Why are you crying, little love?"

"I... I don't know." He shrugged, shivered. "It's all so big, so... not me."

Rivan held him close, hands beginning their hypnotic stroking again. "And what is you, Jewel?"

"Nothing. I'm nothing. I just use, and not even Dean likes me anymore."

"Wouldn't you like to be someone who is something? Wouldn't you like to be someone I like? Someone you like?"

"I can't. I don't know how. I..." He met Rivan's eyes, suddenly angry. "You don't understand. You live here in this place with clean water and no bugs and I've been using since I was little. Da gave me to a man who taught us to fuck and shoot so things didn't hurt and things do hurt and if I use nothing matters." He held his hands out. "Nothing matters and I don't know how to do things that matter. I don't know how to be someone. I don't know how to feel things right."

Rivan took his hands and kissed each one. "I'm sorry,

little love. It sounds like a lousy start to life. But that's no reason not to grab onto this opportunity now. All you have to do is be, we'll work the rest out as we go."

"Don't be nice to me!" He shook, more scared now than ever. "You're supposed to be mad at me and yell and call me names and make me go. You're not acting like people act!"

"Well I'm not people, Jewel. I am Rivan."

He looked over at Rivan, vibrating a little, unsure whether to scream or hit and run around in circles.

Rivan grinned suddenly. "I won't yell or call you names or make you go, but if you'd be more comfortable I can tie you up and fuck you until we're both exhausted."

Jewel blinked.

"You can't be real." He pinched his arm. Hard. "I died. Dean killed me yesterday morning and I'm dead."

Rivan tsked and rubbed his arm where he'd pinched. "I'll apply any pain you need, little love. And I'm real enough. As are you. I'll show you."

He was tugged back close, Rivan's mouth sliding over his, tongue pushing into his mouth. Jewel pushed back, letting himself be mad, letting himself feel. Rivan's hands were strong, sure, and he let himself push against them, let himself fight and need.

Rivan kept kissing, kept holding, not letting him go.

To his surprise, he got hard, the struggle and sensation and fury burning inside him. Rivan purred, mouth moving to suck at his neck, hands sliding, one landing on his ass and pulling him against Rivan, rubbing them together.

"I... I'm mad. I am..." His breath came faster, hips thrusting, rolling.

"Feeling," murmured Rivan against his skin, teeth sinking in next to the existing bite mark.

"Yes!" He arched, seed spraying, hands tangling in

Rivan's hair.

Rivan purred around his skin and began to lick the bite mark, still moving, cock hard against his belly. Panting, shaking, his body felt like it was on fire. Still hard. Still hot. Rivan's mouth took his again, hard and needy. He growled, hands tangling in Rivan's hair.

"That's it, Jewel, give it to me. Give it all to me." Rivan's hands grabbed at his ass, fingers digging in, pulling, slamming their cocks together.

They fought, teeth clicking together, his lip bleeding, Rivan's arms marked by his nails. Rivan tumbled them out of the chair, rolling them and pushing him into the carpet, hips grinding down. He gasped, struggling and growling, unsure what he felt, what he knew, just letting go. Rivan rolled them again, putting him on top, hands hard on his hips, demanding his passion.

He bucked, cock sliding hard against Rivan, the feeling a burn. "Rivan!"

"Give it to me!"

He screamed, coming hard, jerking violently as he came.

"Yes!" Rivan rolled them again, humping hard against him several times before heat splashed against him.

Jewel fought to catch his breath, fought to figure out what he'd just done, why he'd just done it. Rivan collapsed half on him, half next to him, breathing heavily. They panted together, the world slowly coming back together. He didn't know what to say, what to do.

Rivan purred softly. "Mm... little love. Such passion."

"I... Is that what that was?"

"Unbridled and uncontrolled, yes." Rivan focused on his mouth, leaning down to lick at his lip. "You had a little blood."

"I... I'm sorry?" He wasn't, but he wasn't sure what he

was.

Rivan frowned. "Why?"

"I don't know." He giggled, the sound surprising him. "I just thought I oughta be."

Rivan laughed and kissed him. "Don't give me what you think I want or you think you should do. Give me you, like you did when we were making love."

"You... You liked it?" Liked me?

"I did. It was honest, real."

"Oh." He licked at his bottom lip, wincing at the sting. "What do we do now?"

"What do you want to do?" Rivan asked him, checking his lip carefully.

"I... I don't want to be alone."

"You won't be, Jewel." Rivan kissed his nose. "I'm right here next to you and I'm not going anywhere without you."

"Oh." He let his eyes close, let himself relax. "Okay."

Let himself believe.

Jewel pushes and Rivan pushes back

Rivan gave Jewel awhile to relax, and then stood, pulling his little love up with him. "I want to spray your lip. I don't like you wincing while we kiss."

"Spray my lip?" The look was curious, Jewel's fingers curling with his.

"A little antiseptic, it'll take the pain and keep it clean."

They padded down the hall toward one of the playrooms. There would be a first aid kit there.

"Oh." Jewel's eyes moved around, taking everything in, watching, so much sharper and clearer than yesterday.

"This is the playroom." He went to one of the cupboards and brought down the box, finding the spray.

"Playroom? You play?" Jewel laughed, sitting up on one of the tables.

He grinned and winked. "Not that kind of play. Although we do have a swing or two." He moved to stand between Jewel's legs and carefully sprayed the split in Jewel's lip. "That should do it."

Jewel's tongue shot out, eyes wide. "Wow."

He grinned and leaned in, licking as well.

"You like to kiss." Jewel tilted his head. "I don't know anything about you."

"Sure you do. You know I like to kiss. You know I like to watch. You know I have amazing stamina, and I drink sweet water."

"I know you pick whores up, and feed them chicken and salad."

He laughed. "Actually, you're the first one."

"The first whore, or the first one you fed chicken?"

He laughed some more, stopping to kiss Jewel again. "Both, little love. What else do you know about me?"

"I... you have a brother. You sing. You eat ice cream."

"So you know more about me than I do about you."

"You know I'm a whore. I use. I dance. I..." Jewel frowned, then those eyes lit up. "Oh! Oh, I know! You don't know my favorite thing in the whole world!"

"Me?" he asked, teasing gently.

Jewel laughed again, shaking his head. "Nope."

"Tell me then." He needed to know what made Jewel's eyes light up like that.

"Have... Have you ever tasted pink bubble ice candy? It sparkles in your mouth. In the dark."

"I never have. You'll have to show me some time." He was going to have to ask Doc what it was -- make sure it wasn't another drug.

"Oh. Okay. It's fun. I... We don't have lights in the flat, so you can eat it and sort of see. And it tingles in your mouth when you suck someone off. Sorta... kills the taste, yeah?"

"Oh, I've never wanted to kill the taste, but I can understand how you might want to. Still, the tingling sounds like fun." Not wanting to taste... it truly was a shame not everyone could have the life he and Kytan shared.

"Well, you know, dirty guys taste... ew. You didn't. Taste ew, I mean."

He purred softly. "I'm glad to hear that." He leaned in and nuzzled the mark he'd left on Jewel's neck. "Neither did you."

"That tingles." Jewel leaned toward him. "You're warm."

"Are you cold? I could turn up the heat -- each room has its own temperature control. We could go find you some clothes." He grinned down at Jewel. "Although I don't see the fun in that."

"I couldn't wear your clothes, Rivan." Those mismatched eyes flashed up at him, teasing, laughing. "You're huge."

He chuckled. "There's the robe though, your leather pants, the clothes you came in. And of course we can always go shopping without ever having to leave the suite."

"Uh-uh..." Jewel shook his head. "You're teasing me."

"I am not!"

Grinning, he set Jewel down off the table, and then grabbed the boy's hand, leading him to the green suite sitting room. There was a comm that linked to the 'versalnet hidden in a cupboard and he fired it up.

"Where do you want to start?"

"I... I don't know. Where is there to go?" Jewel walked up, fingers touching the screen

"You name it, there's a place to get it on the net. We could start with accessories or footwear, formal, informal, fun clothes. Sexy stuff, provocative, sleepwear."

Those lovely eyes met his, unsure. "I... I don't even know what some of those things are. I... You're sure you want me?"

He pulled Jewel to him and kissed his little love. "I'm sure."

Jewel shivered, tearing up again, hands slapping the moisture away. "I'm sorry. I can't stop."

Rivan wiped the tears away, pulling Jewel right into his lap. "You're still working the Risque out of your system. You'll be sassing me again in a moment."

Sniffling, Jewel leaned into him. "I don't sass. Much."

"No, you don't. Though I think you have it in you -- when the Risque lets you go." He kissed Jewel's nose. "Let's start with Zero -- they carry some of everything, aimed at the younger crowd."

He put in a search, bringing up Zero's catalogue in short order.

Jewel blinked, looking at the clothes, fingers moving constantly, steadily. "Oh. Oh, look at the pretty colors..."

"Choose what you like -- just fill the shopping cart up. Don't worry about cost, we'll go in and pare it down after we've looked at everything."

"Anything?" The clothes Jewel chose were bright, sparkling, playful.

"Whatever your heart desires." Money was no object.

Jewel played for a while, choosing loose, flowing clothes mainly in blues and greens. Then the boy relaxed against him, blinking and scratching, the pale skin turning pink. "What do you like?"

"Peekaboo clothing -- hide and seek with skin and ass and cock."

"Perv." Jewel chuckled. "Lots of lace and torn spots?"

"Oh, Jewel, I'm a perv, but not because of a few bits of lace and some torn clothing." He winked and nuzzled Jewel's neck.

Jewel shivered, still scratching lightly, little spots visible on the thin arms. "I miss the Risque. I miss the way it made things simple, easy."

He took Jewel's hands in his. "I know. But where's the fun in easy?"

He needed to comm Doc, make sure the spots and scratching were normal.

"I..." Jewel tugged against his grip, the motion unconscious. "What do you think is... is fun?"

"Kissing. Watching. Making love. Pushing boundaries." He looked into Jewel's eyes, slowly bringing the tugging hand behind Jewel's back. "Pushing your boundaries."

Jewel's breath came a little faster, eyes flaring with a reluctant need. "Pushing how?"

"Any way you can imagine." He put both wrists in one hand and traced Jewel's lower lip with his fingers. "Any way I can imagine."

"I itch. I... I can't scratch if you have my hands." Jewel's tongue flicked out.

"I don't think scratching's going to help."

"You... I... I don't know. I... Rivan. You're holding my hands."

"I can stop if you'd like. But if I do? I'm going to cuff them instead. I don't want you scratching." He slid his hand down along Jewel's chest.

"Cuff them? I... I don't... I itch. You'd tie me up? What if I said no?" Jewel's cock began to fill.

"You can say no all you want, Jewel, I'll still cuff them."

He circled Jewel's cock; they'd gone over the safeword, he wouldn't do anything Jewel really didn't want.

Jewel's hips moved reflexively, sliding the filling cock against his hand as those eyes went wide. "If I screamed?"

"Mmm... Still cuffing you."

"Why?" Arousal was pouring from his little love, the thin body vibrating against him.

"Because I don't believe that you'll stop scratching just because I tell you to. So I'll have to insist." He kept his eyes on Jewel's, free hand sliding down to tease the hot balls.

"I itch." Jewel's legs spread. "I want to scratch."

"Are we still talking about your skin?" Rivan asked, teasing softly.

"I..." Jewel pulled against his grip, look going stubborn. "Yes. Yes. I am."

He chuckled. "You can't scratch, little love."

"Why? I need to. I do."

"You'll tear your skin. And I said you couldn't."

"It's my skin." Jewel pushed against his hand, so hot, so lovely.

"But I said you couldn't, little love."

Jewel made a soft little sound -- desperation and frustration and passion and arousal all mingling. "You're going to make me mad at you."

He purred softly. "What are you going to do then?"

"I... I'll fight you. Kick. Scream."

"Mm... you promise?"

"I..." Those eyes flashed and Jewel jerked, trying to bite at him. "Yes."

"Good." He pulled on Jewel's arms, forcing the thin body back so he could lick the sweet nipples.

"No! I'm mad at you! Let me go!" Jewel struggled, nipples going hard and tight.

Ignoring his little love's cries, he took a nipple between his lips and began to pull.

The tugs against his hands increased, the scent of Jewel's arousal stronger, flesh heated under his tongue. He stroked Jewel with his free hand as his mouth switched nipples, teeth threatening.

"Let me go. Bastard!" The struggles increased, the fluid leaking from Jewel's cock easing the way.

Purring, he bent Jewel back farther, mouth moving down to lick at the wiry muscles of Jewel's belly. Such sweet, warm skin.

Jewel was kicking at him, such perfect fury, such heated need. The way the boy was sitting and bent, Rivan was in no danger of being hurt, so he didn't stop to bind the flailing legs. He just kept stroking that hard, leaking cock, mouth playing over Jewel's chest as he held Jewel's wrists tight.

"I'm going to scream, going to get free and scratch and find my stuff and shoot up and you can't stop me..."

"Go ahead," he murmured, nipping Jewel's navel.

Jewel screamed, head thrown back, body struggling, cock throbbing in his hand. It was arousing, furious. Real. So beautiful and passionate.

Rivan shifted until his cock was rubbing against Jewel's ass as his little love moved. Jewel jerked, ass rubbing against him, driving him crazy. He turned his head down, hand slowing so he could lick at the tip of Jewel's cock.

"I'm not going to come for you. I'm not. I'm mad. I itch. I'm not going to come."

He purred and licked again. "I think you are."

"Am not." Jewel was panting, almost sobbing, a flush crawling over his belly, Jewel's flavor sharp on his tongue. "You can't make me."

"I'm not going to make you, Jewel. You're going to do it yourself."

His hand slid away from Jewel's cock as his mouth surrounded the tip.

"Oh..." Jewel went still for a long heartbeat, body shuddering.

He did no more than suck, not trying to pull Jewel in deeper or let him go. His little love would take his own pleasure as soon as he stopped fighting his body.

Soft little cries filled the air, Jewel vibrated, wrists twisting in his grip. He squeezed Jewel's wrists -- there would be bruises, beautiful bruises -- and fondled the hot, soft balls with his other hand.

Come on, little love, take what you need.

A sharp cry sounded as Jewel's need overcame anger, cock pushing deep into his lips, over and over, balls slapping into his chin.

He moaned around the hot flesh, sucking hard, letting Jewel have it all. It didn't talk long before Jewel gave him what he wanted, bitter-salt seed filling his mouth. He swallowed it down and then pulled off, rubbing his own cock against Jewel's ass. Jewel spread for him, thin legs wrapping around his waist. Purring, he rubbed his prick along Jewel's skin, the head of his cock bumping the soft balls, making him moan.

The hands in his own relaxed, stopped pulling as the aftershocks faded. He pumped his hips furiously, crying out as he came, come splashing over Jewel's skin.

Jewel was relaxed and still against him, watching him, eyes huge and dark.

He murmured happily, letting Jewel's wrists go and nibbling his way up the sweet belly and thin chest, moving slowly toward Jewel's mouth.

Jewel didn't move, just watched him, lips parted. "Rivan."

"Yes, little love." He brought their mouths together, pressing a warm kiss on Jewel.

A soft sob pushed into his lips, then Jewel was kissing him back, responding. He wrapped his arms around Jewel, pulling the slender body tight against him, bringing them together.

The touch of Jewel's hands sliding over his shoulders to hold him was sweet. He settled back in the chair, holding his little love close, nuzzling and kissing. Jewel relaxed against him, cuddling close, falling into a deep sleep once again, fingers periodically returning to scratch, stopping as he brushed them aside.

He leaned in and hit the link for the Doc's. He'd check a few things and then take Jewel to bed.

It was going to be a lovely voyage of discovery for them both.

Hinton Begins to Learn Pleasure

Kytan grinned over as Van's new boy started screaming, caterwauling like he was going to die. His brother did have the strangest luck with people. "My brother's sub. Trying to come off Risque."

Hinton was bound again, this time suspended from the ceiling, swaying gently, skin bare to touch.

"It sounds painful," murmured Hinton, eyes watching him.

"I imagine it is. You both will have surviving your pains in common." He offered Hinton a smile. "Would you like me to brush your hair?"

"Oh. Yes, please." Hinton smiled at him. "You keep making me feel good."

He picked up the brush, coming to stand behind Hinton, slowly brushing, careful not to pull. "I am here to assure that you heal, that you feel. Did you enjoy your breakfast?"

"Yes. It's been so long since there weren't drugs or pain making the taste go away." Hinton's head fell forward as he started to brush.

He nuzzled one shoulder, then continued brushing, intent on teaching pleasure and control to the abused nerves. Hinton's eyes dropped closed, soft moans filling the air.

"Tomorrow, we will have a masseur come and exercise your muscles, relax them." He periodically kissed a spot on Hinton's body, tongue sliding out to taste.

"Oh. You're. I'm."

"Yes, Dove? Tell me what you're feeling. All of it." He would have nothing held back.

"I'm getting hard again. You're making me feel things... good things." Hinton shook his head. "I keep waiting for the pain to come back, but you make it pleasure instead."

"Good. I want to fill you with pleasure, allow your nerves to relearn the paths." He brought the brush down, sliding the bristles gently along Hinton's skin.

Hinton gasped, jerking. "Oh."

"Tell me, do you like that?" He stroked down further, brush moving along the fine skin.

"Y...yes." Hinton rippled, swinging gently.

His lips brushed along the soft, sweet skin. "What do you feel?"

"It's prickly, almost not good, but it is good."

Kytan chuckled, let his hair drag along Hinton's skin. "And this?"

Hinton gasped. "Soft!"

"More?" He repeated the caress.

Hinton shivered. "Not enough."

He swung his hair, letting it land harder against Hinton's skin.

Hinton moaned. "Oh, Kytan..."

"Yes, Dove?" He swung again, letting the tail hit harder still.

"It's... it's good."

Again and again he covered Hinton with the blows, sensitizing that pale, fine skin.

Hinton whimpered and shook, cock hard and leaking, nipples tight for him.

"Tell me what you feel, Dove." It wasn't a request; he would know.

"I can feel every strand of hair hit me, Kytan. Oh..."

"Yes. Is it hot, your skin? Do you burn?"

"It consumes me."

"Shall I whip your cock with it? Make you come again?" His own prick was aching, throbbing in his loose trousers.

Hinton gasped, eyes wide. "Yes. Please."

Kytan purred, hair slapping against the boy's dark, straining cock, the soft, velvet balls.

Hinton cried out, body jerking in its bonds.

"I want you to come for me, Dove. I want to see your pleasure." Another blow, hard and quick.

"Kytan!" Hinton shouted his name, come splashing from the swollen cock, spraying his hair.

He purred, quickly moving to taste, to lick the seed from the sweet, flat belly. Hinton shivered and shook, grey eyes watching him.

"Tell me what you feel, Dove. I will have all of you." He would repeat the request as many times as it took for Dove to learn to share automatically with him.

"You're so... amazing. Every touch is so big, so much." Hinton shivered again. "Your tongue is hot."

"Your seed is, too. Would you like to taste?"

"I... I don't know. Okay."

He brought his lips to Hinton's, kissing long and deep, tongue sliding in to offer a taste. Hinton's mouth opened wide, lips so soft and warm. The kiss was sweet, heady and he was loath to let it end, enjoying the connection between them.

Hinton's tongue touched his, softly, hesitantly. Kytan hummed, encouraging. Come, Dove, kiss me.

Hinton's tongue slid over his and into his mouth, a low moan vibrating between them. The kiss continued until both of them were panting, breathless, his hands stroking through Hinton's soft hair.

Those grey eyes were huge, Hinton staring at him.

"Tell me what is in your mind, Dove." He licked Hinton's lips.

"No pain. There's no room for it. You just keep giving me pleasure."

"And how does that make you feel, my beautiful dove?" His heart was stolen and he suddenly wanted Van to meet this strong, dear boy, to see the pleasure in those grey eyes.

Hinton frowned slightly, looking confused. "I feel pleasure."

He chuckled, nuzzled Hinton's mouth. "No, I meant does the lack of pain make you happy? Proud? Confident?"

"Oh!" Hinton looked sheepish for a moment before smiling at him. "Happy, I guess. I keep waiting for it to come back."

Kytan nodded, bringing a cup of cold juice up for Hinton to sip. "It has been only a day. Eventually your heart will be more used to pleasure than pain."

"Thank you," murmured Hinton, sipping at the juice, a smile lighting his Dove's face.

"Lime and berry." He winked, letting Hinton have his fill. "It is time to turn you. Do you need anything while you're loose?"

Hinton's cheeks flushed.

"No hiding, Dove. None." He stroked Hinton's nose. "No more hiding alone for you."

"I like it when you touch me. I want to know what it's like to touch you. Is that allowed?"

"Yes, under certain conditions." He started easing Hinton upright, slowly letting the slender body bear its own weight. "You may touch me, but not yourself. If you touch your own skin or attempt to hurt yourself, I will have to punish you. Do you think you are ready for that?"

Hinton bit his lip and then shook his head, tears in his eyes. "No."

He released the bonds and drew Hinton into his arms, holding him close. "Very good, sweet Dove. It will be a reward, yes? For both of us. Your hands, soft and warm upon my skin, learning me, feeling me."

Hinton nodded. “I’m sorry.”

“For hearing your own heart? For being honest?” He laughed softly, hugging Hinton, pleased all through. “Never be sorry for that.”

Hinton’s arms went around him, the soft mitts making his Dove’s hold a little clumsy.

“Thank you, Kytan.”

“Mmm...” He wrapped one leg around Hinton, rocking them together, giving the boy all his strength, his care.

Hinton melted into him, trusting him, needing him.

They relaxed together, Kytan humming softly, singing old songs until his Dove fell into a relaxed rest again. Soon. Soon they would find Hinton’s center and they would fly together.

Jewel Feels Plain and then Jewel Feels

Jewel woke up, blinking, trying to figure out why he was cold and why his hands weren't moving and why he was itching and... He lifted his head looking around, pulling at the bonds around his wrists he couldn't remember having put on.

"Hey! I want loose!"

"I'm sorry, Jewel, I can't do that." Rivan moved from the armchair to the bed, stroking his cheek. "You were scratching in your sleep, little love. Tearing your lovely skin."

"I itch. Let me go. I need to." He shifted, shook, nuzzling into Rivan's hair automatically.

Rivan pet him softly. "You need to what, Jewel? You don't have to hide from me."

"I need to scratch. I need to get up." He needed to pee and to get something to drink because he was so thirsty.

"You're not allowed to scratch. You can get up though." Rivan even helped him get to his feet, hands strong and sure on him.

He pulled at the cuffs, holding them out. "Unlock me? I gotta go."

"Have to go where? Oh!" Rivan grinned and winked. "I'll hold it for you."

"What?" He backed up a little, shook his head, surprised. "I can do it. Just let me go."

"Are you going to scratch if I take them off?" Rivan's hand was on his leg, stroking, warm.

"I... I'll try not to. I itch. I do." His toes curled, thighs parting just a little.

"Your choices, Jewel, are to leave the cuffs on or to have them taken off. But if you scratch, I'll have to punish you, so make your choice carefully."

"I... I won't." Not with you watching, anyway. God,

he itched. "Please. I have to pee and wash my mouth out. It tastes bad."

Rivan took off the cuffs. "We'll go have something to eat once you're done. That should help the taste."

"Okay." He headed to the bathroom, not the slightest bit hungry, groaning as he got to piss. He brushed his free hand through his hair, wincing at the way he looked.

Pale.

Spotty.

Plain.

Ew.

Rivan had followed him, those golden eyes watching him, not missing a thing. "Problem?"

"Huh?" He shook his head, fingers sliding over his belly. "You going to follow me everywhere?"

"Yes."

"Why?" He couldn't decide whether to back up a step or step forward and get to the sink, wash his face.

"Because you're coming off Risque and I don't want you to hurt yourself."

"I'm not hurting myself. I just like getting high." He stepped toward the sink, washing his face, scrubbing.

"It's a crutch. You can be so much more without it. Feel so much more."

"I itch without it. Sleep all the time. Cry. I'm ugly." He cupped his hands under the faucet, drinking deep.

"Ugly? You, little love? Never. You've got dark circles under your eyes from never sleeping, but they'll disappear with time." Rivan chuckled softly; man that sound was sweet. "So will the itching."

He wet his hair and stood, fingers rubbing against his arm, feeling the urge to dig in, scrape. "I hope so."

"Careful, Jewel, that's almost scratching." Rivan came to stand behind him, hands sliding around his sides to stroke his belly.

"Not scratching. Touching." He rubbed against Rivan, against those hands, skin tingling and itchy and maddening.

"The doctor sent up some cream for your skin. He said it would help with the itching, but it would turn your skin pink." Rivan kissed his shoulder. "So which is worse -- the itching or pink skin?"

"Pink?" He looked at himself in the mirror, shook his head. "I'm ugly enough without my makeup. I don't wanna be pink."

"Interesting choice." Rivan's hands slid over his skin, not scratching, but touching. It was something else to focus on.

"Interesting? Why?" That hand felt good and why wouldn't he pick the itching? What if the pink didn't go away? The itching would eventually -- he'd scratch or find some Risque and then he'd be fine. It was just a matter of time.

"Most people don't have the discipline to ignore something like an itch. It makes me wonder what else you have the discipline for," murmured Rivan, eyes intent on his in the mirror.

"Discipline?" Those eyes made the itching worse, made him want to run. Or move closer. Something.

"Strength. Control. The ability to do things because they must be done even when you don't want to."

"I don't have any of that." At least he didn't think so. It didn't sound like very much fun.

"Of course you do." Rivan dropped a kiss behind his ear. "And one day you'll realize it."

He snorted, stepping forward, a little unnerved, hands sliding over his arms, rubbing hard. "You act like you know me. You don't."

His hands were taken, Rivan stopping him. "No rubbing. And I may not know you, but I'm a very good read of people and I want to know you."

"You didn't say no rubbing before." Gods, he was tired of being angry.

"I changed my mind. I don't want you scarring your skin or making the itching worse." Rivan frowned. "What we need is a distraction."

Rivan went to the comm unit in the wall by the door -- a fucking comm unit in the bathroom. "Kytan?"

A low voice sounded, rumbly, deeper than Rivan's. "Yes, Van?"

"Mmm... brother." Rivan's cock went from half hard to hard. "Are you ready to meet my boy?"

"Oh, I would love that." A warm purr sounded. "Where, beloved?"

"The main sitting room is neutral territory. And has that lovely love seat we could all sit in together and the deep soft chairs."

"Yes." The commlink clicked off, the voice gone.

"Where are my clothes?" Jewel looked around; he wasn't going to meet that voice naked.

"We don't need clothes, little love. There is nothing to hide from my brother." Rivan held out his hand. "I've been looking forward to you meeting each other ever since I found you."

"No clothes? But..." He slipped his hand into Rivan's, blushing dark. "I don't even have any makeup on."

"I would have him see you as you are. And if this meeting goes well and you don't rub or scratch, maybe we'll go visit the inking parlor and see about some permanent coloring."

He didn't like it -- not at all -- but the temptation go get permanent color, a mask that would be for always was too strong to resist. Jewel followed Rivan into the sitting room, choosing a single chair to curl up in, legs drawn up under his chin.

Rivan pouted at him, but sat in the chair next to him, hand stroking his arm as they waited.

It didn't take long before a strong man, a blond and tawny version of Rivan came out, dressed in loose clothing, carrying a beautiful boy bound in what looked like soft cloths. The two settled together on one sofa, the large hands stroking and arranging the bound one.

Rivan smiled, sitting straighter in his chair, eyes on the pair. "Brother. You're a sight. And this is your Dove?" Rivan slid a hand along his arm and around his back, stroking his neck. "This is my Jewel."

Jewel ducked his head, curling farther into his chair. Look at them -- Rivan was tall and dark and perfect. His brother was like a big cat and the dove guy was all big eyes and fine skin and big money.

"Lovely." Kytan's voice was all rumble.

"Isn't he?" Rivan's fingers stroked his neck. "It makes me happy, having him here."

He arched an eyebrow, just swallowing his snort. Right. When there were guys like over there available? Jewel wasn't sure what Rivan's deal was, yet -- maybe the man liked saving people, maybe he liked a challenge. Who knew? Better yet? Who cared? Eventually it would be over.

"What about your boy -- is he settling in, Brother?" Rivan's fingers stayed on him.

"He is, Van. Very honest and giving. He is sleeping well, eating." Kytan nuzzled one of the guy's cheeks. "I couldn't be more pleased."

Well, good for them. Assholes.

Rivan turned to him, one eyebrow raised, as if Rivan had heard what he'd said.

"Jewel is detoxing from Risque. He's doing very well, really."

"Yeah, I haven't chewed off my own arm yet and only

tried to run away once."

Kytan chuckled at his words. "Only once? That is impressive."

"You should see him dance, Brother. It's like magic."

"He has lovely eyes. Are you going to let his hair grow? It would move with him, flow."

Let his hair grow? What the fuck? It was his hair...

"It would, wouldn't it?" Rivan's fingers slid through his hair. "I haven't decided yet. Later we're going down to see Paul. Get his eyelids inked and his lips. Dark red to complement his pale skin." Rivan leaned in and kissed his shoulder.

Kytan nodded. "He would look most exotic. Oh... your own little gyspy, yes? In gauze and chains, dancing for you?"

Rivan purred. "You paint the most beautiful pictures, my brother."

The guy in Kytan's lap seemed oblivious to their conversation, curled in Kytan's lap, eyes almost closed.

"You got him drugged?" Jewel pointed to the dove guy with his chin. Man, if that brother's guy could be stoned, so could he.

"Not drugged," the dove guy murmured, shuddering. "Happy."

Oh, fucking hells.

This was silly.

Ridiculous.

Stupid.

Kytan obviously didn't think so, though, a soft purr sounding, hands petting the thin body.

Rivan gave him a look and then sighed.

"I think, brother, it is time to take our leave. It's hard for Jewel to watch your happiness when his own remains elusive. Doc said things should be settled back to normal within a week, even if he's been using as long as he claims."

Standing, Riven went over to Kytan. "I miss you brother." Then their mouths went together in a kiss.

It was beautiful and passionate and, fuck. Fuck, he was angry again. Angry at Riven for being upset with him even when he didn't say anything. Angry at the stupid bird boy for being all purry and smooshy and stupid.

Angry about itching.

Angry about being the ugly one, the poor one, the unhappy one.

He moved down the hall to the blue room, then the bathroom inside, shutting the door and locking it before trying to figure out the shower. The door opened quietly – Rivan's palm obviously was keyed in to open the lock. Then Rivan came over and turned on the water for him, making it hot, all without a word.

Jewel stepped into the water, letting it burn his tears away, arms wrapped around himself. Rivan joined him, arms coming around him, holding him against the solid warmth of Rivan's body.

Jewel closed his eyes, hiding, thinking about nothing but the water.

"We'll find our way, little love, have faith."

"You could have someone like the guy your brother has."

"I could have anyone I wanted, Jewel. I chose you."

"I'm not nice."

"I don't remember saying I was looking for nice."

Through their entire conversation Rivan never drew away, just stayed solid against him.

He began to relax, eyes closed. "I don't know what to do. Your brother acted like I was yours, like I wasn't real."

"You hid yourself when I introduced you, Jewel, he was merely reacting to your lead."

"You all are beautiful. What was I supposed to do? Be proud of being the plain one?" The anger rose in him again along with the tears, unhindered by the drugs.

"Where did you get this idea that you were plain?" Rivan sounded honestly confused.

"Oh, don't fuck with me. I'm a whore, I'm not blind. I'm little and pale and my eyes don't match and -- look at you! You're beautiful!"

Rivan turned him suddenly, slamming him up against the wall. "I like little. I like pale. I love that your eyes don't match. And you're my whore now and I will not have you belittling yourself."

His breath came quick and fast and he shook, unable to decide whether to cry or scream, tongue stinging where he bit it.

Rivan growled and then their mouths were pressed together, the kiss hard and wild, Rivan's body pressing up against his own. He met Rivan's passion head-on, crawling up the strong body and holding on tight, nails digging in.

Rivan humped against him, pushing him against the wall over and over again, making noises and pushing them into his mouth.

"Feel you." Jewel moaned low, eyes fastened to Rivan's, begging. Needing. Make me feel. Please. More.

"Good," growled Rivan, hands sliding down to his ass, a finger from each pressing into him.

"Yes." He nodded, fingers tangling into Rivan's hair, tugging them closer together. "Yes."

Rivan nodded, his fingers disappearing. They were soon replaced by the hot of Rivan's cock pushing into him, stretching him wide.

"Oh..." He nodded, something inside him spreading, needing. "Yes. More. Please. Make me feel."

"Yes, Jewel. I will." Rivan set up a hard pace, fucking

him against the wall.

It burned, pulled his skin as he slid against the tile, tugged his hair, was everything he needed. Rivan's fingers dug into his ass, holding him spread, that cock spearing him.

"Rivan..." He met those eyes, toes curling. "Don't stop."

"Not stopping, little love."

"Promise you won't drop me?" His heart was pounding, chest heaving as he fought his sobs.

"I'm not going to drop you, Jewel. Or make you leave. Or get tired of you. Or leave you alone." Thrusts punctuated the words, the promises, for that's what they were, he could see it in Rivan's eyes.

"Why?" The tears started, the heat inside him breaking them free.

"Your eyes," murmured Rivan, beginning to lick at his face.

"My eyes?" He kept moving, sobbing, needing so badly.

"Yes."

Rivan thrusts got faster, harder, pounding into him.

"Please. Please. I need." He buried his face in Rivan's throat, jerking, hand reaching to tug brutally at his cock.

Rivan's hand wrapped around his, squeezing his hand and his cock. Harsh breaths came from Rivan's throat. He screamed, letting his emotions out, letting them pour out along with his seed, hot and fierce and emptying him.

That big cock kept pounding into him, hard and fast and then suddenly filling him with heat.

He took a deep breath, then another, sobs slowing. "Oh. Rivan."

Rivan nuzzled him. "Jewel."

He nodded, relaxed, humming softly. "Feels good."

Rivan hummed and nodded, one hand sliding over his

skin.

"Don't let me go. I n... Please. Just don't let me go." He didn't want to be scared anymore, didn't want to have to worry anymore.

"I've got you, little love."

"Okay. Okay, good." He just let go, trusting those arms to hold him, trusting Rivan's words.

Rivan held him, nuzzled him, kissed him.

"Rivan?" He blinked, tongue sliding over Rivan's skin. "I... I'm hungry." He grinned a little, almost enjoying the sensation. "I am. I'm hungry."

Rivan grinned back at him. "The club makes the most amazing food. What do you like?"

"I don't know. I... What are our choices?" He reached out, stroked Rivan's smile.

Rivan sucked his finger in, nibbled at the tip before letting it go again. "Anything you want. I'll bet Moffat could even come up with your pink tingley stuff."

"Can I have oatmeal with honey?" He'd had it once, snuck into some place and stolen a bowlful. It had tasted warm and filled him up.

"You can have anything you want, Jewel. Anything."

Rivan's cock slid from his body and he was gently lowered.

"I want..." He swallowed hard, unable to meet Rivan's eyes.

Rivan's hand tilted his chin. "What?"

"I want to..." He closed his eyes, hiding. Ashamed. "I want to sound like the dove-boy sounded. Like I belong here, too."

"Jewel. You belong here. I promise."

Jewel nodded, trying to believe. "Okay. I want oatmeal, please, with honey, and I want to be with you."

"All right. Let's go order your oatmeal and..." Rivan looked him straight in the eye. "I'll get my collar. I want you to wear it."

He swallowed and nodded. "Is...is it pretty?"

"Not as pretty as you, but I made it myself."

"You did? Can I see?" Something in his belly was churning -- excited, scared. Pleased.

"Of course."

Rivan turned off the water and grabbed a towel wrapping him in it. He cuddled into the softness, rubbing himself dry, nerves firing, skin so sensitive. Rivan dried himself quickly and then took his hand and led him to a door they hadn't gone through before. "This is my and Kytan's bedroom. The collar is in here."

"Oh... That bed is huge..." It smelled different in here, not bad, different. "I can smell your brother."

Rivan nodded and smiled. "I love him very much. You'll get to spend more time with him and hopefully you'll grow to love him, too."

"He... You think he'll like me?" He almost smiled back, the happiness on Rivan's face addictive.

Rivan nodded. "I do. But you know, Jewel, you're here because I want you to be, not because of anything Kytan feels."

"If he didn't like me, you still would." It wasn't a question, not really.

"That's right." Rivan gave him a quick kiss and then turned to a dresser, picking up a fancy box and bringing it over. "This is where I keep my special things. Well. The smaller ones anyway."

"Fancy." He looked at Rivan, surprised that someone would show him their special things, show him where the important things were kept.

Rivan smiled. "Kytan gave it to me."

The box was opened and Rivan pulled out a thin collar made of ice blue and dark brown leather twined together. It was handed over to him.

"I'd like you to wear it."

"Oh!" He smiled, turning it over and over in his hands. "Oh. Oh, Rivan! Rivan, look! It's my eyes!"

Rivan nodded. "I made it a few months ago."

"Yeah? Do..." He met Rivan's eyes. "Do you think you made it for me? I mean, really? Just for me?"

Rivan took the collar and turned several times, fingers sliding over the braided leather. "I made it thinner than collars usually are. Malachi teased me mercilessly that my sub would look silly with it, except you won't because it fits your size. And I made it the color of your eyes. Even the blue is light rather than dark. Yes, Jewel, I'm sure I made it just for you."

"Oh. Can... Will... Put it on me? Please?" He was bouncing a little, heart racing again.

Rivan nodded and put the collar around his neck, fingers ready to snap it closed. "A collar isn't something to be given or accepted lightly. It means that you are mine, that we declare that to all who see you. I'm offering you my collar. Will you wear it?"

"Does that mean... That means you have to keep me, you won't let me fall?" His fingers traced the collar, trembling. "That I get to be home here?"

"Yes, Jewel, that's exactly what it means." Rivan stroked his cheek. "Can I close it? Will you accept my collar?"

"Yes. Okay. I... I'll be yours." Tears started falling and he pushed them away with a groan. "I never cry so much. I'm not sad, honest."

Rivan snapped the collar closed and leaned in to kiss away his tears. "It's all right, Jewel."

Rivan closed the box and put it back on the dresser, and then came back and took his hands. "Often the collaring is done as a ceremony in front of friends, family, the community. But I was impatient and you needed to know I was sincere. Maybe we can go the party route when we get it soldered closed."

"Soldered? What's that? Can I see it on? Do you like it? Do you like it on me?" He had a thousand questions and he still wanted his oatmeal and... He stopped short. "You'd let your friends meet me?"

"Of course." Rivan frowned. "Why wouldn't I?"

"Because I am... I used to be a whore?" His fingers trailed the collar again. "I'm not anymore, though, right? I'm not for sale." He liked that thought. Not for sale. Not. No.

"My friends don't judge. And no. You aren't for sale anymore." Rivan growled. "You're mine and I don't share. Well. Except with Kytan, but that's entirely different"

"I'm not for sale." He nodded, pushing into Rivan's arms. "Not for sale. And if someone hurts me, you'll tell them no and you won't let rats bite me and I won't have to fuck strangers on the street, even if you're mad at me and..." Oh, he was giddy.

Silly.

"No rats, no streets and if someone hurts you, I will hunt them down and hurt them back." Rivan was growling.

He nodded, hands cupping Rivan's face, bringing their noses together for a quick, quiet touch that he'd only ever shared because he wanted, not because he was paid to.

Rivan smiled at him, fingers stroking his cheeks and then the collar. "Are you happy, little one?"

"Yes, but don't tell anybody. I don't want it to stop."

Rivan chuckled a little sadly. "All right. It will be our little secret."

"Well, you can tell your brother." He pushed into Rivan's arms, cuddling as hard as he could. "Thank you. Please don't be sad. Please, Rivan."

"I'm not sad, little one. I just wish you had more confidence." He got a sudden wink. "You will soon enough."

"Are you going to fill me up with it?" He giggled, daring to play a little.

Rivan waggled his eyebrows. "Among other things."

"Oooh!" He laughed and tossed his head, playing. He could feel the collar, warm and resting on his throat and it made him feel settled. There. "Promises, promises."

"Yes, Jewel, they are." Rivan was still smiling, but his eyes were serious, intent.

Before he could convince himself otherwise, Jewel launched himself into Rivan's arms, holding on tight. "Okay."

Okay.

Hinton Discovers He Likes Focus

Hinton watched as Kytan and Rivan kissed. If his hands weren't bound he could reach right up and touch where their mouths met. It was obvious they cared for each other very much; he could feel it as well as see it. Plus they were sexy and his penis was getting hard again.

Again. Wow.

It was like Kytan had made the pain mostly go away and now the rest of him was waking up, alive and eager and wanting.

The other guy -- Jewel -- took off and the kiss broke apart. Kytan's brother, who looked so much like him, rubbed their cheeks together and Rivan smiled down at him.

"It's hard for him. I'm sorry, I have to go." With that Rivan went and Hinton curled against Kytan, alone again. He liked being along with Kytan because it was quiet inside him when it was just the two of them.

Kytan purred for him, hands sliding and petting him. "Poor Jewel. Hopefully soon they will be more settled."

"What's wrong with him? Why was he a risk?"

"A risk?" Kytan sounded confused for a second, then chuckled, hugging him close. "Risque. It's a street drug. Kills pain, sensation. Keeps you awake and numb all at once. Van's trying to help him learn to feel again."

"Oh. Kind of like you and me." He looked up at Kytan, who was making him feel again, and smiled.

Kytan nodded, leaning in for a long, soft kiss. "Yes, Dove. One day, the four of us? Will be a family. Feeling, laughing, together and happy."

"Oh." The pain surged with that word. Family. He had one once, before the car accident and the fire, and suddenly it all slammed through him again, hard and sharp. He shrank back into himself with a whimper.

Kytan's hands stretched him, refusing to let him hide. "No, Dove. You can't hide from it. Let yourself feel, and then let it go. Do you miss them?"

He nodded, tears leaking from his eyes. "Everyone should have a family."

"Yes. Everyone should. You will have two. Your birth family, who were stolen from you and your chosen family." Kytan sounded relaxed, calm, sure. Accepting. Strong.

He couldn't stop the tears, couldn't keep the pain inside his head from jabbing and making him cry. "I keep trying to remember them before the fire, but that's all I can see. Them burning up."

"That is normal, understandable." Kytan nodded, lips sliding over his cheeks. "What where their names?"

"Basil and Julia." More tears fell, their names strange on his lips -- had it really been so long since he'd spoken them -- aloud or in his heart?"

"Julia is a lovely name. What color were your mother's eyes?"

He closed his eyes. "I can't remember. Brown I think, but all I can see is the flames in them."

"What color are my eyes, Dove?"

"Brown," he murmured, looking up to confirm. "Like dark honey."

"That's right. Your focus, Hinton. Remember? I will watch you for always."

He nodded. "Not alone with the fire anymore."

"Never alone again." Those warm eyes watched him, held his attention. "I will not let the pain steal my Dove away."

"Promise, Kytan?" Oh please, promise. He didn't want to get stuck in the pain again, not now that he knew how good it could be.

"I swear to you, Hinton, never alone again." Nothing had ever sounded so sure, so absolute.

He smiled up into Kytan's eyes, the pain already fading, blunting beneath Kytan's confidence.

"There. There is my dove. See? Even with the pain, we were together this time. Whole." He could feel Kytan's pride, Kytan's pleasure. "You did beautifully, my dove."

The words were like a caress, making him feel good, making him hard.

"I think my sweet dove has earned a reward, pleasure to sweep the pain away, yes?" Kytan slid down, lips brushing and kissing, tongue flicking out on the way to his shaft.

He whimpered softly, breath catching. "Oh please, Kytan."

Kytan smiled for him, lips dropping over his prick, surrounding him in a perfect, wet heat. His mouth opened but he can't make a sound. He never imagined, never thought. How could anything be so good? So good it almost hurt.

A gentle, firm suction started, sending him higher and higher, pleasure making a heavy, heated ball in his belly. Without thinking he reached out for Kytan, but the bindings held his hands fast against his sides and a shudder moved through him, body rippling with pleasure.

His sacs were held, stroked, balls rolled as Kytan's hair pooled on his hips, his thighs. So many things Kytan showed him, so many ways to find pleasure. Such overwhelming, wonderful pleasure that proved itself to be stronger than the pain, more real than the pain.

He made soft noises, unable to keep silent now.

Kytan purred for him, the vibrations filling him, sliding along his shaft.

"Oh, Kytan! So big!"

His hips moved of their own accord, pushing, needing. He pushed deeper, his entire shaft buried in Kytan's mouth, being licked, loved. His whole body undulated, arms tight at his sides, legs bound together. The pleasure consumed him, filled him absolutely everywhere.

All the time, Kytan's eyes were on him. Watching.

Brown. Kytan's eyes were brown.

He came, body shaking as heat poured out of his cock.

Kytan sucked and swallowed, drinking from him, sending more and more sensations shooting along his spine. He whimpered and shook and felt, the pain driven so far away it was barely a thought.

He was taken in Kytan's arms, held close for a long moment before he was lifted, heading back to their rooms. "Come, my dove. A nap, I think, then food."

"Whatever you wish, Kytan."

Anything. He would do anything for his focus.

Jewel, Rivan and the Collar

Rivan petted Jewel, holding his little love close. His fingers strayed to the collar around Jewel's neck. His collar. The one he'd made months ago, letting his instinct guide him. It had guided him well. The colors were a perfect match for Jewel's eyes.

He turned up Jewel's face, smiling into those eyes. Jewel looked happy for the first time. Purring softly, Rivan brought their lips together. Jewel opened easily, kissing him back, tasting him, there.

Rivan knew once Jewel was settled in his skin, once the boy was sure of him, they would have such fun exploring the boundaries of pleasure and pain together. For now, there would be making love until Jewel believed he belonged, believed it wouldn't be snatched away.

He deepened the kiss, drawing Jewel down onto the bed he shared with his brother -- let Jewel see that he would keep nothing in his life from his little love. Jewel purred, the sound happy, warm, the relaxation and peace inside his Jewel delicious. Almost steady hands stroked his hair, his face, exploring him, feeling him. Wanting him.

"Yes, little love, making love to me." He slid his hands down along Jewel's back, fingertips moving on the warm, smooth skin.

"Making love..." Jewel moaned, shivered, voice a whisper. "Oh... I like the way that sounds."

"It feels even better," he murmured, lying back and bringing Jewel on top of him.

Jewel nodded, entire body sliding against his. "You're beautiful. M...my beautiful Rivan." Those eyes flashed up at him, making sure, checking.

He purred. "You think so, little love?"

"Oh, yes. Yes, Rivan. You..." The slender hands

spread, sliding over him. "You're beautiful."

He smiled, pleased Jewel thought so. One day Jewel would believe that he was beautiful in his own way as well.

Jewel leaned down, licking at his nipple, hands stroking his belly. He groaned, letting Jewel know how much he liked it, how he was enjoying this. He felt Jewel's smile, fingers sliding around his cock, petting him, feeling him.

"Feels good, little love." Rivan slid his fingers through Jewel's short hair.

"Yeah." Jewel cuddled, eyelashes tickling his chest. "It does." Those fingers weighed his balls, stroked his inner thighs, dipped into his navel.

"Mmm, don't stop." He lay back, reveling in the touches freely given.

"Okay. It feels good to just... well... feel, I guess." Jewel curled up, fingers tangling in the dark curls above his cock. "Tell me about you? You and your brother? Do you work? Have you lived here a long, long time?"

"Kytan and I started a business together and three years ago we sold it for a lot of creds. We've lived here every since." As he spoke, he slid his fingers over the soft skin.

Jewel hummed, stretched. "Oh, that's nice... Are you oldest or is he?"

"He is. My big brother." Rivan chuckled, he could hear Kytan's protests, 'Only a few minutes, Van, that's hardly older.'

Jewel grinned. "He seems like a big brother."

Rivan laughed. "Yes. Yes, he does." He nudged Jewel. "Do you have any brothers?"

"No." Jewel shook his head. "Not that I've ever met. My Da got taken when I was just little and I got sold off to work the corners."

"I'm sorry, little one." He kissed Jewel's forehead, fingers finding his collar. "No more corners for you."

He got another smile, Jewel's frown dissolving like cloud hit by sunshine. "That's right. I'm not for sale."

"Never again, little love. You're mine now."

"Yours." Jewel nuzzled, hummed. "What happens next? What do we do now?"

"We get to know each other, our likes, dislikes, our bodies, our needs. Then we see where we can push ourselves."

"Oh. Are... are there rules? Do you have rules?"

"There might be. We'll make them together if we need them. You remember what you're supposed to say if you need me to stop?"

"I... Bir... no. No. Chicken. Like the salad. Chicken."

"Good. Use it if you need to. I expect you to obey me and you will not use Risque again. But otherwise no, no rules yet."

"I can go outside?"

"With me, yes. I want us to be together all the time." It was important for both of them.

"Why?" Rivan was surprised not to get an argument, just the question. Maybe Jewel was tired. Maybe something in Jewel understood how vulnerable his little love was, was beginning to trust the security.

"Because we are a unit now. You and I. There is no privacy between us, no space. Later when we can recognize each other's breath in the dark, then we might separate for short periods of time, but for now." He shook his head. "We are as one."

"Oh." Jewel blinked, then cuddled into him, holding on tight. "Does it scare you, too?"

"I suppose it does." He would not hide from Jewel, to do so would be to give them an imbalanced relationship from the start. "The only person I have opened myself up to so completely is my brother. And he is my brother -- I knew he would not hurt me. You, I must have faith in."

"I'm not a very strong person, Rivan, but I'll try to be good. I will."

"I believe there is strength in everyone. It only needs to be found, encouraged." He tipped Jewel's face up and kissed his little love softly. "I have faith in you."

Jewel snuggled in, rubbing them together, offering another gentle kiss. He purred, need a slow heat in his belly. Jewel's cock and balls slid along his shaft, warm and smooth.

His hands slid down along Jewel's back, finding the sweet little ass and guiding Jewel's movements until his little love picked up the rhythm on his own. Then he was free to explore, fingers searching out sweet spots on Jewel's body.

Those sharp little teeth settled around one of his nipples, biting carefully then soothing the sting with that hot tongue.

Jerking, his hips pushed up, sliding them together harder. "Jewel... 's good."

Jewel nodded, moving faster, a moan brushing against his chest. "I... I want."

"Good." Yes, good. That Jewel wanted, the Risque's hold on his little love fading.

Jewel shuddered and started rocking, cock painting trails on his belly, his pubes, sweet, soft pants filling the air. Rivan met the thrusts, matching Jewel's movements, letting his little love set the pace. His fingers wandered, traveled up and down along Jewel's spine.

"Oh..." Jewel's head lifted, eyes bright, hungry, Rivan's collar on the slender throat.

Leaning up, Rivan licked at the collar, tasting where it met Jewel's skin, the flavors of leather and salt mingling in his mouth.

"Rivan!" Jewel jerked, come spraying along his belly,

hot and slick.

He purred, hands finding Jewel's ass and pressing his little love down as he humped up. He slid against Jewel, their middles slick with Jewel's come. Jewel pressed down into him, giving him the friction, the pressure he needed. With a shout he came, more heat spreading between him and Jewel.

Rivan's hips settled, his arms circling Jewel, holding his little love close. Jewel's eyes were closed, body relaxed, dozing almost immediately, body trying to heal, to detoxify.

With the scent of them mixed together all around him, Jewel's pliant body in his arms, Rivan believed they were on the right track and that his faith in Jewel was exactly as it should be.

He closed his eyes and dozed with his little love.

A New Family Comes Together

Kytan floated in the huge whirlpool tub, Hinton on his lap, arms around his neck, mitted hands crossed on the edge of the tub. They had invited Rivan and Jewel to join them, to let the heat and comfort of the water ease the integration of their family.

His dove was progressing beautifully, skin healed, good food and pleasure turning his sorrowful waif into a laughing, bright-eyed young man.

The door opened to let Rivan and Jewel in, both naked but for the collar that Jewel wore about his neck.

He smiled, beaming at Van, so pleased. "It looks perfect."

Van smiled back at him, giving Jewel a one-armed hug. "Did you hear that, little-love? Kytan approves."

To his surprise, Jewel gave him a grin, or at least a close approximation. "Thank you. It... It means I'm Rivan's."

He nodded. "It suits you, Jewel."

Hinton turned to look, nodding. "It's pretty."

Van looked proud enough to burst, his brother's happiness a palpable thing. Van and Jewel settled in the water, Jewel in Van's lap, fingertips stroking over the bubbles. He smiled at his Van, wanting a kiss, wanting to make love. Aching. He hadn't had his Dove yet, wouldn't until Hinton was ready, and the days of restraint were wearing on him.

Van's eyes were caught between watching him and looking at his Jewel, hands sliding on Jewel's back. "I miss you, brother," his Van said softly.

He nodded, allowing his need, his want to show in his eyes. "As I miss you, my Van."

His dove looked from him to Van and back again. "You're both here now. You could kiss again." Hinton's cheeks reddened. "You looked so good together."

He chuckled, nuzzling Hinton's cheek, jaw. "You liked watching us love each other?"

His dove nodded. "It was beautiful."

Van smiled at them and then looked down at Jewel. "What would you say to that, little love?"

Jewel snuggled in, fingers trailing down Van's chest. "I didn't get to see before."

"Would you like to see now?" Van asked. His brother kissed Jewel's lips softly. "Do not be afraid to speak your heart."

"I want to see." Jewel pinked, so lovely, Van's boy, so unique and interesting. "You're both so beautiful."

Van kissed him again. "Thank you, little love. Would you and Hinton like to sit together?"

Kytan nuzzled his dove. "Will you float with Jewel?"

Hinton nodded, looking shyly over at Jewel.

Jewel gave Hinton a smile. "I don't bite. Promise."

Kytan chuckled, helping Hinton move, making his little dove comfortable beside Jewel.

"Not unless you want him to," Van murmured with a wink, making Jewel pink up.

Jewel looked at Hinton's mitted hands. "Are they broken?"

Hinton shook his head. "Not my hands, me. I hurt myself." His brave little dove showed Jewel the pale marks on his arms.

"Oh." Jewel nodded, not looking the slightest bit surprised. "My friend Jump? He does that. Makes cool designs. You trying to stop?"

Kytan looked over at Van, eyebrow arching. Perhaps their boys had more in common than they had believed. Van nodded, his brother obviously thinking the same thing.

Hinton was nodding, too. "It wasn't helping. Kytan is."

His heart swelled with pride even as Jewel answered, fingers petting Hinton's scars. "Yeah? Cool. I... I stopped Risque for Rivan. It's hard, yeah?"

Hinton nodded his agreement. "But it's worth it, isn't it?"

Jewel tilted his head, grinning over at Rivan, eyes mischievous, playful. "I'll have to try it for longer and let you know..."

His Van mock growled, fingers mussing Jewel's hair.

Then those missed lips pressed against his, Rivan not waiting any longer to join their mouths. Kytan growled, tongue pushing in as his body moved against Van's, needing to be touched, to be felt so badly. Rivan's hands slid over him, starting at his shoulders and sweeping down, fingertips teasing his nipples as they passed by.

His hands cupped Rivan's head, tilting his Van so the kiss could grow deeper. With a soft sound Van pushed their bodies together, sliding them easily in the water. Need flared inside him and he growled, reveling in the strength of his Van, of the ability to take and need and not worry.

"I have need of you, brother," murmured Van, hand finding his cock and pumping it.

"Yes. Van. Please." Kytan gripped Van's shoulders, head thrown back in need.

Van's mouth closed over his neck, lips fastening on and pulling the blood to the surface. The sensation was sharp, necessary, bright and he needed more, hips driving his cock into Van's hand.

"You'll make love to me," murmured Van, the words not a question.

"Yes. Forever." Kytan slid his hand down to Van's hip, cupping the curve of that fine ass. "Forever."

Van pushed back into his hand, repeating the word softly. "Forever."

Their mouths joined together again, tongues twining and tasting, his fingers pressing in to stroke Van's hole. His brother moaned, pushing back to take his fingers in.

His need flared and he spun Rivan, chest snuggling up to the strong back. "Please, Van. It's been so long."

"Yes. Please, Ky, fill me." Van reached back, finding his prick and guiding it to the small hole.

"Yes..." He arched, pushing in, purring at the heat, the pleasure. His love.

Van's body fluttered around him, squeezing and rippling. "Ky! Oh, my Ky."

"Yes. Yes, love." He let himself take what he needed, knowing Van would accept him, love him, take him deep.

Van's hands gripped the edge of the hot tub, giving his twin traction as Van moved with him, pushing onto his cock. He heard his dove moaning. His eyes rolled, hips pushing hard, then harder, body knowing nothing but need.

Van was making low, needy noises, body moving with him, pulling him in, holding him so tight.

Kytan reached around, cupping Van's cock, tugging it. "Soon. Brother. Please."

"Ky!" Van moved frantically between his hand and cock, body tight and hard and hot.

His named was called out again, Van's heat sliding over his fingers only to be stolen away by the water. He let himself go, balls tight and aching as he came, pushing heat deep within his Van's body.

Van moaned softly, breathing hard. "Oh, brother. I love you."

"Mmm... love..." He rubbed his cheek against Van's shoulder, purr loud and pleased.

"Wow. That was... wow." His dove's voice was soft, awed.

"Yeah..." His brother's boy sounded needy. "You two should do porno vids."

His laughter bubbled up, low and rich and tickled. "Oh, Van. Your boy is something else."

Van reached over, stroking Jewel's cheek. "He is, isn't he?"

He nodded, noting the pleased look in those odd eyes as Jewel nestled against Van's fingers. He slid free of Van's heat, moving to gather his dove close now that his need was dealt with.

Van gave him a soft look, eyes happy, a silent thank you, and then his brother gathered his own little lover close. "Did we make you need, Jewel?"

"That would have made a near-dead straight woman hooked on Risque need, Rivan."

He laughed again, shaking his head at the matter-of-fact tone, the confidence. Such a mixture of innocence and cynicism.

His Van laughed as well, hands disappearing beneath the water. "What do you want to do about it, little love?"

"Oh..." Jewel shifted, gasping. "Rivan. I feel you."

Kytan cradled his Dove, leaning in to whisper softly, "And you, my beloved one? Do you need?"

Hinton turned those large grey eyes up to him, nodding. "Yes, please, Kytan."

"Of course, dove." His finger wrapped around the hard cock waiting for him. "Do you find my Van beautiful?"

"Y...yes." Hinton's breath hitched, the slender hips pushing his dove's cock through the tunnel of his hand.

"Mmm...I do, too." He licked Hinton's lips. "His beauty is different from yours, my lovely one."

"He's almost as beautiful as you," Hinton murmured, mouth opening for him.

Jewel was moaning, Rivan's hands still out of sight in the water.

He took Hinton's mouth, tongue pushing in, fingers stroking the cock in his hand faster.

Soft sounds were pushed into his mouth, echoed from across the hot tub.

Kytan scooted over, Rivan moving with him, until they sat together, holding their little pets, loving them. Rivan kissed Jewel and then leaned into him, bringing their mouths together, letting him taste the sweetness of Jewel's mouth on his Van's lips.

He moaned, tasting deep before turning to his Dove, completing the circle. Hinton's mouth opened wide, letting him in, the slender hips pushing hard into his hand. He growled low, letting his pleasure and possession show, vibrate through his dove.

Hinton cried out, hips snapping, heat again pouring over his hand before being taken away by the water.

"Mmm... beautiful." He smiled, purring softly, keeping his dove close, held.

Jewel and Van were still making the water move, Van's boy filling the air with sounds, but his dove only had eyes for him, gazing up at him.

"How do you feel, my dove?" His fingers traced Hinton's face, stroking.

"Do you remember what you said about family?" Hinton asked.

"I do." He focused on those sweet eyes, watching for pain, for worry.

"I think I'm beginning to understand."

"Yes? I had no doubt you would, Hinton. None at all."

"Do you think Rivan and Jewel think of me that way?" Hinton asked, whispering.

"As family? As part of us?" He nodded. "I know my

Van does. Jewel accepted your scars without question."

Hinton nodded and nuzzled against him. "Kytan?"

"Yes, Hinton?"

"Would it be okay if I love you?"

His heart swelled, smile undeniable. "Yes, Hinton. I think that would be just fine."

In fact, it would be most glorious.

Temptation finds Jewel

Jewel was curled on the sofa, dressed huge, heavy, warm, soft clothes, watching a vid and drinking bubble-pop.

It was cool.

It was fun.

It was three in the morning, but he'd finally stopped sleeping all the fucking time, so it was okay.

There was a tap at the window and he peeped, completely shocked to be looking up into Dean's eyes, his ex-boyfriend rapping, hanging upside down, grinning.

"Fuck!" Jewel went over to the window, looked up at Billy and some dude in an air scooter, hovering. "Go away! You'll get hurt!"

"We're here to rescue you!"

He tilted his head. This was the same guy who'd thrown him out, burned his stuff. "Go away."

"No. Seriously, J. We got stuff, we got a good deal. Buster there?" The dark haired scooter guy waved. "He makes our stuff, baby. MAKES it. All we want. All the time."

Oh. Oh, fuck.

He shook his head, hands holding onto the rail at the window, forcing his body to stay still. "Go away. I... I'm shutting the window."

"I brought you a hit, Baby." Dean held out an injector, offering it over. "Come on. We'll go flying."

"Rivan..." His whisper was low, too soft for anyone to hear, but he needed Rivan to wake up and shut the window and make them go away.

The best he could manage was to not reach for it.

"Jewel? Little love where have you... " Rivan's voice faded away and then his lover's heat was next to him, Rivan's arms crossing. Rivan sure looked imposing when he wanted to. "What is going on here -- I shall have security called and you all will be taken to a penal colony."

He relaxed, almost collapsing in relief. "Shut the window, Rivan. Please. Make them leave me alone." He hadn't taken it. He had waited long enough. He'd done it.

"You heard the man. I'm closing the window and if you don't leave, I'm calling security."

Rivan closed the window and then waited Dean and the others to go. "Do you think they believed me, little one? Because I will have them removed."

"I hope so. I hope so. I didn't take it. Did you see, Rivan? I didn't take it." He was shaking, so proud and scared all at once.

Rivan turned away from the window and wrapped those strong arms around him. "I know, little love. I'm so proud of you. So happy."

Jewel just collapsed into Rivan's arms, tears falling. "Yes. And you heard me. Thank you. It was so hard, Rivan. My body wanted to so bad and I made my hands be still." He'd done it. He had. And Rivan had seen.

Rivan held him, stroking his back. "It's okay, Jewel, it's over. You did it. You know where your home is now and you protected it. I'm very proud of you."

He nodded, meeting Rivan's eyes. "Yes. I did it. And you heard me." He laughed, pushing closer, chin held high. Proud of him. Rivan was proud of him.

Rivan purred softly, kissing him. "My Jewel."

"Yes." He nodded, fingers stroking through Rivan's hair. "Yours."

Rivan's fingers found the collar, stroking it in a way that was becoming more and more familiar. "Yes, little love, mine."

He nodded, chin lifting. "And they can't have me back. Ever. Because I belong with you."

"Thank you, Jewel. I knew I could believe in you, trust you with my heart and you did not fail me." Rivan kissed him softly.

He couldn't stop smiling, holding on tight. He was floating, flying, heart beating hard.

"Happy looks good on you, little love."

"Does it?" He giggled, tossing his hair, which was getting longer, and so dark.

Rivan purred. "Yes, little love. It does."

He preened, face tilted up for a kiss. "Your love."

"Yes. My love." Rivan's mouth came down on his, the kiss hard and possessive. "Mine."

He opened wide, cock going hard, tingles filling him. Yes. Yours. More.

Rivan's fingers pulled at his shirt, taking it off. "Less clothes, yes, little one?"

"Yes." He shimmied out of his pants, unashamed, prick eager.

Rivan let his robe fall away, body beautiful, muscled, cock hard for him. For him.

"Mmm..." He stepped forward, moving into Rivan's arms. "Beautiful."

"As are you, little love." Rivan's arms slid around to his ass, pulling him in tight, mouth covering his again. Jewel moaned, ass pushing into Rivan's hands, tongue pushing against Rivan's, playing, teasing. "You taste good." Rivan pullled him in closer, rubbing them together.

"Do I? I was drinking bubble-cola."

Rivan laughed. "I meant you, little love." One of Rivan's hands came up and tilted his head, their kisses growing deep. Rivan stole his breath, hips rubbing his cock against one hot, strong thigh. "So hot." Rivan nipped at his lips, hands hard on his ass, encouraging him.

"You make me. You're always so hard..."

"You make me," Rivan murmured back.

He grinned, moving faster, almost climbing up Rivan's body. Rivan growled, hands moving to cup his thighs and pull him up. He gasped and shifted, that sound drawing his balls up, sparking need in him.

"Want you." Rivan moved them to the couch, pushing him down into the cushion, grinding against him.

"Yours." He wrapped around Rivan, arms and legs. "Always yours. More."

"Always, little love." Rivan's fingers pushed against him.

He opened, pushing against Rivan's fingers, meeting that passion head on. Rivan growled again, fingers going in deep, spreading him wide.

"Oh..." His knees drew up, toes curling. "Yes. More."

Rivan's fingers pegged his gland again and again. "Yes, Jewel. More."

"Rivan!" His eyes rolled, electricity shooting through him. "I feel you!"

"Good." Rivan's fingers slid away and his lover's hot cock pushed against him.

"Yes..." He whimpered, spreading wider. "Need. Rivan."

"Yes." Rivan sank into him, cock hard and hot and spreading him wide. "Yes!"

Jewel wrapped his legs around Rivan's waist, hips jerking, body begging for more, now, deep, please. Rivan didn't disappoint, setting up a brutal pace, thrusting fiercely. He could feel it everywhere, even his bones shivering and shaking. He reached for his cock, fingers wrapping around and tugging hard, giving him the slight burn that got him off.

Rivan bent, nipping at his lips and then his jaw before settling against his neck, teeth biting, lips sucking hard.

"Yours!" He arched, shaking hard, body going still as

he just felt.

"Mine," growled Rivan, nipping at his earlobe, cock sliding across his gland.

"Oh. Oh, again." He was so close, so needy.

"Mine." Again and again, Rivan repeated the word, pegged his gland, joined them together.

"Yes." He sobbed, clenching tight around Rivan's cock as he shot.

Rivan shouted his name, slamming into him and filling him with heat.

He took one deep breath after another, focused on the feel of Rivan in him, above him.

Rivan purred, licking at his lips. "Oh, little love."

"Yours." He smiled, chasing that tongue with his mouth.

Rivan chuckled and nuzzled, settling gently down against him. Jewel wrapped around his lover, arms and legs, holding on, hugging tight.

"How are you feeling, little love?"

"Happy. Home." He closed his eyes, lips moving to whisper near Rivan's ear. "Love you, Rivan."

Rivan purred, holding him even closer. "Thank you, little love. I love you as well."

He nodded. He knew.

Hinton is Happy

Hinton was happy.

He wasn't on drugs and he hadn't hurt himself at all since Kytan had taken him in. The pain was still there, but it wasn't sharp anymore, dulled instead by his tears and Kytan's touches. He could think of his first family without becoming crippled by the pain.

More often, though, he liked to think of his new family. Kytan and Rivan and Jewel. He didn't know Rivan and Jewel very well yet, but he could see the connection between them, the connection between his Kytan and Rivan.

His Kytan... oh, he was in love with the most beautiful man he could have ever imagined.

He murmured happily, stretching within the silk bonds that didn't hold him still so much as safe.

Kytan purred, soft lips brushing his belly. "That's a lovely sound, my dove."

"Oh, Kytan. I didn't mean to wake you." He smiled, looking down into the honey-brown eyes. "I'm happy."

"I am too." He got a grin, warm and pleased, tongue sliding out to taste.

"Oh, that feels good, Kytan. I love how you touch me." A month ago he would never have believed gentle touches could be felt and enjoyed as much as sharp, hard cuts.

"Mmm... Tell me, dove, are you ready to touch me?"

He shook, the need like an ache deep inside him. Not sharp and hurtful like the pain of his parent's dying, but he wanted it so badly. "I want to try. I don't think I'll hurt myself."

"You won't. I'll be right here. I won't let you." Those eyes were serious, warm. "You touch only me, Hinton. Only me."

He nodded. It had been so long since he'd touched anything with his hands and the only thing he wanted to touch was his Kytan.

His arms were unbound, hands released, slid free of the mitts and placed on Kytan's chest.

"Oh..." Tears filled his eyes, his fingers stretching, flexing against warm skin. "Oh, Kytan... "

"Mmm... Yes. Feels so good." Kytan pressed into his touch, tongue sliding out to wet warm lips.

"You're so warm." He laughed through his tears, fingers sliding over the smooth skin.

Kyan kissed his tears away. "For you, sweet dove. All for you."

He watched as his trembling fingers slid across Kytan's nipples, gasping as they hardened for him. They drew his fingers again.

Kytan purred, wriggling. "Yes, Hinton. Feels so warm."

"Does it make you feel as good as you touching me feels?"

"Yes." Kytan slid those warm arms up along his spine, drawing them together. "Yes, my dove."

"Even touching you feels so good."

He was almost vibrating, hands sliding up over Kytan's shoulders, holding on for a moment before sliding down again. Kytan was hard for him, cock heavy and hot in the hollow of his hip. His fingers fluttered against Kytan's nipples again, but continued on down, wanting to touch that heat.

Smooth and silken, Kytan's flesh was heavy in his palm, throbbing, burning. "Hinton."

"Is this okay?" he asked, fingers exploring the hot cock.

"Yes, love. Touch me."

"Thank you, Kytan." He circled Kytan's cock, stroking the way Kytan had touched his penis. "Wow."

"Oh..." Kytan moaned, leaning in to lick his lips. "Yes."

He raised his head, wanting a proper kiss, fingers sliding down to the soft skin of Kytan's balls. Kytan took his lips, tongue sliding in deep, spreading his lips. He moaned, discovering that touching Kytan was as exciting as being touched.

They moved together, tongues and hands and hips all sliding and pushing. He slid his fingers over Kytan's hips and around to the tight ass, moaning. Oh, there was so much to touch, so much to feel. Their cocks slid together, Kytan's tongue and hands trailing over his skin, body moving under his hands. He whimpered, pushing hard against Kytan, turned on by the touching, by being touched, feeding noises into Kytan's mouth.

"My love. Make me come. I want your touch."

He gasped, hand wrapping around Kytan's cock, mimicking the movements that always felt so good to him. Kytan's hand copied his motions, making him feel sexy, powerful. Beautiful.

He tried to concentrate on doing the things that Kytan had done to him, thumb sliding across the tip, squeezing, but mostly he just rocked into Kytan's hand and tried to match the rhythm with his own. Not that Kytan's moans and soft cries sounded like it was disappointing. Hot drops slid down over his fingers, easing the way.

His hand moved faster and faster, the slick and hot so good and suddenly he was crying out, almost surprised as he came. Kytan's heat poured over his fingers only a few seconds later, his lover crying out for him.

Hinton wrapped his hands around Kytan's back, holding on as his body shook.

"Oh. Oh, sweet dove. Perfectly. You've done perfectly." Kytan pulled him in closer, holding him tight.

Tears leaked from his eyes and he sniffed hard. "Happy," he murmured. "So happy."

"Good. My sweet love. You touched me and I flew." Kytan kissed each tear away.

He beamed up at Kytan. "I love you so."

"I love you." Kytan's lips covered his again, tongue slowly tasting him. "Shall we go celebrate? Perhaps the hot tub and supper together at the table?"

He nodded, hands sliding along Kytan's back, reveling in the ability to touch. "Are you going to put the mittens back on?"

Kytan tilted his head, considering. "While we sleep or while I cannot see you, yes. But for now, you may touch me."

"Will you still sometimes feed me?" He blushed, he enjoyed being pampered and cared for by Kytan.

Kytan's eyebrow lifted, eyes shining. "Every meal I do not give you permission to feed yourself."

He smiled, pressing close. "Thank you, Kytan."

"I'm proud of you, dove. Very proud."

Oh. Oh, he'd made Kytan proud. He colored, chin tilting up.

Kytan's hand cupped his cheek. "Yes. Very proud. My Hinton. My strong lover."

"Strong? Me?" No, Kytan was the strong one. His focus.

"Yes. My dear, brave strong dove." Kytan took another kiss and another, making his head swim with sensation.

Pride filled him along with the happiness. Kytan thought he was brave and strong and if Kytan thought it, it must be true. He opened wide to his lover, his focus, hands reveling in sliding over Kytan's skin.

He could get used to this. To all of it.

Rivan and Jewel Push Boundaries

It was time.

Rivan believed his Jewel was ready to take the next step in their relationship, to find his next boundary. He made a soft, pleased noise just thinking of his little love in nipple clamps or with weights on his balls.

Ropes and chains. Leather bindings. Blindfolds.

He turned to Jewel who was watching a vid. "Let's play."

"Hmm? Play?" Dark curls bounced around Jewel's face, eyes shining and clear. "Play what?"

"With our bodies." He grinned, Jewel's happiness making him hard.

Jewel grinned back, still confused, but willing to trust him without question.

"Just come with me. You remember the playrooms? We were in one for a medkit back when you were first here."

Jewel stood, frowning, trying to remember. "Itching? No. No. My lip. You fixed my lip."

He nodded and licked Jewel's lip. "Yes."

Rivan took Jewel's hand, leading him down to one of the playrooms. Jewel whistled, following along, hand relaxed and warm in his.

"What's the wildest thing you ever did on the street?" He was curious to see how far Jewel had gone before.

"Wild fun or wild scary?"

"Both," he said as he opened the door the simple playroom.

There was a padded table to one side and hidden cupboards along one wall.

"Wild fun? I liked getting my nipple pierced. A guy paid me to do it; it was like a big thing. Lights and blindfolds and stuff. Bad? I guess taking stuff I didn't know what it was. We'd put a bunch of pills in a bag and pull out how ever many we were supposed to. You could get way sick."

"Did you ever? Get sick, I mean." He settled Jewel on the table and went over to one of the cupboards, searching through the stuff there.

"Oh, yeah. Couple of times. Once or twice it was cool. Mostly, though? I just passed out." Jewel crossed his legs, watching him.

"What about the blindfolds -- you like that?" He found a pair of nipple clamps that weren't too tightly sprung.

"Sometimes. I mean..." Jewel shrugged. "I didn't like when a trick would put something over my face so they could punch me and I couldn't tell who was doing it, but Dean used to do stuff..."

"So you like it if you like the person you're with." He grabbed a blindfold as well and some leather cuffs to attach Jewel to the chains.

"I guess so, yeah." Jewel tilted his head. "Do you want to punch me? I mean, I'd let you, but..."

"Punch you? Heavens no." He shook his head. "Well, I might whip you or paddle you at some later date, but it'll be consensual, I promise." He brought the items over to Jewel, showing his little love the clamps, blindfold and cuffs.

"Oh... pretty." Jewel's fingers stroked over the clamps, making them shine,

"They're going to look lovely on you. Just a little pinch, hmm?"

Jewel nodded, giving him a grin. "Do I need to take my barbell out?"

"It's up to you -- it'll hurt more if you leave it in." He licked his lips, watching Jewel.

"I..." Jewel's fingers unscrewed the end of the barbell, sliding it out and handing it to him.

He took it and pocketed it, leaning in to kiss the suddenly naked nipple.

"Mmm..." Jewel arched toward him, moaning. "Rivan..."

He bit the small piece of flesh, tugged it with his lips.

"Oh!" Jewel's voice was surprised, aroused, the sound settling in Rivan's cock.

He purred, getting the clamp ready in his hand as he kept tugging, pulling until Jewel's nipple was hard as a stone. Jewel was panting, hands tangling in his hair, little noises pouring out.

"Doing it now, little love," he murmured, placing an almost chaste kiss on the little nipple before setting the clamp on it.

Jewel hissed, head falling back, cock hard and wet-tipped.

"Burns, doesn't it?" He slid his hand along Jewel's cock, thumb sliding across the tip.

"Uh-huh. Rivan. Oh."

He groaned, leaning forward and taking the other tiny nub of flesh into his mouth to make it hard. Jewel shivered, anticipation heavy in the air now, body rocking. He tugged the nipple to hardness and then slipped the other clamp on.

"Oh. Oh. Rivan. I... I feel you." Jewel's eyes rolled, tongue sliding out.

"So beautiful." He tugged gently on the chain attached to the two clamps.

"Rivan!" Jewel's toes curled, body jerking.

"Yes..." He purred. Perfect. "Hold out your hands, little love, I'm going to put the cuffs on."

"The... the cuffs?" Jewel held his hand out, shivering. "I want you."

He nodded. "And you'll have me. But first I'm going to hang you from the ceiling. Then, when you're all stretched out for me, I'll take you."

"Oh. Okay." Jewel nodded, relaxing, cock throbbing visibly. So trusting, so responsive.

That trust was so sexy.

He fastened the cuffs and led Jewel over to the chains, attaching them to the cuffs and then adjusting them so his little love was stretched for him. Jewel's head fell back, stretching that slender throat, collar fine against the pale skin.

"Oh, little love, you look amazing. Stunning." He circled Jewel, fingers trailing over the fine skin, tugging the chain as he passed it by, ending with a hand on Jewel's ass.

Jewel pushed back into his touch, a soft cry sounding. "Want."

"I know. Let me just put the blindfold on and you'll look perfect." He slid the leather up along Jewel's skin.

Jewel keened, lips parted. "Oh..."

He leaned in and licked at one of the marks he'd left on his little love's neck before sliding the blindfold around Jewel's head, hiding those pretty eyes away.

"You... you'll stay in here with me?" Jewel's wrists twisted, tugging at the chains.

"I'm not going anywhere, little love. Not without you." He leaned in, licking and nuzzling.

"Oh. Oh, good. Good, Rivan." Jewel tried to move toward his touch, body throbbing.

Reaching around Jewel, he tugged on the chain again, pulling on both nipple clamps together as he rubbed his hard prick against Jewel's ass. "Gonna send you flying, little love."

Jewel arched, body moving beautifully, ass sliding along his cock.

He moaned. "Gonna fly with you." He slid his hands down along Jewel's sides, hands cupping the prominent hip bones.

"Yes. Yes, Rivan. Please. I want. I need."

"I know." He spread Jewel's legs with his knees, moving Jewel to his toes, exposing that sweet hole. He nudged it with his cock, hands pulling back, bringing Jewel onto him.

Jewel's cry was sweet, body pulling him in deep, muscles rippling.

"Does it burn, little love?"

"Yes... More, Rivan. I feel you."

"Good." Using his hold on Jewel's hips for leverage, he pulled out and then pulled Jewel back onto his cock, moaning as it was squeezed tight. Jewel shuddered, head falling back, lips parted. "Beautiful..." He leaned in and lapped at Jewel's neck and shoulder, searching, deciding where to bite.

"Mmm... Yours. Yours, Rivan."

"That's right."

He found his spot, teeth sinking into Jewel's skin, marking his little love as he fucked the tight ass. A sharp, sweet cry filled the air, Jewel bucking, riding his cock. He moaned around Jewel's skin, hand going down to stroke his little love's cock.

"Rivan!' Jewel went still, stiff. "More. Oh, love..."

He kept fucking, kept stroking, free hand going to the chain and tugging. Heat sprayed, Jewel's cock jerking in his hand, hole clenched tight around his prick.

"Yes, little one, fly... fly." He kept thrusting, making Jewel shudder and shake for him.

Jewel's cock filled for him again, low moans filling the air.

"That's my little love."

He closed his eyes and fucked, hands sliding over the now familiar lines of Jewel's body, knowing where to touch to pull the most sensation out of his lover.

"Yours. Rivan. Feel you. Love." The soft words filled the air, Jewel moaning.

"Yes, feel me." He kept moving, pushing with his hips, fingers tugging off the nipple clamps.

"Oh!" Jewel jerked, ass jerking.

He found the abused nipples with his fingers, massaging them, tugging on them.

"Rivan. Rivan. Hurts. Feel you. Oh..." Jewel was crying out, rocking furiously.

He grabbed one of Jewel's hips, helping his little love come back hard on his cock, the other stayed with Jewel's nipples, working them. "That's it. Feel me."

"Yes..." Jewel hissed, come spraying, the scent heady and sharp. His little love's pleasure pulled him into his own orgasm. Crying out, he filled Jewel with his heat.

Jewel relaxed, panting, shuddering for him. He moaned, pulling out of Jewel's body and working to release his lover from the chains. Jewel slumped against him, moaning softly, nipples hot against his chest.

"So sweet, so good. My sweet love." He got the cuffs off and started to massage the thin wrists, the slender arms.

Jewel purred, relaxing. "So good."

"I thought you might like that," he murmured, lifting Jewel, cradling his lover. He headed for Jewel's suite. Jewel curled in, resting easy. He kissed his little love softly as he lay the boy down on the bed. "You did so well and we flew."

Beaming, Jewel held out a hand for him. "Stay with me?"

"I always do." He wrapped around his little love, one hand resting possessively on Jewel's hip.

A warm, relaxed body cuddled close, Jewel's lips hot and soft on his throat. "Love you."

"Mmm. I love you, too, Jewel."

He pulled the covers up over them, wrapping them in a warm cocoon. Jewel's fingers rested against his belly, eyelashes tickling his skin.

"How do you feel?"

"Hmm? I... Warm. Melty. Safe."

"Perfect." He nuzzled Jewel's neck. "Just perfect."

"Just yours."

He nodded. "Yes."

Just his.

A New Family Comes Together

Kytan smiled over at his little dove, the thin hands mitted and bound to the chair. There was a soup bubbling on the heater, thick slabs of bread toasting, a choco cake waiting with cream. They were going to share a meal, perhaps go downstairs to one of the private pools and swim together as a family. Play together.

It had been too long since he had spent good time with his Van.

"I have lime and berry juice for drinks. Do we need a salad, Dove?"

"Whatever you like, Kytan. I like to watch you move." His little Dove's voice was soft, sweet, eyes watching him.

"Do you? We should go dancing. Move to the music." He wiggled and boogied, letting his hair sway.

"Oh, you're beautiful. I would love to move with you."

"I'd like that." He smiled over. "Rivan says his Jewel dances. We could all go."

"Oh, I don't dance, but I could... well you would make my movements match yours." The grey eyes gazed at him with such faith.

"You would be beautiful, so fine. My dove." Kytan walked over, drawn by those curved lips, needing a kiss.

His Dove's head tilted back, lips opening eagerly, anticipating him. He brought their mouths together, tongue pushing in deep, tasting the sweet flavors of need. Hinton whimpered and opened even wider. So responsive. He cupped the back of Hinton's head, tilting his love further, taking those lips with a passion. Hinton's arms strained at their bonds, his Dove reaching for him, even when tied down.

Kytan slid his hand down, finding the hard prick unerringly, pumping firmly. Dove keened softly, body pushing up into his touch. Yes. Yes, pretty dove, give me everything. He purred, pumping harder, eyes open and watching the pleasure in the beautiful face. Hinton's grey eyes clung to him, the slender body moving with him, tongue sliding along his. Such a beautiful dove. So fine.

He could feel Hinton's cock become harder, knew his Dove was close. He knelt down, lips wrapping around the hard shaft, tugging, sucking. His Dove cried out, hips snapping Hinton's cock into his mouth, seed pouring down his throat.

He drank Hinton down, purring happily. "Mmm... appetizer."

Hinton giggled softly.

"Do I get an appetizer too?"

Kytan stood, winked as he unfastened his slacks. "Is my dove hungry for me?"

Hinton licked his lips, straitening. "Yes, Kytan."

He freed his cock, pumping slowly, teasing them both. Moaning. His little Dove whimpered, stretching toward his prick. He took a step forward, bringing his prick to the sweet open lips. Whimpering, Hinton's lips closed over the tip, tongue swiping across his slit.

"Yes..." He arched, pressing in. "Dove."

Hinton didn't reply, just sucked harder on his cock, head bobbing eagerly. Kytan let himself go with it, hips moving, balls tight and aching. His sweet Dove didn't balk for a moment, sucking and humming, grey eyes gazing adoringly up at him.

"Sweet love." He ran his fingers through Dove's hair, pushing in deep.

Hinton's eyes widened, but his Dove's throat opened to him, let him in.

"Yes. Yes, love. So good." He moaned, backing off,

hips pumping faster.

Hinton followed him, head moving to keep him deep. Oh, so good. So strong. So fine. His dove. His head fell back, throat working as he panted. Soft sounds vibrated around his cock, Hinton's suction increasing, tongue sliding over his skin.

"Hinton!" He cried out in warning, then came, hips jerking, eyes rolling wildly.

His Dove swallowed hard, drinking him down. Several drops slid from the sweet mouth. He leaned in, licking at Hinton's face, moaning low. Hinton's face turned, his Dove searching for his mouth. The kiss was sloppy, soft, both of them moaning and lazy and happy.

"Tsk, tsk, you started without us!"

Van's complaint didn't sound terribly serious, but he could hear his brother's pout.

"Ew. Sloppy kisses!" Jewel's voice was teasing, playful. His Van's little bit of a love had proven to have a wicked sense of humor, a quick mind.

Hinton flushed, color high on the pale cheeks, but his little dove lingered nonetheless, obviously taking much pleasure from their kiss.

Kytan lingered, too, then stood, gave his Van a smile. "We were having appetizers. Next time, don't be late."

Van grinned wickedly. "We enjoyed our own appetizers... in private." His brother winked. "If I'd realized they were meant to be a part of dinner, we would have come here before coming."

Hinton giggled softly.

Jewel snorted and wandered over to the heater. "What's this?"

"Soup." He winked at Van. "Do you like soup?"

Jewel shrugged. "I don't know. It smells good."

Van grinned and began to set the table for four. "I smell choco, brother."

His sweet Dove sat quietly, happily bound to the chair, watching them carefully.

He nodded, stroked his dove's hair. "Cake with cream and I reserved a private pool for after."

"Lovely. Will you take off your little dove's mitts so we can all swim together, brother?"

Kytan nodded again. "If he feels he is ready. Hinton?"

His Dove nodded. "I would like to try."

"Wonderful!" Van beamed. "And may I kiss you hello, Hinton?"

His Dove's eyes flashed to him.

He smiled, nodded. "Answer as you wish, my dove." He winked at Van. "And be wary that I might ask the same of your jewel."

"I hope you do, brother. For I would taste him in your mouth."

Van's hand lingered a moment on his shoulder and then his brother bent, tilted Hinton's face up. The kiss was soft, but long, lingering, Van taking his time.

Kytan met Jewel's odd and lovely eyes. "May I?"

Jewel blinked, watching Van and Hinton, then nodded, raising up on tip-toes to offer the kiss-swollen lips. Sweet and sharp, Jewel was fiery passion where his dove was sweet yielding. Delicious.

Van purred, coming to him. "Jewel, go kiss Hinton while I kiss my brother."

"Oh. Okay, yes."

Jewel scooted over and Kytan pushed into those warm arms. "Beloved..."

Van's mouth closed over his without a word. He could taste his Dove there, his own seed, Jewel and Van himself under it all. They pressed together, passion flaring, rich and deep and undeniable as his fingers pushed through Van's hair. Van moaned, hands grabbing his ass, tugging them together harder. Their kiss was deep and encompassing, Van's want tangible.

"We could skip the food..." He was hard again, empty, needing.

"Feed on each other," Van agreed.

"Yes, Beloved. Bed." He licked and sucked on Van's lips. "Shall we let our boys watch?"

"Shall we let them join in?" Van's voice was low, growly, need clear.

"Yes. Yes, beloved. Our bed. Our love. Our family."

"Yes. It is time we loved each other four on four."

Kytan nodded, stepping away to remove Hinton's hands from the mitts, from the bonds. "If you touch yourself, Dove, I will punish you. It is time to love each other."

"Yes, Kytan, I won't disappoint you."

"Oh, brother, look at the love he has for you. Beautiful."

"He is all I hoped for." He bent and took a kiss. His Dove kissed him back eagerly, hands soft and tentative upon his shoulders.

Van purred in his ear, hand sliding down his back to his ass, goosing him.

He chuckled, lifting Hinton in his arms and heading toward their bed. "Come, brother, and take what you need."

"I need you, brother. And our sweet boys all together. Making love." Van had Jewel's hand, leading his boy.

"Yes." He began stripping Hinton quickly, eager to sink into the pleasures of laughter and flesh.

"Jewel. Undress Kytan." Van's voice was low, husky as he ordered the pretty boy.

"Oh. Oh, okay." Little fingers worked his clothes off, bared him as he bared Hinton. He offered Van a grin. "So obedient."

"He knows there are rewards in obedience, brother. Just as I learned at your feet."

Kytan smiled. "And you learned beautifully, Beloved." Van purred, need flaring between them.

His brother stripped quickly, pushing him back onto the bed as soon as Jewel had the last of his clothes off. He arched, wrapped his legs around Van's waist. "You're going to take me."

"I am, brother." Van brought their lips together in a fierce kiss.

He could feel his Dove's sweet touch on his face, small, warm hands sliding along his skin. Jewel was curled up behind Hinton, mouth and fingers making his dove cry out. The grey eyes watched him and Van, glazed with pleasure.

His brother broke the kiss and turned with a wanton smile. "Do you know how to prepare for penetration? Help me get my brother ready for my cock." His dove's eyes widened. Van's smile grew sultry. "Jewel can show you how, help you."

Kytan reached up, fingers finding the bottle of lube and handing it down, Jewel working to slick Hinton's fingers.

Hinton watched, wonder in his eyes. "I'm going to... inside of Kytan?"

Jewel nodded. "Yup. Slick him right up so Rivan can fuck him. It's cool. "

He looked over at Van and smiled. "He's blunt, your jewel."

"Refreshing, isn't it?" Van gave him a wink and moved slightly, giving their little loves room between his legs.

Jewel's fingers guided Hinton's, his little dove trembling.

"S'okay, Hinton. I'm here." He grinned at Jewel's words, Van's eyes fierce and proud. His own voice was a gasp as the gentle fingers circled his hole.

Two fingers slid into him, his own Dove's and Jewel's, sliding slowly, opening him gently. Kytan moaned, the sound vibrating throughout him, low and rich and wanton.

"Oh." Hinton's breath was hot against his inner thigh as Jewel guided two more fingers in. Two of Jewel's, two of his Dove's, preparing him for the girth of his Van's cock.

He squeezed and stretched, a low cry falling from his lips as his pleasure grew.

"Find his gland, Jewel, teach Hinton."

Their fingers shifted, searched, found his gland and slid across it.

"Oh..." His eyes fell closed, thighs parting again. "Again."

Jewel moaned. "See? So beautiful?"

"Yes," breathed his little Dove, the small fingers stroking him inside again.

"Hurry, little ones," murmured Van. "My need is great."

"Yes. Yes, I need." Kytan twisted, body gripping their fingers.

His sweet dove called out, fingers moving more freely inside him now, separating from Jewel's, truly allowing him to know the fingers inside him were from two and not one.

"My turn," growled Van and those slender fingers slid away, his brother's heat and girth pressing against him, demanding entrance.

He bore down, needing to feel that heat, that stretch. Van gazed down at him, pushing in slowly, controlling the penetration. He could feel Hinton's fingers still, gently touching where he and Van were joined.

"Oh..." He smiled, pleasure and want twining within

him like a braid. "Van. We have our family with us."

"Yes. Your Dove has a sweet and curious touch, brother. It makes me need."

Van moved faster, fucking him in earnest now, filling him again and again as Hinton and Jewel both slid their fingers against ass and cock and balls. Jewel's hands found his cock, the touch sure, practiced, intended to drive him mad, so different from his sweet dove's. He could feel his Dove's breath against his hip, the sweet touches continuing, as did Jewel's pumping and Van's thrusting.

"Let go, brother. Let us feel your pleasure. Please." Van's voice was husky, thick with want.

His answer was a deep purr, a growl that spoke of need and joy as his seed burst from him, pleasure soaring through his body.

"Yes!"

Van pounded into him, sending aftershocks through him and then coming hard, seed pushing deep.

He heard a soft gasp from Jewel, looking over to see the little hand working, full cock red and urgent. Van kissed him gently and slid away from him, settling next to him to watch Jewel. His own little dove gazed up at him, eyes needy, but the slender hands were on his thighs, moving restlessly.

He reached out, fingers wrapping around his dove's prick, moving in reward for such perfect obedience. Hinton gasped, pressing close against him.

Van leaned in and whispered into his ear. "Let them kiss each other as they come, brother."

He purred, nodded. "Kiss Jewel, my pretty dove. Taste him."

Jewel gasped, opening, moaning into Hinton's lips. The boys kissed, both humping hard, Jewel into his Rivan's hand, Hinton into his hand. His Dove spent first, crying out into Jewel's mouth as heat spilled over his hand. Jewel's cry was harsher, fingers harsh against his own flesh, driving himself to orgasm.

Van whispered again into his ear as the kisses between the two boys gentled, grew lazy and sated. "He accepts pain beautifully, brother, finds exquisite pleasure in it."

He purred, nuzzling close. "Oh, lovely... Mine glows when he is bound, submits completely. They complement one another."

"They do. As do we, my brother."

Van hugged him close. "Our family is finally complete, my brother."

Kytan smiled, happy and whole all through. "Yes. Yes, Beloved. We are whole."

New Brothers Play

Jewel looked in the cooler, frowning.
He wanted...
Something.
He'd watched all the movies.
Bathed.
Wandered.
Napped.
Eating was the only thing left he hadn't done.

Hinton was in the kitchen when he got there, trying to work the ice cream scoop with those mitts of his.

"Want some help?" He gave Hinton a grin, thankful that Rivan didn't make him helpless.

"Oh. Jewel. Hi." He got a shy smile and Hinton nodded. "I didn't want to wake up, Kytan. I should have just called down to the club kitchen. But I knew there was a pot of butter pecan up here."

"S'kay. I don't mind helping." He scooped out some ice cream, nodding at the mitts. "Want me to take them off for you? They look uncomfortable."

"Oh no, only Kytan can take them off." Hinton sounded shocked that he could even suggest it.

"Oh. Are they locked?" He pushed over the ice cream and found the big bent spoon Hinton sometimes used. "I'm pretty good with locks."

"No, they aren't locked." Hinton took the spoon from him, less awkward with it than he'd been with the ice cream scoop. "Thank you."

"Oh. You're welcome." He wandered aimlessly, taking a random bite of this or that. "Where did you live before here?"

"Different places. The hospital for the last year or so." Hinton shrugged. "My family has lots of places on different planets. But this is home now."

"Wow. I've never seen a hospital. They don't have those where I'm from." You lived or you died. That was it.

"No? Where are you from?" Hinton was still having some trouble with the ice cream.

He reached out, helped Hinton take a bite. "Nowhere. Everywhere. I sorta came up from downstairs."

"Downstairs? You worked as a sub in the playrooms?" Hinton handed his spoon right over.

"No. No. I..." He shrugged and fed Hinton a bite, refusing to be ashamed. "I worked the street in front. I'm a whore, a good one."

"Isn't that dangerous? I mean isn't it safer to work in a place like the Glove, isn't it?"

"Sure, but you gotta have creds and id and shit. You know, stuff and this dude that owns the place don't like Risque users and... well, I do. Did. Used to. Use."

Hinton nodded, liking away ice cream from his lips. "I used to cut myself. They were worried I was going to kill myself."

"Did you want to?" He tilted his head, curious.

Hinton shook his head. "I just wanted the pain to go away. The cutting helped."

"Oh. I knew guys that did that. I liked the Risque, it made everything... easy. Quiet. Um... sorta dull, I guess." He shrugged again. "Rivan doesn't let me anymore."

Hinton gave him a small smile and waved his mitted hands. "I know all about that." Hinton looked around and leaned in, whispering. "They're something else, aren't they?"

He nodded. "Does it scare you sometimes? How they know?"

Hinton smiled and shook his head. "No. It's... reassuring. Like I don't have to worry about it anymore."

"Yeah? I... I'm still trying to get used to it all." He

lifted his chin, grinned. "It's still my home though."

"Yeah. Home. Family." Hinton returned his grin. "I've never had a brother before."

"Really?" He offered Hinton another bite. "Me neither. I really wanted one, though. To have a brother."

Hinton licked the ice cream off the spoon and gave him a shy, bright smile. "Brothers like them, yeah?"

"Yeah." He chuckled, nodded. "Yeah."

"I like the way you kiss." Hinton's voice was soft, but sincere.

"Oh. Really?" Jewel scooted a little closer. "'Cause kissing you was fun."

And hot.

Sexy.

Sweet, sort of.

Hinton pushed his chair over a little closer. "Yeah. You make me feel good."

"Oh. Oh, good. Wanna kiss again? I bet you taste like ice cream."

Hinton nodded, eyes wide. "I bet I do, too. You should find out."

"Okay. Yeah." He leaned over, licking Hinton's lips. "Yep. Ice cream."

Hinton pushed their lips together, tongue softly meeting his own. Sweet. Warm. He smiled and took one little kiss after another, their tongues sliding together, heat filling his belly.

"Oh, it feels good," murmured Hinton, moving closer, chair squeaking across the floor.

"Uh-huh." His hand brushed over Hinton's belly. So warm and soft.

Hinton murmured and licked at the inside of his mouth. Oh. Oh, this felt... He moaned and scooted closer, lips opening. Hinton's mitted hands slid along his arms, the fur soft against his skin. That made him groan, pushing closer, almost crawling into Hinton's lap. Hinton's arms slid to his back and up under his t-shirt, tugging him closer still.

Jewel finally just gave up, straddling Hinton's lap properly and pressing close, looking into soft grey eyes. "Am I too heavy?"

"No. It feels good -- you feel good." Hinton smiled at him, tugging him in and he could feel Hinton's cock, hard and hot inside his pants.

"Yeah. Good." He reached down, unfastened Hinton's pants, fingers stroking Hinton's prick. "So hot."

"Oh! Oh! Jewel." Hinton pushed into his touch.

"Uh-huh. 's good." He got his own cock free before diving back into the sweet kisses, scooting to rub their cocks together.

Hinton groaned into his mouth, hips pushing, helping.

"Oh, good. More." He wrapped his hand around them both, pumping hard, panting into Hinton's mouth.

Hinton's soft-mitted hands moved over his skin, stroking and petting as Hinton's kisses grew more and more breathless. Pleasure filled him, not loud and furious and bright, but soft, gentle, warm. Good. So good.

Hinton was moving faster, hips pushing up against him, hands stopping their petting in favor of holding him close. He jerked as his own thumb slid over the tips of their cocks, so hot, so wet. So good. So close.

"Oh! Jewel!" Hinton called out, jerking against him, heat splashing over his hand and cock.

His toes curled as he came hard, almost laughing it felt so good.

Hinton was smiling at him and then kissing him softly again. "That was really nice."

"Yeah. Really, really." He grinned, licking the corner of Hinton's mouth.

There was a soft purr from the door, Rivan standing there, smiling. "Really, really, really nice. Such pretty boys you are."

Another purr, this one low and deep, Kytan's head appearing beside Rivan's. "Indeed. Most beautiful. Pleasure and happiness suits them."

Oh. Oh, wow. Hinton's cheeks flushed, but the soft mitts stayed on his back, kept holding him.

"We..." He nuzzled against Hinton, meeting Rivan's eyes. "We decided we're going to be brothers, me and Hint."

Rivan's smile was warm and he nuzzled back against Kytan. "Most excellent."

He nodded, arms sliding around to hug Hint tight.

Yeah.

Most excellent.

Lovers and brothers and home.

Really most excellent.

End

Sean Michael

Made in the USA